M. Sean Coleman

·

A HOLLOW SKY

An Alex Ripley Mystery

RED DOG

UK

For Richard, my rock.

"And all things, whatsoever you shall ask in prayer, believing, you shall receive."

Matthew 21:22

October

DARK. DARK. DARK. She'd always hated the dark. It used to scare her, but she'd been alone in the dark for so long now she'd almost got used to it. *Almost.*

She wasn't actually alone, of course. There were often voices around her, outside the darkness. Mummy mostly. She always knew when Mummy was there, even before she spoke. Mummy always chatted to her these days. Telling her what was happening in the world, singing to her while she fixed her hair, saying how pretty she was—all the things she'd never said or done before the dark had come.

Some days, like today, the darkness was cold, too. It made it more difficult to breathe. Like icy water all around her again, creeping inside her, filling up her mouth and lungs. She had been floating in the dark for so long now. She was sick of it.

Shut up, silly. Don't be such a baby.

She felt Mummy come in—just a small, faint light in the corner of her mind. *Hello Mummy.*

"Hello my love."

Far away and right there. Bright and cheerful as ever.

"Are you awake?"

Always. And never.

Warmth suddenly, blossoming on her forehead. A kiss. She focussed on it, willing the heat to spread, wishing the light would grow and she could finally wake up. But the light faded again, as it always did, and the cold returned.

Someone else was there too. Sad. Broken. Tired. Mummy often brought people to visit her. People who needed her light. Whoever this was, was in a lot of pain. A woman, definitely. She was holding her hand now.

Can I help?

So much pain, spreading from her hand, up her arm and across her back. Up and down her spine like little electric shocks, or tiny needles stabbing at her.

This is too hard. I can't do any more for you.

But she had to do more. She had to fix it. Mummy's hand on her shoulder, giving her strength.

This woman's pain was blue. White. Jagged and sharp. Stabbing at her. Slicing her. Pricking her skin. And she was fighting it with all her strength.

Don't give up. Not long now.

She could already feel the warmth spreading down her neck, into her arm, towards her hand. It was happening.

There you go. All better.

And just like that, the warmth left her and the cold swallowed her up again. Back underwater. Back into the dark.

Night night.

THIS QUIET, ORDINARY street in a coastal village in North Wales was as unlikely a place for a miracle as you could imagine. The sky was grey and flat, blending into bland pebble-dashed houses, drab net curtains. Even the broken concrete paving slabs were the same dull grey.

Jane Hewitt gazed at the front doors as they slid past her passenger window, half-counting the numbers. She had a nervous, excited tingle in the pit of her stomach. Was she being stupid? She didn't think so. So many events, coincidences maybe, had come together to bring her here today. Call it fate. Call it divine intervention. Call it serendipity. Jane knew—absolutely, categorically knew—that this was God's will.

Her husband, Ian, sighed as they reached a T-junction. The indicator clicked monotonously. She resisted looking at him, not wanting to give him any excuse to ask her again—as he had at least ten times already in the last few days—if she was sure she wanted to do this.

He didn't share her faith. He only went to church because it made her happy, and if—*when*—she was gone, he would probably never go again. She wished it was different, but she understood. He'd lost what little faith he'd once had the day they'd been given her diagnosis. Two little words: Terminal Cancer.

She had tried to convince him that these things were sent to try them. That this was all part of a bigger plan. But she had seen it in his eyes. He no longer believed. It made her sad to know that he wouldn't have faith as a comfort when she was gone. And that's why she was here. That's why she was sure she had to do this. Even if it was too late for her, she wanted Ian to believe again. Even for one day.

She winced as the car jolted over another drain cover. So much pain coursing through her, constantly challenging her strength. She hadn't taken her full dose of pain relief today. She wanted her mind to be as clear as possible. For once, she wanted to feel everything.

They turned into a newish housing estate. Wider streets, with broad pavements framing neat front lawns. In one garden, a cheeky gnome was bending into a small pond with his bare bottom pointing at the street. It made Jane smile.

"That must be the place," Ian said.

Jane looked ahead at a large bungalow, on the end of the cul-de-sac, and felt her stomach hitch. It was the house she'd seen on the website when she'd looked Megan Shields up. *This is it.* She let her eyes linger on the building, drinking in the detail, as Ian pulled up at the curb and climbed out.

The house was freshly painted, with a vibrant red door, wide and welcoming, at the end of a neat, paved pathway. A double garage stood separately off to the left. Two matching new model Range Rovers, black and elegant, were parked either side of a converted minibus. The bus was painted in soft blues and whites, blended to look like clouds, with pleated curtains framing its windows and the words *God's Gift – The Power to Heal* emblazoned on the side.

Jane took a deep breath, forcing that niggling little voice down again. *Was she right to challenge God's plan for her?* She had asked herself the question over and over. Finally, she'd come up with an answer she could live with: God wouldn't have given Megan Shields the power to heal, and he wouldn't have led Jane to discover her, if it hadn't been part of His plan. This was a reward for her lifelong undying faith. This was His gift to her. *One more night.* That's all she was asking for.

Ian opened her door and bent down beside her, the wheelchair angled against the side of the car. He looked tired. His eyes, usually so bright and smiling, now looked dull and sad. His thick, dark hair had a peppering of grey she was sure hadn't been there six months ago. Even his arms, so lithe and strong from years of running and cycling, looked thinner.

"It's not too late to change your mind," he said.

She didn't want to rake over the same arguments again. Not now.

"You promised," she reminded him.

His judgement was wrong on this. She was sure. This was what she needed to do, and he had promised to support her. She wasn't backing out now. He took her hands in his and looked into her eyes. Pain and love. She smiled beseechingly: *You promised.*

Ian sighed, lifting her gently, easily, as he had done so many times over the past months, and placing her into the wheelchair. He gave her shoulder a little squeeze as they set off up the path towards that wide red door.

A young man, handsome to the point of angelic, opened the door before they could reach it. His blonde curls bobbed as he half-bowed in greeting. His watery blue eyes danced happily across Jane's face and his smile warmed her.

"You must be Jane," he said, his voice smooth and soothing, deeper than she'd expected.

She smiled as he stepped behind her chair and took the handles, wheeling her over the threshold. Love and power emanated from the building, already wrapping her in its warm embrace.

IAN HEWITT TIGHTENED his grip as the young man closed his hand around the handle of Jane's wheelchair. For just a moment, Ian resisted letting go. He caught the tiniest flash of defiance in those cold blue eyes. At odds with the soothing, affected voice this young man had greeted them with. When he conceded, the young man smiled at his tiny victory. As he wheeled her away, Ian couldn't help but feel that Jane was being taken from him.

He knew he was letting his own prejudices cloud his judgement. While he had no evidence that Megan Shields was a fraud, he couldn't help but voice his cynicism. He simply didn't believe in faith healers. Jane had shut him down straight away. Megan Shields was different, she'd told him. She was special.

When he'd researched Megan, he'd been shocked. Not by the hundreds of glowing reports of incurable diseases and terminal conditions the girl had supposedly cured, but by Megan's story itself.

Megan, aged eight, had been on a Sunday School trip to a holy site in North Wales when she had become separated from the group. By the time they found her, she was floating face down in a small pool of water in the ancient bathing chamber. They thought it was too late—that she had drowned.

Miraculously though, the little girl didn't die. She even came round briefly in the hospital and spoke to her hugely relieved mother. Megan had declared it just hadn't been her time to die—she still had things to do. Megan had fallen asleep shortly afterwards and, with her mother resting in a chair beside her, she'd slipped into a coma, and there she stayed.

As days turned into weeks, and months became years, young Megan's condition remained unchanged. She had simply fallen asleep, and all doctors could do was wait and see if she would ever wake. Her mother, Anne, a single-mother of three, had spent every moment she could at her daughter's bedside, praying for a change. Waiting for a sign that her little girl would come back to her. Promising to be a better mother if she could only have the chance.

Over time, Megan became something of a celebrity on the children's ward. The girl who wouldn't wake up. A real life sleeping beauty. Children on the ward would take it in turns to sit with her, playing with their dollies on the end of her bed, reading her stories in broken, stuttering little voices, or telling her about their own treatments, fears, and breakthroughs.

Anne's mother, meanwhile, found comfort in prayer, her faith encouraged by a kind young priest who had moved to the village. Reverend Francis Rodwell would visit the hospital as a volunteer and bring flowers and gifts from well-wishers in the local community. He and Anne would talk for hours and struck up an unlikely friendship. According to Anne, it was he who had first opened her eyes to what was happening.

Anne had come from a religious family, but her own faith had slipped, and, even by her own admission, she had led a wild life. Until Megan's accident. That's when she'd started praying again. It had taken the Reverend Rodwell to point out that Megan's affliction may serve a greater purpose than Anne had considered.

With each child who visited Megan, and later left the hospital cured of their ailments, Anne's conviction grew stronger: Megan's life had been interrupted so she could help others. And it wasn't only children Megan helped. Soon, people from other wards would appear at the door, a small gift in hand and a gentle request to pray with Megan on their lips. How could Anne refuse them? It was God's will, after all.

And it was Anne's part in the whole enterprise that troubled Ian the most. He couldn't understand how, as Megan lay trapped in her coma, her own mother could allow countless strangers to invade her daughter's space, lay their hands on her and claim her gift had healed them. While Megan herself had no voice, no choice. What kind of mother would do that?

Ian had been even more appalled when he'd then discovered that Megan's healings had become something of a business for her family. After three years in the hospital, Megan showed no signs of coming out of her coma, though doctors remained convinced that she would wake up. Her brain function was still normal, and scans showed she seemed to respond to the stimulation of company and conversation around her. And she certainly got plenty of that.

The Reverend Rodwell had taken it upon himself to run a fundraiser to help Anne buy a house suitable for Megan to come home to, whether or not she woke. The appeal had raised hundreds of thousands of pounds, which, coupled with the generous donations that satisfied visitors made to Anne's purse in exchange for a little time with her daughter, meant that Megan could leave the hospital, and move into a specially designed room in a purpose built house, with round-the-clock care.

Over the next three years, Megan's healings became a growing business. People flocked from around the world to see this special young girl, who was quietly becoming a young woman, and pray with her in the hope of healing themselves. The donations continued to roll in. Newspapers, magazines and television companies paid for exclusive stories. Generous benefactors left legacies to Megan in their wills.

It made Ian sick. He couldn't stomach the idea that Megan's mother was cashing in on her daughter's condition, and using people's faith to lure them to her side, with vain promises of hope, and miracle cures, in exchange for so-called donations. He smelled a scam. But then, even by his own admission, he was a huge cynic. Besides, Megan certainly had enough testimonials to support her mother's argument that she *could* heal. Whether or not Ian believed it, Jane did, and it was one of the few things she had left to believe in.

Although he hadn't wanted her to come, and he'd tried to talk her out of it several times, now they were here, he would keep his misgivings to himself. For her sake. After all, there was no financial obligation on them. What real harm could a little prayer do?

He reluctantly fell in behind the young man, hearing the squeak of the wheelchair tyres on the wooden floor as they moved up the broad hallway. The house was quiet. A faint smell of disinfectant—medical and clean—lingered beneath one of those musky room fragrances.

The unmistakable sound of a children's cartoon, all American accents and loud music, carried from somewhere in the house. The lights were dim, the hallway sparsely decorated.

It reminded Ian of visiting his mother in the care home in the years before the Alzheimers took her. Noises off. A respectful hush. That same sense of clinical cosiness that always made him feel anxious about his own future.

He peered through the open doors left and right as they passed. A large kitchen, white and modern. A huge American-style fridge. As red as the door. Surfaces clean and clear. No evidence of ongoing family life.

Further down the corridor was a small lounge where two young children, eight or nine years old, sat side by side on a huge cream leather sofa. Brother and sister—twins by the look of them—their faces reflecting the technicolour glare of the television set in the corner. The girl looked up, eyes narrowed in a small frown, before returning her attention to the cartoon as her brother broke into a peal of laughter. Such a normal, happy sound. It jarred here.

A tall, elegant woman in her late thirties emerged from a doorway at the end of the corridor. Immaculately and expensively dressed, with perfectly coiffured hair and too much make up. Her posture seemed guarded though she'd spread her hands in a welcoming gesture. The smile on her lips did little to mask the hardness behind her eyes. She was wary. Ian wondered whether she could sense his discomfort. He smiled back at her, but her eyes were already fixed on Jane.

"Welcome," she said, her voice tinged with a smoker's rasp. "I'm Anne. Megan's mother."

She bent awkwardly forward to shake Jane's hand.

"Thank you so much for letting us come," Jane said. She sounded unnaturally cheerful. Nervous and excited, Ian realised. Anne looked at him as she straightened up, her smile frozen on her lips. He extended his hand over Jane's shoulder, having to reach around the young man still holding on to Jane's chair. Her handshake was limp and soft. Meaningless.

"Megan's ready for you," Anne said, directing her focus to Ian in that annoying way people do when they encounter a person in a wheelchair. It rankled every time. If Jane had noticed, she didn't give any sign.

"Great," she said. "I'm looking forward to meeting her."

Anne's smile twitched.

"Good," she declared, her fingers fidgeting with the buttons on her jacket. "Before we go in, though, I'll need you to fill in some paperwork. Just for our records, you know?"

"Of course," Jane beamed.

Anne must have caught Ian's frown.

"It's nothing to worry about," she said, dismissively. "We like to keep a record of Megan's visitors, so we can keep in touch. We're all family in God's eyes."

It was all Ian could do to stop himself rolling his eyes as he followed them into a small waiting room. A large wooden desk dominated. Two chairs. A water cooler. A small red sofa and a coffee table, littered with brochures.

The young man wheeling Jane moved one of the chairs aside and pushed Jane up to the desk.

"Thank, you Simon," Anne said, sitting down behind the desk and clearing her throat.

She gestured for Ian to join them and, as he hesitated, Jane turned awkwardly in her chair to look at him. Her expression nearly broke his heart. Silently willing him to toe the line and not make a fuss. *Just do what they ask so I can have this.* He would do anything to make her happy. Especially now. He sat down beside her and took her hand in his, giving it a little squeeze.

Anne had been right, the paperwork was light. Ian filled in Jane's name and their address, details of her condition and a contact number. There was a disclaimer at the bottom about healing not being guaranteed, which Ian dismissed as a statement of the obvious.

He handed Jane the pen and let her sign it herself. Her hands were so thin now. Her grip strength almost non-existent. He could see the bones and veins through her papery skin. It hurt him to see her labouring now over something which had once been so automatic.

"Right," Anne said, tucking the paperwork into a folder. "Shall we?"

On cue, Simon stepped forward to open a set of double doors on the far side of the room, revealing a bedroom decorated in bright, childish colours. Ian stood up before the young man could come back, and turned Jane's chair, wheeling her towards the door.

Simon hesitated, clearly uncomfortable with this part of his role being removed. Ian noticed the firm nod from Anne to her young helper. *Let him do this.* Simon smiled insincerely as they passed.

The room, though brightly decorated and full of youthful expression, felt creepy and oppressive. Macabre almost. Megan lay propped up on pillows, painfully thin and almost translucent white, eyes closed, hair in dark ringlets. Someone had applied a little colour to her cheeks, and Ian couldn't help thinking she looked like a doll, dressed and painted and waiting to come to life. None of it could mask the tubes and drips feeding her, keeping her alive in ways that her body was no longer capable of. *What kind of life was this for her?*

Ian stopped, unable to walk further into the room. Jane looked up at him, her eyes full of questions and fear. *Are you going to stop me?* He shook his head. They'd been married long enough to know each other's minds. He wouldn't stop her, but he didn't think he could be part of it.

"I'll just..." he stuttered. "I'll just wait for you out here. Okay?"

"I'll be fine," she replied, still reassuring him, even now.

He wheeled Jane across to Megan's bedside, pausing long enough to see her face soften as she tentatively reached out and took the young girl's hand.

He caught a strange look on Anne's face when she realised he was leaving. It was the first time he had seen anything like genuine emotion in her eyes. She looked hurt. Not angry or sad, but hurt. She could obviously sense his cynicism and it clearly pained her that he didn't believe in her daughter's gift.

He shut the double doors behind him and retreated into the waiting room. As soon as they clicked shut, he questioned his decision. Should he at least try to be more supportive? He took a deep breath. No, he was right. Having him in the room would distract Jane. This was her thing. Her last hope. If he was honest, he knew he was reluctant to be there because he didn't want to see the disappointment on her face when nothing about her condition improved.

He turned to the water cooler, poured himself a cup and downed it. Choral music started up from a set of speakers set high on the wall. Ian caught himself sneering. It was all so choreographed. Like those hideous New Age retreats, or massage parlours with whale song and incense, all designed to create the perfect mood. A placebo, rather than a real cure.

He'd better snap out of this negative funk before Jane came back out. She would need his support, not a smug 'I told you so'.

He sat down on one of the sofas and glanced at the collection of leaflets and magazines on the coffee table—all of them either advertising a local church or promoting Megan's work.

He picked up a glossy pamphlet for a group prayer meeting with Megan. *A unique experience. Open to everyone.* He tossed it back onto the table, shaking his head. What would they do? Wheel that poor girl out in front of a baying crowd? How much money would that rake in? Judging by the cars in the drive and the equipment he'd seen, none of this was being done on the cheap.

Ian checked his watch, straining to hear anything through the closed doors. The choral music had reached a stirring crescendo, and from the hallway outside, the sound of the two young siblings bickering, followed by a loud wail drifted over the music. *What kind of life was this for them, either?*

He stood and paced back and forth in front of the door. He hated waiting at the best of times, and it felt like they had done a lot of that over the past year. Waiting for consultants, x-rays, chemotherapy, radiotherapy, therapy, counselling, more consultants, nurses, doctors, specialists. Bad news heaped upon bad news, all delivered with that same, measured calm. Difficult, yet familiar to those giving out the news. Devastating for Jane and Ian.

Through it all, Jane had remained strong and stoical. She had kept praying for the strength to fight the cancer that was eating away at her. Ian had tried to stay strong for her too, but he knew she could feel his growing frustration. It wasn't fair! Why her? Why was this happening to his beautiful, caring, wonderful Jane? *Only the good die young.*

When they had told her that the last round of treatment hadn't worked, and there was now nothing more they could do, Ian had felt the last bit of fight drain from him. She was terminal. They talked of end-of-life planning. Palliative care. Hospices. He couldn't listen to any of it.

Jane had spent a lot of time talking to the hospital Chaplain, who gave her strength, if not hope. Ian had only met him briefly and found him to be upbeat and charismatic. Friendly and supportive. Exactly what Jane had needed, and just what Ian was afraid he was failing to provide.

It was through him that Jane had found this place. He had introduced her to Reverend Francis Rodwell, who had told her about Megan, dangling that irresistible hope of a cure in front of her. Ian couldn't help worrying how Jane would feel when she realised that this, too, would fail to save her.

He poured himself another cup of water, pressing the plastic to his lips. A strangled cry echoed from the bedroom beyond. *Jane!* He dropped the cup, water splashing on the floor and up his leg. He shouldn't have left her alone in there.

Bursting through the doors, he stopped dead in his tracks. Jane was standing beside the bed. She was holding herself up on the bed frame, but she was standing! On her own. She hadn't stood unassisted for over six months. Her cry had been one of pure happiness. Tears were streaming down her cheeks, but she was laughing. Ian couldn't believe his eyes.

"Janey? Are you okay?"

It was a ridiculous question. She was standing up! He couldn't remember the last time she'd looked this okay.

"Megan darling," Anne intoned, still gripping her daughter's hand, and wrapping her other hand over Jane's. "Give Jane the strength she needs to cast out this illness for good. In the name of God, Megan. Use your gift to heal her pain."

Ian took a step towards Jane, arm outstretched to offer support, but she shook her head. She wanted to do this alone. She reached up to her side and unclipped the rigid, plastic back brace.

"Jane, no," Ian said, unable to hide the panic in his voice.

The brace was the only thing that was giving her cancer-weakened spine any support. Without it, her vertebrae could collapse into each other. She shook her head again as the brace dropped to the floor beside her feet. She didn't even flinch. If anything, she stood a little taller.

She smiled at him, eyes wide with joy and relief, as though her pain had fallen away along with the back-brace. Even Ian had to admit that something miraculous had happened to his wife.

He walked towards her, hands outstretched as she took a tentative step away from the bed. She lifted and placed her feet with cautious precision. She laughed. An explosion of delight as she took his hands in hers, looking him in the eye.

Her eyes glistened, dancing over his face. She looked radiant. She took another step. And another. Ian stepping slowly backwards, leading and encouraging her like a toddler taking her first steps. They both laughed. They both cried. Nothing else existed but this single beautiful moment.

"It worked," she half-whispered. "I've been healed."

And Ian believed her.

JANE AND IAN had talked all the way home in the car. An excited buzz of disbelief, amazement, and elation. Every time Ian had glanced across at her, she'd been glowing, radiating happiness. Her whole demeanour had changed.

Of course, they had no way of knowing yet what medical reaction her illness had actually had to the encounter with Megan, but Ian couldn't deny that something had happened. She had walked out of that house on her own two feet, resting on his arm, stepping slowly, but she had done it.

He didn't want to jinx anything by asking how she felt every few minutes. He was just enjoying seeing her so serene and so happy at the same time. Perhaps she had been right to believe. Maybe he needed to have a little more faith himself. If anything would convince him of an Almighty power, this would do it.

Now as they sat at their dining table, a delicious dinner devoured between them, a glass of wine in hand, old favourites playing on the stereo, Ian felt a sense of contentment he could scarcely define. He'd given up hope, and now he had his wife back. It felt more than he deserved. He was happy to sit back and listen to her give thanks for her miracle.

He'd even cast aside his cynicism and left a donation for Megan's foundation as the smallest thank you for the gift she had given them. Perhaps he had been too harsh in judging Anne's actions. What if there was some great plan, and Megan's gift was part of it? It would mean she'd always been destined to fall into a coma and use her life force to help others. He couldn't help but wonder if all of those that she helped were as deserving as his Jane. Were there that many good people out there?

"We could go back to that little house in Paris," Jane said, excitedly.

She'd been running through hundreds of possibilities all evening. Places and things they'd given up on ever seeing or doing again.

"That would be perfect, wouldn't it?" he replied.

It felt so strange, talking about a future the doctors had assured them was no longer theirs to enjoy. Wonderfully strange. Ian felt the long-held tension easing out of his body, too. He hadn't realised quite how much of his energy was being absorbed by worrying about Jane. Or rather, worrying about life without Jane.

She used the corner of the table to help her stand up. A movement so sudden and yet so cautious. She grinned at him.

"Come here," she said, holding a hand out to him.

For a moment, Ian wondered whether he was imagining all of this. This couldn't be happening, could it? He stood up and took her hand, realising now that it was their wedding song playing.

They slipped into an easy, slow dance, his arms around her waist, supporting her, just in case. As Etta James sang about her love finally coming along, he thought; *At Last. How appropriate.* He couldn't remember ever feeling happier.

She lifted her head to face him, and he leaned down, kissing her gently at first, and, when she responded, more passionately. Kissing, intimacy, passion. These, too, had all been off the cards. Ian felt his stomach tighten as though it was their first time.

When he lifted her and carried her to bed, she didn't complain. She was still painfully thin and light as a feather, but she felt more real than she had for a long time. She smiled as he laid her on the bed, lifted her own hips to help him undress her. Sensual again, this time, rather than the functional, clinical way he had been preparing her for bed since she had lost the ability to undress herself comfortably.

He lay beside her, naked, excited, but feeling cautious. Was this the right thing for them to be doing? Shouldn't they wait for her to build her strength? She reached up and pulled him into another kiss. There would be no more waiting.

JANE WOKE HIM in the early hours, her body rigid with pain, too agonised to even cry out. It was just coming up to five in the morning. They had been asleep for hours, but he leapt straight out of bed, dialled the ambulance and got her a shot of morphine. The response was automatic. As though the events of the previous day and night had been nothing more than a dream. This was the way they knew things to be—Jane in inconsolable agony, and Ian desperately trying to help, but knowing it was no use.

He dressed her in loose-fitting clothes, doing his best to console her as he lifted her body. She felt frail again. Broken. Destroyed. What had happened? He had genuinely felt a change in her; he was sure it wasn't just wishful thinking. They had made love, for God's sake! Had he done this to her? Had he made it worse?

As they waited for the ambulance to arrive, Ian held her hand in his, whispering over and over again:

"I'm so sorry."

Whether he was sorry for her pain, sorry that nothing had changed the way they believed it had, or sorry for himself and his own shattered hopes and dreams, he couldn't say. He was just so very sorry.

Ian only let go of Jane's hand briefly as they loaded her into the ambulance. Grabbing their bags, still packed and ready from countless overnight stays in the hospital, he joined her in the back, bracing himself as the vehicle lurched into action, the muted sound of the sirens piping overhead.

Once they were underway, he sat by her side again. There was nothing for the paramedics to do apart from get her to the hospital quickly.

"I'm sorry, Janey," he said again.

"Shh," she replied.

A tear trickled down her temple from the corner of her eye. He wiped it away gently. In all the time she had been ill, through all the treatments and every indignity they brought, he had never seen her cry. He knew she must have done, but she had never let him see it.

That single tear broke his heart. Because she wasn't crying about the pain, or because she knew she was dying. She was crying because God had deserted her. She had given herself wholeheartedly, and He had abandoned her. Her faith counted for nothing in the face of this cancer. She would die anyway. And it was this understanding that had finally broken her spirit.

"I love you so much," he whispered, close to her ear. The familiar smell of her illness was back, lingering on her skin, stealing her from him.

Her lips opened, as though she might reply, but she didn't. A long, slow breath rattled through her teeth. She would die tonight, and there was nothing he, nor God could do about it.

He had been preparing for this moment for months, ever since the doctors had sat them down together and told them that there was nothing more they could do. And now it was time. He wanted to curl into her. Go with her. Hold her close and give her every bit of life that still coursed through his own body. He had promised himself that he would be strong. He'd sworn to her he'd be fine. But, right now, he was neither.

A fierce, burning anger consumed him. Not because he was losing her. Nor because of cancer's indiscriminate destruction. But because they had stripped her of the one thing she held so dear: her faith. She had believed she was healed, they both had. And those frauds had let her believe it.

As he gripped Jane's hand, resting his head on her chest, listening to the faintest breath struggling in and out of her wracked body, he vowed he would make them pay for their deceit if it was the last thing he did.

1st December

ALEX RIPLEY HAD never thought of her flat as unwelcoming, but she'd had the strangest feeling since she'd arrived home after her last case. Somehow, it didn't feel like home anymore. It was empty and cold. A stark reminder that she was still alone—still waiting for news either way of her husband, John, missing in action in Afghanistan.

She'd been back for over a week now and still hadn't worked up the energy to get on with even the simplest things. She hated food shopping anyway, but there was only so long she could survive on what was in the cupboards.

Besides the domestic banalities, she also had work to be getting on with, calls to return, a book to promote. And yet, she couldn't find the motivation to do any of it. Whether it was fatigue, lethargy, or the lingering complications of her ordeal in the Lake District, she didn't know.

The haunting echoes of the strange case she'd just finished up in the Cuckoo Wood still disturbed her sleep. Perhaps coming so close to dying herself had thrown too harsh a spotlight on her current situation. What if she had died up there? She would never find out what had happened to John.

As lucky as she'd been to escape her near-drowning, the residual damage to her lungs was giving her trouble breathing, especially at night. Maybe she should have listened to the doctors and stayed in the hospital a little longer. She had insisted that she would recover quicker at home, but ever since she'd got back she'd felt unsettled here. Like something was missing. And of course, it was. Not something, but someone.

Lying on her sofa, clutching a photograph of John to her chest was not helping her state of mind, but she couldn't put it down. She had been so sure she'd seen him up there in the Lakes, and the strange vision of him still haunted her. She'd imagined the whole thing, of course, but he'd felt so real. It had given her a glimmer of hope that John was still alive and made her miss him all the more.

The whole case had unsettled her more than most. An old friend and forensic officer in the Lake District, Emma Drysdale, had called her in to help them understand why a spate of teenage suicides in a deeply religious, old-fashioned village were being attributed to a series of angel sightings. Within a week of arriving in the remote village of Kirkdale, Ripley had discovered a community so caught up in their faith and their past secrets, and so fearful of so-called contagious sin, that they had refused to see what was going on. It had taken an outsider to uncover the truth, and Ripley had nearly died doing it. Maybe it was time for a change of career.

Her phone rang again, startling and shrill in the silent room. She let it ring through to the answer machine, listening to the message, in John's voice, declaring that neither of them were there. It was only true for one of them. She knew she should change it, but she hadn't been able to bring herself to delete his voice yet. Superstition, perhaps.

The caller hung up without leaving a message. She'd been inundated with calls from journalists about her new book, which had hit the shelves the week before she'd gone up to the Lakes. It felt like a lifetime ago. The culmination of two years investigating various angles on healing miracles and faith healing.

As usual, her sceptical point of view had ruffled a lot of feathers on the way. Judging from the reviews so far, and the number of messages on her answer machine still waiting for a reply, this book was causing as much of a stir as her previous ones. Her reputation as a no-nonsense debunker of miracles was intact, as proved by the now familiar outpouring of hate and abuse on social media.

The answer machine had barely reset when her mobile phone rang. Someone was keen to speak to her. She levered herself up on an elbow, checking her mobile on the coffee table in front of her. The screen told her the caller was Neil Wilcox.

She snatched the handset up. Neil had served with her husband, John. He had been one of the few from

John's squadron who had visited her after they'd all come home without their Captain. He and his wife had shared enough dinners, barbecues and drinks with them to call him a friend, though she'd only seen him a handful of times since John had gone missing. She knew he blamed himself. She also knew that he was one of the few who was convinced that John had been taken alive.

"Neil, I'm here," she said.

"Alex," Neil said, relief and urgency in his voice. "Thank god. I just tried your home number..."

"I was screening calls," she admitted. "What's going on?"

She could already feel that familiar flutter in her stomach. The fear, which always accompanied a call from one of John's colleagues, that this would be the moment that she found out he was gone for good.

They had counselled her early on to prepare for the worst and, though she would swear she was expecting to hear of his death, she couldn't deny that she still clung on to the hope that he would come home alive.

"We've had a communication," Neil said, tentatively, as though sensing her anxiety. "We can't say for certain that it's from John, but it's looking increasingly likely."

Ripley felt her legs crumple beneath her, sliding her back down the wall until she was sitting on the cold tiled floor, the plastic handset creaking in her tightening grip, her stomach turning somersaults. She'd had a similar call once before, and it had turned out to be a false alarm, so she was wary of getting her hopes up. But Neil Wilcox, of all people, knew what she'd been going through, and she was sure that he wouldn't have called unless they felt there was credibility to their intelligence.

"We were wondering if you'd heard anything yourself? Over the last couple of weeks?"

She was his wife. Of course he'd try to call her if he could. But John was a military man. If his resources were limited, he would prioritise getting a message to the people most likely to save him.

Ripley couldn't help thinking that she *had* heard from John in the past couple of weeks, just not in a way she could share with Neil. She had believed so strongly that he had been with her in the Cuckoo Wood. She'd heard his voice calling her name.

"No, I've heard nothing," she said. "But... he's alive? I mean... What kind of communication?"

"Short. Just a few seconds. We're sure it was him." Neil sounded urgent. Excited and nervous. Ripley felt the same energy catching her, too. The faint call of hope. "You're sure you've heard nothing? No strange messages? Even if he didn't speak..."

She felt like he'd punched her in the gut. There had been a message on the machine when she got back. No one had spoken. Just background noise from an unknown number. She'd dismissed it as an accidental call.

"There was something. A message while I was away. But it sounded like a pocket call."

"Do you still have it?" Neil asked.

"Yes," she breathed. She'd deleted none of the messages yet. "What's going on, Neil? What did he say?"

"It's classified," he said, sounding frustrated. "But we're sure it's him, and if it is, then as of two weeks ago, he's still alive."

His voice slid off towards the end of his sentence as though he'd suddenly remembered who he was talking to.

"I don't want to get your hopes up unnecessarily," he said. "But we've got a good feeling about this. That's why I wondered if you'd heard anything that may help us. Obviously we're chasing it up with the intelligence unit on the ground out there. If there is even the slightest hint we've found him, we're going in."

"Jesus," said Ripley. "I don't know what to say, Neil."

"Just check that message again and call me back, okay?"

She hung up and breathed out, trying to calm her racing heart. The indicator on the answer machine told her she had twenty-two messages to get through and she couldn't for the life of her remember where in the sequence the mystery call had been. She reached up to start playback but stopped short. Her hand was shaking.

She stood up, feeling a slight rush of blood to the head, and headed to the kitchen. She splashed water on her face and pulled a bottle of white wine out of the fridge. Carrying the bottle and a large glass back into the lounge, she slumped down on the sofa, filled the glass, and put the bottle on the side table beside the answer machine.

Her finger rested on the play button, summoning the emotional strength to press it. Had that message really been from John? Had he tried to reach her first? She had skipped past it as soon as she realised it wasn't an intentional call. What if he'd said something? Taking a deep breath, she pressed play, pen poised over the notepad balanced on her knee.

The first couple of messages were from her agent from before she'd gone away. She deleted them almost as soon as she heard who it was. She'd already responded to those. The next three were from journalists, which she skipped through too.

Another beep followed by the automated voice telling her that this message had been left at ten fifty p.m. on Monday the twenty-third of October. The day she'd driven up to the Lake District to meet Emma Drysdale.

"Dr Ripley? I hope you don't mind me calling so soon. This is Ian Hewitt. From the television show yesterday."

God, she'd meant to call him back and had completely forgotten. Ripley had met Ian Hewitt on a Sunday morning debate programme about faith healers, and he had told her a rather disturbing story about a young girl in Wales who could, according to her mother, cure people of the worst illnesses, despite the girl having been in a coma for eight years herself.

It was exactly the kind of case that Ripley would have loved to feature in her book and, though it had come too late to include, Ian Hewitt's plight and Megan's story fascinated her. She wrote his name in capitals on her notepad and circled it twice. She would call him back later.

The next message made her heart leap into her throat. The automated voice told her it had come in on the thirty-first of October. Halloween. The night Ripley had nearly drowned. And the night she thought she'd seen John in the wood.

The message began after the beep, and Ripley leaned closer to the machine to hear. Crackling static. A pulse-like buzz getting louder. Shuffling. Voices in the background. This was the point that Ripley had skipped the message on before. Now she held her breath in anticipation. A staccato rat-tat-tat of what sounded like automatic gunfire burst out and a distant voice shouted something in a language she couldn't understand. Her heart was pounding. Then a voice she recognised. Just one word. *'Lexi?'* It's what John always called her. It's what she thought she'd heard that night in the woods. A click followed by another long beep signalled the end of the message.

She listened to it again another four times before she called Neil back.

"It was him," she told him. "He said my name. It was him."

"I'm coming over."

NEIL WILCOX LOOKED older than she'd remembered, his hair greyer, his eyes more tired. It had only been a couple of years since she'd last seen him and the transformation came as something of a shock. It hadn't crossed her mind before, how John might have changed in the time he'd been missing, but if Neil Wilcox had aged this much, so must John have. She quickly shut down the thought of other changes John might have suffered. It didn't bear thinking about.

"Come in," Ripley said, opening her arms to greet him.

He kissed her cheek as they embraced. She should have made more of an effort to keep in touch with John's friends, but she found it too hard to see them without him by her side. The elephant in the room made every encounter almost unbearable.

"How are you doing, Alex?"

She smiled. Ordinarily, the inquiry had undertones of other, unutterable questions. 'How are you coping without John?' or 'How can you just carry on as normal, knowing your husband is missing?'. Ripley hated the concerned expression that usually accompanied the enquiry, too, but tonight was different. Because tonight there was hope. Hope of finding John alive. Hope of bringing him home. If ever she was likely to call anything a miracle, it would be seeing John again. Waking up beside him. Being allowed to live again.

"I'm trying not to get too excited," she said, closing the door behind him. "But this is the closest thing I've had to good news since John disappeared. I'm not sure I can take it in."

"We're a long way from getting him home, yet," Wilcox said. Ever the pragmatist.

"I know, I know," she acknowledged, as he followed her through into the lounge. "But I've just heard my husband's voice for the first time in over three years and I think that constitutes a glimmer of hope."

"Absolutely," he replied.

His eyes, despite the new lines, were still the same vivid blue, fading to pale grey around his pupils. Ripley had always found them stunning. He smiled, resolutely.

"Let's have a listen then."

She queued up the message on the answer machine and pressed play. Despite the quietness of the room, they both huddled close to the machine, looking at each other as the message played. When it ended, he leaned across and played it again.

"I'll need to take this with me," he said, tapping the answer machine. "Get our specialists to analyse the message, see what they can pull out of that background noise."

"It's not much to go on, is it?" she asked, fearing that, in the end, it wouldn't get them any closer to finding him.

"You'd be surprised what these guys can do," he said.

She unplugged the machine and bundled the cables up with it, but hesitated to hand it over. The greeting message was the last recording she had of John's voice, and she was suddenly gripped by an irrational fear of losing it. It was why she'd never got rid of the machine in the first place.

"I'll get it back to you exactly as it is now," he said, as though reading her mind. "Don't worry."

"What if he calls again, and I miss it?"

He dug into a small backpack at his feet and produced an old and basic replacement.

"Got you covered," he said, triumphantly. "But you really should think about dragging yourself into the modern age, you know. Nobody uses these things anymore."

He declined her offer of coffee, both of them acknowledging the urgency of getting what information they could from the message.

"We'll have a drink when John's home," he said. "Okay?"

It was intended to reassure her that they would handle it, but Ripley still couldn't quite believe it would happen. As with everything in her life, she'd believe it when she saw it.

"Thanks, Neil."

She stayed in the doorway watching him until his car turned out of the end of the street. The evening was already drawing in. Short days, long nights. More time to think. Never a good thing. Perhaps she should call a friend and head out. She needed a distraction, or she would go mad thinking about John.

The loud ringing of her landline startled her. Her breath caught in her throat. *Could it be John?* She slammed the door and dashed for the handset, trying to compose herself as she snatched it up.

"Hello?"

"Good afternoon," a voice said, official and flat. "Would it be possible to speak to Dr Alex Ripley?"

Ripley bristled. If this was another journalist trying to get a quote out of her to go in one of their reviews, they could get lost.

"Speaking," she snapped.

"This is Detective Dylan Harding from Rhosfaelog Police," he said.

Ripley felt herself relax. She'd never heard of the Rhosfaelog Police, but she was pretty sure this was nothing to do with John, nor was it likely to be about her book.

"What can I do for you Detective?" she asked politely.

"I've got a gentleman by the name of Ian Hewitt in one of our holding cells."

"Ian Hewitt?" she asked, surprised. "What's happened?"

And what does it have to do with me?

"He's fine," the Detective said. "It's just, well, there's been an accusation against him, and he's currently helping us with our enquiries."

"Right..." said Ripley, waiting for more.

"The problem is, Doctor Ripley, he's asking for you. He says he won't talk to us unless he can see you first."

2nd December

EVEN THOUGH SHE had assured Detective Harding that she would come down first thing in the morning, Ripley had spent most of the previous evening deliberating whether to go to Rhosfaelog at all.

She was still feeling battered from her last case, and she didn't think she had the energy to help anyone else right now. Finally, in the early hours, she'd decided it would be a good distraction while she waited for news from Neil Wilcox. Besides, she had promised Ian Hewitt that she would help him when she'd first met him and she felt guilty that she hadn't followed up on that promise.

Detective Harding hadn't been able to go into too many details over the phone, apart from that they'd brought Ian Hewitt in for questioning after Anne Shields had accused him of harassing them and breaking in to her house.

From her brief conversation with Ian when they'd met, Ripley knew he was angry and upset about his wife's death and blamed Anne Shields and her daughter for the way she'd died. She couldn't help worrying that he'd gone seeking his own justice. If only she'd called him straight back when she'd got his message, maybe she could have stopped him. Though she couldn't blame herself for Ian Hewitt's predicament, she could at least try to help him now.

And, if she was honest, Megan Shields's story fascinated her, and she was keen to see her in person. Especially in the light of her past two years' research.

Ripley had come across some totally outrageous claims and some equally baffling ones. Some outright frauds and some almost convincing examples of unlikely cures. In most cases, misdiagnosis, unexpected reactions to medical treatment, or a simple placebo effect could explain even the most convincing miracle cures. Ripley had found no proof of divine intervention. But then, she'd found no evidence against it either.

The business models surrounding faith healing were both controversial and emotive. Of all the types of miracle that Ripley had been asked to investigate over the years, this was the one that most demanded unwavering faith from all participants, regardless of the outcome. It was also the most difficult to prove— there were so many extenuating circumstances, other influences, and plausible explanations for seemingly impossible change. It made bringing charges against fraudsters difficult and often saw people placing their full trust in a practitioner's gift at the expense of genuine medical treatment.

Ian Hewitt's accusation against Anne and Megan Shields was simple. He believed that they had hastened his wife's death through their deception, and they had broken her heart in the process. There was no question that Ian's wife, Jane, had been dying. But he believed she would have lived longer, as the doctors had promised, had she not believed in Megan's gift and tried to walk. Jane had died so quickly after her alleged healing, there could be no other explanation.

Having met him, Ripley couldn't believe that Ian would actually harm them. He was a slight, gentle man, over-cautious in his movements and mannerisms. The idea of him breaking into their house seemed ludicrous, but she didn't really know him or what he was capable of. Why did he want to speak to her before he'd answer the police's questions?

Ripley had seen plenty of cases where people felt angry that they had been duped or that a so-called healer had taken advantage of their faith to con them out of their hard-earned cash, but Ian had told her already that there had been no compulsion to pay for a meeting with Megan. In fact, he'd admitted that they had made a sizeable donation because they had been so happy that Jane had appeared to be cured.

From the little she'd heard, Ripley had already warned him that he would have a hard time proving fraud, or making any legal charges stick. All he could really do was publicly discredit Megan and perhaps make others question a mother who would use her sick daughter for financial gain. Ripley couldn't deny that she was excited to meet them both.

The drive to Anglesey was fairly straightforward. She'd waited for the rush hour to calm down in

Manchester before hitting the road, and now, just under two hours later, she was crossing the Four Mile Bridge which connected Anglesey to Holy Island. It was fitting that she would find a case like this in a place so steeped in religious history.

Holy Island was so named because of the high concentration of stone circles, burial chambers, standing stones and other religious sites housed there. Ripley had never visited, but it had been on her list for a while. Another good reason for agreeing to see Ian Hewitt, she reasoned.

The salty tang of the sea hung in the air, mixing with the cold drizzle and blurring her windscreen. According to her sat-nav, she wasn't far from Rhosfaelog now. It had been so long since she'd seen the sea and she had to admit she was looking forward to striding out across a long beach, with the cold wind whipping her hair around her face. She loved beaches in winter. When they were empty and quiet and not full of holidaymakers.

She'd booked herself into a cosy looking holiday cottage with an unpronounceable Welsh name on a secluded bay for a couple of nights. Just enough time to see Ian Hewitt and meet Megan and her mother before heading home again. The sea air might even be good for her ailing lungs, which were still recovering from her near-drowning up in the Lake District.

The road was a narrow single track, bordered by low hedges over which the landscape opened out onto vast fields, dotted here and there with white-walled houses, all with the same grey slate roofs.

The sea filled the horizon, white horses dancing on solid grey. A small church on the right, with a few cars lining the slip road leading to its gate. On the left, a sign on a garden wall advertised a cottage and studio to rent. *Nice idea*, she thought. *In a different life.*

She passed the pub she'd considered staying in, before she'd found out they were full. The White Horse. An appropriate name given the panoramic view of the choppy sea they'd boasted about on their website. According to her instructions, the turning to her little cottage would be a few hundred yards further down the road. It was a bumpy drive down a very narrow track, but the blurb had promised that it was a short, easy walk back along the cliffs to the pub where Ripley had planned to eat that evening.

She almost sailed past the turning, it was so narrow. She swung the old Audi onto the tracks at the last moment and the suspension gave a disgruntled squeal.

As she slowly picked her way over the bumps and holes, the cottage come into view, with a battered green Land Rover Defender parked at an angle in front of it. A short woman in a yellow sou'wester hopped out and waved cheerily, beaming as Ripley pulled up beside her.

"You must be Dr Ripley," she said, her voice had a wonderful sing-song Welsh lilt which made Ripley smile. "I'm Bron."

"Alex," said Ripley, shaking the woman's hand.

"How was your journey? All right? You found us okay?" Bron didn't wait for an answer, or stop to draw breath. "Good, right then. Follow me, let's get you in out of the cold. I've had the heating on. Tried to warm the place up a bit. We rarely have guests in the winter, look, so I usually turn everything off. It's no problem, like. Just may need to get a fire going. If you feel the cold that is."

Ripley smiled to herself as she slung her bag over her shoulder and followed Bron up to the heavy wooden door, waiting whilst she struggled with the lock, providing a running commentary throughout.

"It's stiff, the lock. You've got to wiggle it, see? I've told Roger to get it fixed, but he doesn't bloody listen, does he?"

She nodded dismissively over her shoulder at the man in the driver's seat of the Land Rover—the much maligned Roger probably gave up listening years ago, when he realised he'd never get a word in edgeways, anyway.

"There we are!"

The door swung open inwards with a low creak, scuffing on the stone floor. Ripley followed Bron into a narrow hallway, with two doors leading off it, and a small flight of stairs straight ahead.

"Right, front room through there, kitchen through here. Bedroom upstairs. There's a loo out the back, but don't worry, we've had a bathroom put in upstairs, too. We're not quite in the dark ages! There's wood by the fire. First bag is free. If you run out, just shout and I'll get Roger to drop some in. Five pounds a sack. Extra blankets are in the cupboard in the bedroom."

Ripley poked her head through the lounge door. It was a cosy looking little space, dominated by a huge old fireplace, with a tatty but clean sofa on one side and a battered leather armchair pushed into the corner.

"I've left some leaflets, for days out and so on. And there are maps on the shelf for walking. Are you a walker?"

She looked dismissively at Ripley's black jeans and soft shoes. Not exactly rough weather gear.

"No," Bron answered her own question, almost managing to hide the eye roll. "Well, never mind. There's loads of old boots and coats out the back if you fancy an adventure."

Ripley smiled.

"You passed the pub on your way, did you?" Bron continued. "They do a good supper in there. Bit fancy for my liking, but good for you visitors. Tell them Bron sent you and they might even give you free pudding. It's pricey, mind. For round here, anyway. City prices. Right. Look. Lovely. Here's the key. My number's on the board in the kitchen. Shout if there's anything else you need. There's nothing goes on around here that I don't know about. I'll leave you to it."

"Thanks," Ripley said, as Bron bustled back out through the front door in a whirlwind of cold sea air. *Hectic.*

Ripley dropped her bag and set about exploring the cottage. It was exactly as she'd imagined it from the pictures. Small. Quaint. Rustic. A nod to guest luxuries, but not enough to force the price up. It was perfect. Even if was on the cold side and had an old, damp smell that reminded her of childhood holidays in her grandparent's beach house in Cornwall.

Having checked the rest of the place out while the kettle was boiling, she stood in the bay window in the lounge, looking out at the rolling waves clasping a steaming mug of instant coffee, and smiled. She was looking forward to striding out over those cliffs later, battered by the wind, with the fine spray from the sea settling on her hair and face. And she was also looking forward to arriving in the warm pub and eating a hearty meal with a nice glass of wine. She was doing everything she could to stop herself thinking about Neil Wilcox, and the call from John, and what it could all mean, but she needed more distraction than this.

She checked her watch. Time to talk to Ian Hewitt.

THE POLICE STATION was small, but easy enough to find. A compact stone building nestling between two old houses, each of which had dates inscribed above them of 1900 and 1905, respectively. The police station looked like it dated from around the same time.

Inside, Ripley found a clean-cut young desk-sergeant struggling with a sudoku puzzle, tongue clamped between his teeth, brow furrowed. He looked up and shuffled the puzzle book under some papers as she approached the desk.

"Can I help?" he chirped.

"I'm Dr. Alex Ripley," she said. "I had a call from a Detective Harding asking me to come down."

"Oh. Righto," he said, running his finger down a handwritten list on a clipboard in front of him. Ripley resisted the temptation to point out her name.

"Ah, right, yes," he said. "Dr. Ripley. Gotcha. Take a seat, will you? I'll give him a shout now."

Ripley retired to a standard issue plastic chair while he scuttled off through a door at the back. She heard him shouting the detective's name, before coming back in and straightening his jacket.

"He'll be down in a minute," he said with a formal little nod.

Ripley smiled. A series of missing persons posters pinned to the noticeboard beside her showed photographs of a handful of men and women who had disappeared in the last few years. Some of the posters were old, yellowing and dogeared around the edges— cases that had lingered unsolved for too long, the photographs unlikely to bear much resemblance to the missing anymore.

A newer, cleaner sheet showed a smiling woman in full walking gear. Sally Anne Jones. Last seen on the seventh of November according to the poster. She'd been on a walking holiday on Holy Island, apparently. Not even a month ago, but the poster was already partially covered over by another flyer—an advertisement for a group prayer meeting with Megan Shields, to be held at the All Souls Meeting House. 'All Welcome!' it shouted in bold type. *I bet.*

Ripley pulled out her phone and took a quick photograph of the flyer so that she could check the details later. The Desk Sergeant looked up sharply at the fake shutter sound her phone made.

"No photography," he said flatly, frowning at her.

"Sorry," she said. "I don't have a pen and I wanted to get the details of this event."

She pointed to the board. He raised an eyebrow, but went back to his work. Ripley checked the photo and tucked her phone away just as a tall man in a charcoal suit ducked through the door, smiling at her.

"Dr. Ripley," he said, stretching his hand out. "I'm Detective Harding. Thank you so much for coming over."

His voice was deep and scratchy, his unmistakably Welsh accent lyrical but dry. When Ripley stood to shake his hand, she realised quite how tall he was. Unusual for a Welshman. She was no slouch herself, and yet she only came up to his shoulders. His hands were like shovels, but his grip was gentle. He obviously had no need to prove how strong he was.

"That's okay," she said. "I'm not sure how I can help. I'm afraid I don't actually know Mr Hewitt very well."

"No. So I understand," he said, as he held the door open for her to follow him through into the back of the station. "It's just that he's refusing to comment on any of these accusations unless he's spoken to you first."

"Can you tell me what he's supposed to have done?"

"It's probably best you talk to him," Harding said. "I'll put you in an interview room. It's nicer than the holding cells."

"Has he been charged?"

"Not yet, but he has been arrested."

"Has he asked for a lawyer?"

"No," he said. "Only you. To be honest, he needed to sober up first, anyway."

He showed her into a small, windowless interview room, with a metal table and a pair of plastic chairs. Ripley took off her coat and folded it over the back of one of the chairs.

"I'll get him for you," Harding said. "Can I bring you a tea or coffee? Some water?"

"Coffee would be lovely, thanks," Ripley replied. "Milk, no sugar."

She sat at the table, hands folded in front of her. Doors slammed out in the corridor beyond. A camera mounted in the corner of the room pointed down at the table. She wondered if it was recording. Surely they would have to tell her if it was? Probably not.

She knew she'd promised to help him, but this was outside her skill set. If Ian Hewitt had been arrested, he needed a lawyer, not a doctor of theology. Too late to leave now. That would be even worse. She would just have to advise him to get some proper representation and see if she could get him to talk about what had happened.

When the door opened again, Ian shuffled in behind Detective Harding. It had been less than a month since she'd seen him, and he'd noticeably lost weight from his already slight frame. He had obviously made an effort for the television show she'd met him on, but he looked smaller than she remembered him. Grey skinned, hair thin and lank, dark bags beneath his eyes, a cold sore on his lip. He looked fragile and lost, and her heart broke for him. The change in him was made all the more evident because he was being led in by the man mountain that was Detective Harding.

Ian lifted his bloodshot eyes to meet hers and smiled weakly. He had been crying in his cell, she had no doubt.

"Thank you," he mumbled. "Thank you so much."

He tried to approach, hand outstretched, but Harding put an arm out to block him.

"Take a seat please, Mr Hewitt."

Ian looked crestfallen, but sat down obligingly. The young Desk Sergeant pushed the door open and delivered a polystyrene cup of scalding coffee and another of water to Ripley. Nothing for Ian.

"Thanks," she said as he placed two miniature containers of milk beside the coffee cup.

"No bother," he said.

"I'll leave you both to talk," said Harding. "And then perhaps we can get on with this interview, Mr Hewitt."

He pulled the door closed, the soft click of the automatic lock hanging in the still air.

"I'm so sorry to drag you into all this," Ian blurted out. "I didn't know who else to call."

"Mr Hewitt, I—" Ripley began.

"Ian, please. Call me Ian," he said.

"Okay, Ian," she said. "What's happening? Last time I saw you, you were talking about pressing charges, and now you've been arrested. What's going on?"

He sighed, shoulders slumped.

"I didn't do what they're accusing me of."

"Which is?"

"Anne Shields claims that I broke into their house and tried to interfere with Megan's life support machines."

"You went back to their house?"

"No!"

He closed his eyes for a moment. She let the silence hang there. He wanted to talk.

"Okay. Yes, I went back. A few times."

"Oh Ian," she couldn't help feeling disappointed in him. Harassing them in their own home would not help any charges he may bring to stick.

"But not like she's saying," he said quickly. "I didn't go inside. They would never let me in."

"I can't say I'm surprised, given what you said about them on television."

Ian shrugged.

"So what happened on the day they say you broke in?"

"I was supposed to meet someone there. A woman. Caroline Clifton," he said. "She wanted to bring her own charges against them. We thought we might be able to work together. Anyway, we'd arranged to meet at their house and have it out with them, but she obviously got there first because by the time I arrived, she was already being thrown out."

"Thrown out?" Ripley asked.

"Yeah, they've got a guy on the door now. It wasn't like that when Jane and I went. There was just a young assistant to greet us. Now there's a proper doorman. Like a bouncer."

"Right. Okay," Ripley said, taking this in. "What happened then?"

"Well, I went after her," he said. "She'd driven off quickly, but I could see she was upset, so I followed her. I caught up with her on the road out of town. She'd pulled into a lay-by and she was just sitting there crying. She wouldn't talk to me, but she gave me her number and told me to call her later."

"And then?"

"Then I went back to the house. Their house. I tried to see Anne Shields, but they said she wasn't there. Which was a lie. So I stood outside, shouting at her. I knew she could hear me. I told her they wouldn't get away with it. Her henchman told me to leave, or they'd call the police. So I left. Eventually."

"Did anyone see you leave? Apart from members of the household or their staff?"

"Yes, there was a neighbour at her window. She'd have seen me walk away."

"So she'll also be a witness that you were harassing them."

"And I don't deny doing that," he protested. "But I didn't go back later. I didn't break in!"

"And can anyone vouch for you?"

"No," he muttered. "I don't think so. I was on my own most of the night."

His voice caught and Ripley remembered that he was still grieving for his wife and he would be feeling the keen bite of that loneliness. She knew how he felt.

"Did you call anyone? Send any texts? Perhaps you could use your phone records to prove you didn't go back."

"I honestly don't remember what I did." He hung his head low. "I know I tried to call Caroline Clifton again a couple of times across the evening, but she never answered. I haven't spoken to her yet. But it's all a bit hazy, if I'm honest. I've been drinking a lot recently."

"I understand," Ripley said. And she really did. "But you're sure you didn't go back there?"

"I don't think I could have got there even if I'd wanted to. I was far too drunk."

"So why don't you just tell the police your side?"

"I didn't know what to do for the best," he admitted.

"Refusing to talk just makes you look guilty."

"I know that, but I didn't want to incriminate myself."

"You need to get a lawyer."

Ian looked up at her with a mix of pleading and fear. "Can't you help?"

"Even if I could, you'd still need a lawyer. These are serious charges, and the police have good grounds. Unless you can prove what you were doing, you'll need someone to help you plead your case."

Ian's shoulders sagged, head hanging low again. His hands shook slightly where they rested on the table.

"Do you think I have a case?" he asked, quietly, without looking up.

"Well, at the moment, it's your word against theirs," Ripley replied. "And you don't remember what you were doing and they have witnesses to place you there earlier..."

He stood up quickly, frustrated, chair clattering backwards, table shunted enough to spill some of her coffee.

"I don't mean this..." he waved his hand dismissively. "I mean Jane. Do I have a case against them for what they did to Jane? Because, as I see it, they're the ones in the wrong, not me. All this break-in nonsense is just them trying to make me look like I've lost the plot."

He held up his hands before she could interject.

"I know I stood outside their house, shouting the odds. I was drunk. And I'm sorry for that. But I didn't do this. Not what they're saying. I wouldn't even know how to start breaking into a house. Besides, that place is sealed up tighter than a gnat's chuff. Cameras inside and out. And alarmed doors. I know, *I'm sure,* I didn't do what that bitch is saying I did. They're just trying to shut me up."

He collapsed back into his seat, clearly not knowing what to do with the roiling emotions. Ripley could see his point. If he hadn't gone back and tried to assault Megan why would they be bringing charges? Unless it was to make him stop shouting his own accusations up and down the street. If they could discredit him, or, even better, get him restrained from coming anywhere near them, then he couldn't really harm them in court. His very tenuous case would simply be thrown out, and he'd be dismissed as a vengeful customer.

She studied him, trying to assess his state of mind. Was he lying to her? Was he lying to himself? Had he tried to hurt Megan? The truth was, Jane had been going to die anyway, and while Ripley didn't think Ian should be blaming them for her death, she remembered the fire in his eyes when he'd described how the whole incident had made his wife feel that her faith in God had been unjustified. She reached across the table and took one of his hands in hers, trying to bring him back into the moment.

"I can definitely help with your case against them," she said. "And I want to. But I can't promise it will come to anything. And in the meantime, you've got to deal with this properly. These are criminal charges you're facing here. If you're sure you did nothing wrong, get a lawyer in, and get them dropped or settled. I'll visit the family and see what I can find out, but I'm not promising anything."

"You'll help me then?" he asked.

"I'll look into it," Ripley replied.

RIPLEY LET DETECTIVE Harding guide her out of the interview room. He'd been at the door almost as soon as she'd signalled, so she was sure he had watched the whole conversation. And why not?

"You saw all that then?" she asked.

The question came out sharper than she'd intended. Harding nodded, no hint of contrition.

"So you know he's denying the charges?"

It was a rhetorical question, though Harding tilted another nod, before leading her off down the featureless corridor. One of the strip lights buzzed and flickered. The scuffed tiled floor worn thin down the middle. The awful bland paint colour that existed only in government buildings.

"For what it's worth, he's been through a lot recently," Ripley said.

"That's no excuse for breaking the law," Harding sniped.

"I agree." Her lip curled as she stared at the back of his head, already feeling protective of Ian Hewitt. "*If* he did what they said, of course. But he's denying it."

"Of course he is," Harding huffed.

"Listen, I'm not saying he hasn't been harassing them, he admits that. But there are extenuating circumstances. I just want him to get a fair hearing."

"He's caused nothing but trouble since he arrived in the village," Harding said. "I understand that he's grieving, but I've still got a job to do."

"Are you going to charge him?"

"I'd far rather he promised to go home and leave them alone, but from the sound of it, he's got no intention of doing that, so I think I will have to charge him, yes."

"His wife died, and he blames them," Ripley said. "He's angry and upset."

"Yes, but his wife died of cancer, Dr Ripley," he said. "It's no more Megan or Anne's fault than it is mine or yours. And, like I say, it's no excuse for his recent behaviour."

"I know," she agreed. "I just feel bad for him. This is the last thing he needs right now."

"Well," Harding said, opening a door and letting her pass through it. "If you can persuade him to drop his own claims and go home, I'm sure I could get them to drop theirs. It would save me a lot of hassle."

Ripley got the distinct impression that the young detective was trying to get out of a lot of tedious paperwork, but she wasn't quite prepared to convince Ian to drop his case. If Anne Shields *was* using her daughter's condition to defraud people, she wanted to be the one to expose it.

"I've promised to help him," she said. "I'll do my best."

She was being deliberately vague—she needed to see things here for herself first.

"Thanks," Harding said.

"In the meantime," Ripley said. "I've told him to get a lawyer, and I've advised him not to say any more until one gets here."

"Honestly," Harding said, "I don't care anymore. I called you over because I thought you might get him to see sense and go home. But if he insists on bringing this case against them anyway, then I've got no choice but to press the charges."

"What will happen to him?"

Harding stopped in front of the double doors at the end of the corridor and turned to face her, his expression one of weary resignation.

"It's his first offence, so he'll get bail. Conditional on him not going anywhere near that property or the family before his hearing. I'm sure they'll want a restraining order, anyway. We'll need to release him into the care of someone who can stop him doing anything stupid."

He looked at her, waiting. It took a moment for the penny to drop.

"Me?" she asked, surprised. "I was only going to stay for a day or so."

"It won't take more than two days to get a hearing," said Harding. "It's just, if he's a danger to the family, I'll have to keep him here on remand unless you're willing to look after him. He's got no one else. Besides, you might be able to talk him down, you know, with a bit more time. They aren't bad people, I swear."

Ripley had the sense that she'd been stitched up from the very first call. Why wouldn't she agree now? After all, she'd already driven across Wales to help. She obviously felt some kind of responsibility for Ian. Did she know him well enough to vouch for him? No, but it would certainly give her time to investigate Megan Shields more thoroughly.

"I'd like to help, but I've only rented a one bed cottage for a couple of days and I can hardly have him there, can I?"

"Where are you at? Bron's place, right?"

"That's right," Ripley said, trying to hide her surprise. She should've known. There are no secrets in small communities.

"Oh, she won't mind," Harding said. "I'll clear it with her, if you're happy to take him."

"But there's only one bedroom," Ripley protested.

"What, in Llan Y Barra?"

"Yes." *So that's how you pronounce it.*

"Nah, there's that whole bit out the back," Harding said, smiling. "The Doghouse, we call it. Only poor old Roger doesn't get sent there when there's guests staying."

Ripley couldn't help but smile herself. She'd walked right into this one. She'd only briefly wondered why they'd been so willing to wait for her to turn up and talk to Ian before they'd charged him. Now she knew. They needed a babysitter.

"You had this all planned, didn't you? You just needed someone here to look after him."

Harding smiled properly for the first time, all the way to the eyes.

"But not just anyone," he said. "Someone he would listen to, who would see all this for what it is, and make him see sense."

"And you think that's me?"

"You'll do."

"Fine," she shook her head at his impudence.

His smile was just the right side of cocky. He was pleased with himself. He held the door open and followed her through, walking side by side with her through the small reception room behind the front desk.

"We did check though," Harding said, suddenly serious. "He's genuinely got no one else. Even if he didn't break in, he's got no one to stand up for him."

"Do you think he did it?"

Harding shrugged.

"I can only go on the evidence, and at the moment it all stands in Mrs. Shields' favour. She's got a lot of support around here, too. People get protective when some stranger comes in levelling threats, especially against a defenceless child."

Ripley heard the veiled warning for her in that statement too. She had seen more than her fair share of small communities rallying themselves against the interfering stranger. Few quite so dramatically as the one she had just found herself investigating in the Lake District. She hoped this place would be different, but she feared her enquiries may be as unwelcome here as they had been in Kirkdale.

It made her more determined to help Ian if she could. If there was any evidence that Anne Shields had deliberately deceived Jane, at least it would constitute mitigating circumstances for Ian's actions.

Ripley made her excuses and left Detective Harding to his work. He'd promised to bring Ian over to her cottage later that evening, and she wanted a chance to explore the place before she found herself babysitting the poor guy.

RIPLEY WAS GRATEFUL for the stupid woolly hat she'd shoved in her bag at the last moment. Colourful candy stripes with a pompom on top, it was an unwanted and unexpected gift last Christmas from a friend who obviously didn't know her as well as she'd thought. She felt it made her look unnecessarily cheerful and quirky. But at least it was warm, and no one knew her here, so let them judge.

It was a bitterly cold, crisp day. Ice in the air made her nose run and her eyes water. She shoved her hands deep into the pockets of her long coat and tucked her chin into her collar. The arctic wind coming off the sea brought a familiar smell of salt, seaweed, and sand. A big gust caught her full in the face as she rounded a long bend in the narrow road.

She'd left the car in the pub car park, intending to head back there for lunch after she'd had a wander around the village. The houses closest to the pub were all large and detached, set back from the road in gardens enclosed by tall stone walls and high fences. No pavements out here, just a narrow road heading past the pub towards the car park by the beach. She'd set off in the other direction, towards the church.

A narrow pavement grew up out of the verge as the road straightened out. A neat row of cottages, small-windowed and compact, ranked along it. Their white-washed walls all stained grey with the years of being battered by the elements. Weather-beaten.

Short, mossy paths led from the pavement to each narrow front door, all painted that ubiquitous seaside blue. An old man in a heavy coat and flat cap, raking leaves from the small patch of grass in front of his cottage greeted her with a cheery 'hello'. *So far so pleasant.*

The church loomed into sight, steeple first. A small building in a small town, though its dark, flinty walls made it seem imposing against the grey sky. The whole church, including the small surrounding graveyard, was above road level on a grassy slope, forcing the observer to look up at it from any angle, lifting their eyes to the heavens in the process. Clever.

A stone wall which protected the graveyard from the road was mostly obscured by a long canvas banner with the words *God's Gift – The Power to Heal* printed across it. The same logo she had seen on the poster in the police station, advertising the group prayer meeting with Megan Shields. Sure enough, beside the words this time was an image of a young girl, seemingly asleep. *Megan.*

Ripley shook her head as she passed the banner— such cynical commercialism should not be on a church wall. She walked up the stone steps to bring herself up to ground level with the church. The door was ajar, and she could hear a gentle burble of voices within. Chatter, rather than worship. A high, joyous peal of laughter made her smile.

She pushed the door open a little further and peered into the body of the church. A handful of round tables nestled in the space behind the pews. Some kind of social morning was in full swing, complete with fat sponge cakes and the rich smell of coffee.

There were only a handful of empty seats, with the rest filled with well wrapped-up parishioners, pinkie-fingers held aloft as they sipped from fine cups. Some women knitting as they chatted, a couple playing dominoes, another reading a faded-covered, well-thumbed, romance novel.

A man in a thick-knit, heavily patterned jumper looked up at Ripley and smiled. He waved happily.

"Come on in," he said, his voice loud enough to carry clearly over the hubbub, which showed no sign of abating. The world was being put to rights here, just as it doubtless was every week.

Ripley pushed the door closed behind her and stepped into the church as the man headed over towards her, his arm outstretched, low and welcoming.

"Don't be shy," he said. "Everyone's welcome. There's coffee or tea in the urns, and there's plenty of cake left."

He shepherded her in without waiting for an answer, steering her towards a low trestle table, decked in a check cloth. A pair of silver catering urns sat side by side, radiating heat. China cups on matching saucers lined the table beside them, and a selection of cupcakes and sponge cakes sat beneath transparent plastic lids. Ripley's stomach rumbled spontaneously. The cakes looked great.

"Help yourself," he said. "They're all handmade. Not by me. There's no charge. Apart from a little friendly conversation and a smile."

"What a nice idea," Ripley said, as he handed her a cup. His hand trembled ever so slightly. His smile revealed yellowing teeth, overcrowded enough to overlap in places, forcing their way over each other at strange angles.

"Gets people together, doesn't it? I'm Colin, by the way. Can I tempt you?"

He lifted a plate of cupcakes towards her, and she chose a small one.

"Of course, if you feel compelled to make a contribution, we have a local fund we like to collect for, but there really is no obligation. We love new faces."

Ripley noticed that the collection box he was talking about also bore that same *God's Gift* logo. She filled her coffee cup and added a splash of milk. She fished a pound coin out of her pocket and dropped it into the container.

"Yes, I've seen some of her posters while I've been wandering around today," she said, treading carefully. "It must be quite a thing to have someone like her right here in the village."

She'd made her voice sound enthralled, excited by this miracle girl. She wasn't sure of Colin's role here, but she'd bet he was very much in favour of Megan Shields and her so-called healings.

"We are all very proud to call Megan one of our own," he said, leaning in too close, his hand patting her arm just briefly. An awkward gesture. His breath smelled of stale coffee, lingering cigarettes, bad gums.

"I'm sure."

"Are you in town for an audience yourself?"

"Not specifically, no," Ripley said, truthfully. "Although I would love to meet her. We all have something that needs fixing, don't we? Maybe I should look her up while I'm here."

"Oh, you definitely should," he gushed. He dashed across to a table near the door and came back with a leaflet which he thrust into Ripley's hand. "We will be holding a group prayer the day after tomorrow. At the All Souls Meeting Hall, just through the back there. We're very excited."

She looked at the leaflet, turning it over to glance at both sides.

"Having come all this way, I would far rather see her in person, if I could," Ripley said, folding the leaflet and dropping it into her pocket.

"Oh, but you will see her," Colin said, looking at her like she was stupid. "She will be right here in the hall, otherwise what would be the point?"

Again Ripley questioned how Anne Shields could wheel her daughter out in front of all these people, in her condition. It was barbaric. The poor girl.

"Oh, great," she said, masking her surprise with false enthusiasm. "Well, in that case, I may well drop in."

"Please do," said Colin. "It'll be busy, but we'll make room for everyone who wants to come. One way or another."

"Are you the vicar here, then?" Ripley asked.

"Oh, Lord no," Colin laughed explosively, and Ripley leaned back to get some clean air between them. "No, they let me do the odd sermon now and then, at peak times, you know? But no, Reverend Rodwell is your man. He'll be here this afternoon, if you were looking for him."

"Great," said Ripley, thinking it would be as good an excuse as any. "Perhaps I'll pop back then. Thanks for the coffee."

"Not to mention the cake," he said.

She waved the cupcake aloft in acknowledgement as she headed for the door.

Ripley took one bite of the cake as she strolled away and dropped the rest into a waste bin as she passed. It had a strange flavour she couldn't quite pinpoint. Mostly cheap margarine and sugar.

The rest of her walk was fairly uneventful. Apart from a fascinating array of gargoyles and grotesques which seemed to adorn even the plainest of buildings here, the village was quiet and unassuming. She passed a handful of people, all of whom greeted her with smiles and a cheerful 'afternoon'.

The clouds crowded the sky, making it seem later than it was, and Ripley cut back along the coast path to reach the pub in time to get lunch before they stopped serving. Out on the exposed cliff top the wind was particularly icy, burning her cheeks and rifling through her clothes. She stopped briefly to examine an ancient stone chamber rising out of the ground only fifty meters or so back from the cliff edge.

She had read about the many burial chambers, barrows and cairns dotting the coastline here, covering over four thousand years of history. This was one of the Neolithic ones, and though she'd read its name in the blurb about the town, she couldn't remember it now.

The chamber looked like a small, uniformly shaped, grassy hill from behind, but as she walked round it, she found two huge slabs of granite rock which formed an opening tall enough for Ripley to stand full height in.

She stood for a moment, touching the cold stone, feeling the history. These ancient structures always reminded her how fleeting our time on earth was. How much had come before and how much would follow.

Like so many of these monuments now, the entrance had been closed off by the council in latter years. A strong metal gate and a heavy padlock, doubtless stopping the local teenagers using it as a hangout and drinking den. Ripley used the torch on her phone to peer into the gloom beyond the gate, grateful to be out of the wind for a moment.

She could make out a large open chamber inside, with smaller rooms carved out around the perimeter. The floor was uneven, stone and sand, trodden down over the years into a shiny, gently undulating surface. There would be bodies beneath that ground. Ancient, venerated souls.

In the centre of the main chamber, a tall pillar reached all the way from floor to ceiling. Ripley could see the shadows of carvings on the pillar, but couldn't make out any of the detail. She wished she could get a closer look.

On the far right, a newish pair of double doors—like pub cellar doors—covered an entrance to a lower chamber. A shiny new padlock secured them, too. Health and Safety gone mad. A damning indictment of modern society that we couldn't be trusted to keep our historical monuments safe without having to be locked out.

It was sad the chamber was closed up now, though the smell coming from inside was hardly inviting—a combination of stale urine, mould and something rotten. Doubtless the final resting place for at least one luckless seagull that had flown into the open chimney and become trapped.

She turned the torch off and stood in the gloomy entranceway, listening to the echoes of the wind and waves bouncing around inside the chamber, creating an eerie low howl that sounded like a caged animal. She could almost believe there were still souls trapped in there, calling out for help. A sudden piercing scream startled her—a seagull, swooping in low over the cliff edge.

"You alright?"

Ripley jumped, turning to find a young man just outside the entrance of the chamber. He was beautiful in that symmetrical, androgynous, almost elfin style that fashion magazines favoured these days. His eyes were pale blue. His hair a short crop of fine, natural, golden curls.

"Just trying to get a better look inside," she said, smiling. "Amazing place, isn't it?"

He shrugged.

"I suppose it is," he said. "Been locked up for years though. I thought you might be one of those nuts who likes to throw offerings in. Makes the whole place stink, does that."

She noticed the accent. Northern. Not local, then. He looked at her quizzically, staring for a moment too long, as though assessing her. He stood a little too close, almost barring her way back out of the chamber's entrance.

"There's an information board over there," he said helpfully, suddenly bright and cheerful again. "Got pictures and everything."

"Great," Ripley said, squeezing past him. "I'll go take a look."

With that, he shrugged again and headed off towards the car park, just beyond the information board he'd pointed out. The only car there was a large, expensive looking Range Rover. Black. Tinted windows at the back. It didn't suit him, but he climbed in nonetheless and reversed out quickly, kicking up the small stones as he sped away. Strange boy.

Ripley shuddered, bracing herself to step back into the wind. From the entrance of the chamber, she could see a pair of standing stones, angled so that one of their broad faces looked out over the sea, and the other back at the chamber's opening. Sentry stones, perhaps? Or markers of an ancient, sacred pathway along which the dead were once processed?

She walked across to the faded information board cemented into the ground beside a bench about a hundred yards from the chamber. According to the yellowing text, partly obscured by a water stain, excavations had revealed a long history for this particular burial chamber, having begun as a henge, or ritual enclosure, around five thousand years ago. Towards the end of the Neolithic Era it had been used as a passage tomb of the kind also found along the Irish seaboard.

What made this chamber special, according to historians, was its bathing well. A separate, smaller chamber, with a stone seat built into it, which had been used at one time for baptisms. Apparently the chamber filled with water on high tides via a narrow chimney which led from the sea below all the way to the chamber.

The surface entrance to the chimney was now closed off with a metal grill, but the howling sound the waves made as they pushed up through the cave was still a big draw for tourists. Thanks to its direct access to the sea below, the chamber had also been used over the years as a smugglers cave, but not since it had been closed off due to the risk of drowning.

There was some explanation of the markings on the central pillar, but most of it was too faded to read. Ripley promised herself she'd look it up when she got back to the cottage. These ancient monuments were fascinating, but it was far too cold to linger out here any longer.

WHEN RIPLEY ARRIVED at the pub, windblown and red-cheeked, the place was buzzing. It seemed strange that it would be so busy, given how remote Rhosfaelog was, but the pleasant hum of conversation and gorgeous smell of home-cooked roast lamb gave the place a great vibe, and made her realise how cold and hungry she was.

"Have you booked, love?" the barmaid asked when she requested lunch for one.

When she confessed she hadn't, the barmaid flashed her a conspiratorial smile and checked her book.

"I'm sure we can work something out," she said. "Since it's just you."

Ordinarily, Ripley would have found the comment jarring, highlighting her unwanted single status, but she sensed no malice in the barmaid's observation.

"We've had a walking group in, but they're on coffees now, so the kitchen can cope," the barmaid said. "Sit yourself down at the bar for a moment, and I'll get something sorted for you, all right? Can I get you a drink while you're waiting?"

"A dry white wine and a glass of water please," Ripley replied.

The barmaid grinned and turned away to get the drinks. She called something through in Welsh to another colleague, presumably about serving a new customer, and he looked up and called back, smiling at Ripley. The barmaid placed the water and wine on the bar in front of her.

"All the ingredients for a good miracle right there," the barmaid said, "Water and wine."

She laughed at her own joke in a way that told Ripley it was neither directed at her specifically, nor the first time the barmaid had used it.

"You seem busy today," Ripley said.

"Yeah, weekends we're always run off our feet," she said, casually unpacking glasses from a dishwasher below the bar, automatic and efficient. "You should see us on a Sunday lunchtime."

She was a short woman, broad shouldered and dark haired, with a friendly smile and hands that had worked for years. Ripley sat back and sipped her wine, taking in the clientele.

A rowdy group of walkers, all colourful waterproofs and muddy boots, occupied the longest table in the main part of the bar. A tall, long-bearded man, at the head of the table, regaling the rest with a tale that involved much arm waving and a lot of hilarity.

On a low table beside the fire, a young couple shared a dessert—a spoon for you, a spoon for me. It was more competitive than romantic, and they, too, laughed well together. Gatherings of friends dotted some tables, families laughed and bickered at others. A handful of waiters skimmed between them all, efficiently delivering and clearing plates of hearty-looking food.

Ripley had not expected to find such a vibrant, popular pub in Rhosfaelog. After the hostile reception she'd recently had in the Lake District, she'd almost come to expect these small rural communities to have an innate suspicion of strangers. Perhaps having a celebrity like Megan Shields in the village made all the difference to their attitudes to outsiders.

"You on your holidays then?" the barmaid asked, polishing a glass and stretching to hang it up above the bar.

"Just here to see a friend," Ripley replied.

She wouldn't exactly call it a holiday, and he was hardly a friend. Even though she had been keen to get away from her flat and distract herself from waiting for more news of John, babysitting an unstable man she barely knew who was facing criminal charges and drinking his way through his grief was probably not the best way to get away from her own worries, and she was beginning to regret agreeing to be his chaperone until the hearing.

"Anyone I'd know?" the barmaid asked.

"Oh I shouldn't think so," she replied. "He's from the mainland."

"Oh right, weekend away is it?" she said, immediately jumping to the wrong conclusion. "Well, your secret's safe with me."

She winked, tapping the side of her nose. Ripley couldn't be bothered to correct her assumption. What did it matter if the barmaid thought she was having some kind of secret liaison? It was probably better than the woman knowing she was here to help someone who'd been accused of trying to hurt Megan. Perhaps they would be better off both going to Ian Hewitt's house instead, rather than staying in the village. She would bring it up with Detective Harding when he brought Ian over later.

By the time her lunch arrived, the bar had emptied a bit. The walking group had just trooped out, sticks in hand, mud-covered gaiters pulled up tight. The young couple were still there, sitting in their armchairs in front of the fire, red wine in hand and stockinged feet casually intertwined. Ripley envied them the idyllic simplicity of their Saturday afternoon. Even before John disappeared, they'd rarely lingered for hours over lunch just enjoying each other's company. They were one of those busy couples. Always had been.

Ripley had settled at a table in the window before her food came, and she watched the retreating group of walkers head off along the cliffs, tilted forward into the wind and striding out against the cold. The ever-changing seascape was fascinating. Big waves crashing over black rocks. Seagulls swooping and arcing, buffeted by the wind, their loud cries evoking memories of summers by the sea.

The few trees which had found purchase in the inhospitable landscape were bent into twisted, stretched shapes by the constant wind, as though they'd been frozen mid-struggle—a permanent reminder of the harsh climate. The pair of standing stones were just visible from Ripley's seat. Strong and ancient. The only things refusing to bend to the will of the wind.

"I thought I'd find you here."

Ripley turned, mid-mouthful, to see Bron standing beside her table, smiling benignly. The cold of the outdoors hung from her clothes.

"Great stuff," Bron continued, as Ripley hurried to swallow. "Don't mind me. I won't disturb your lunch. Just to say I had a call from young Dylan Harding earlier, down at the station, he told me you're going to be having a guest. So I wanted to drop you in the key for the doghouse. It's not as rough as its sounds. It's just a nickname. It's quite nice, really. Amanda over there at the bar told me you were in for your lunch, so I thought I'd catch you here. Save me coming all the way down the track later, see?"

She placed an old fashioned, over-sized key on the table beside Ripley's plate as she spoke, nodding all the time.

"I hope it's not a problem," Ripley began, conscious that everyone had obviously been talking about her since she arrived.

"No, love. Don't you worry. Dylan says you're doing him a massive favour, so it's fine by me. Besides, I feel a bit sorry for your friend. He seems quite lost."

"I think he is," Ripley replied.

"Listen," said Bron, laying her hand gently but conspiratorially on Ripley's arm. "You'll have to be a bit careful, all right? I'm happy for you both to stay, of course, but I can't have it become too big a thing, if that makes sense. Can't really afford to fall out with the family, see? They put a lot of work my way. And for my boys, too. So if you could try to keep a low profile, and see if you can get your friend to back off from them, I think everyone will be happy."

Ripley had already surmised that Megan's charity provided work for most of the village in a roundabout way. It wasn't as though this part of the coastline was a particularly tourist friendly resort, so they could do with all the trade they could get.

"I don't want to cause any trouble," Ripley said.

"I'm sure you don't love," said Bron. "Thing is, we've all come to rely on Megan in one way or another. People are very protective of her. So if there is any trouble, I'm afraid it'll be you two who come off worst. Not that there will be, of course. Everyone's very welcoming."

She fell silent a moment, thinking.

"You let me know if anyone gives you any grief though, all right?" Bron continued. "I know everyone in this place, so if any of them starts on you they'll have me to answer to, okay?" She patted Ripley's shoulder reassuringly. "Just think of me as your guardian angel."

Bron had said her whole piece in the same helpful, matter-of-fact tone of voice that she'd used to explain how everything worked in the cottage. And yet, despite Bron's encouraging smile and continual nodding, Ripley felt she'd just been gently warned to keep her nose clean. Perhaps the suspicion of the outsider presented itself behind a smiling face here. One thing was certain, Ripley rarely heeded those kinds of warnings.

"Understood," she said, keeping her voice flat, and trying not to sound defensive.

"Right then," Bron said, bright and cheerful again. "I'll let you finish your lunch."

She patted Ripley's arm and bustled off to chat to a tall, broad-shouldered young man at the bar who looked enough like her to be related. He stared at Ripley from beneath a fringe of curly, dark hair as Bron spoke to him. He nodded once, and Bron patted him on the shoulder before heading off again, greeting almost everyone she passed on the way out of the pub.

By the way the young man settled back on his bar stool, drink in hand, dark, brooding eyes fixed on Ripley, she was sure he'd been told to keep an eye on her. She also guessed that he wouldn't be the only one to have been given that instruction. Her appetite gone, she felt the overwhelming desire to get some fresh air. The legendary cheesecake would have to wait.

Leaving enough cash to cover her bill, Ripley slipped her coat back on, tucked the heavy key into her pocket and strode out of the pub. She locked eyes with the young man as she passed him, holding his gaze long enough to let him know she wasn't easily intimidated. He smiled back disarmingly.

Outside she walked around the side of the pub and out onto the path towards the cliffs. There was a bench tucked away behind a heavy clump of gorse, the old wood battered by the elements and the memorial plaque long since illegible. Ripley sat for a moment, breathing in the cold, salty air. Without warning her lungs forced another paroxysm of violent coughing. There were times recently when she thought she might cough so hard she'd loosen something.

"You all right?"

She looked up, mid-cough, to find Bron's young man standing in front of her, his demeanour more concerned than threatening.

"You shouldn't ought to be out here with that cough," he said, sitting down beside her uninvited.

Ripley's coughing subsided enough to let her draw in a rattling breath.

"Mum said to make sure you had everything you needed," he said. "Over at the cottage."

So he was Bron's son. That made sense.

"I'm Gareth," he said, reaching into his pocket and pulling out a hip flask. He unscrewed the top and handed it across to Ripley. "Here. This might warm you up a bit."

His smile was as bright and charming as his mother's, but his eyes were darker and more brooding. Ripley took the flask and sniffed, wary of taking drinks from strangers. He chuckled.

"It's all right," he said. "It's not a cheap one! I find a tot of good whiskey every now and then keeps some of this wind out of your bones. Don't tell my mum though, she'll think I've gone soft."

Ripley smiled and took a small sip, letting the warming alcohol coat her raw throat. He was right. It was a good whiskey.

"Thanks," she said, handing the flask back to him.

"No problem," he said. "I've always hated this wind. Cuts right through you, doesn't it?"

She smiled, unsure why he was being so friendly and feeling slightly exposed out here alone with him. She hadn't been able to see this bench from the window she'd been sitting near and she wondered now if anyone else could.

"Listen," he said.

Here it comes.

"Mum told me to keep an eye on you while you're in the cottage. She's told me who you've got staying, and she thinks it may land you in some trouble. She likes to think she's some kind of pillar of the community, with her fingers in all the pies, but really she's just nosey. And she's pretty good at making a mountain out of a molehill. If you keep on the right side of her, you should be fine, but if you find yourself in any bother with anyone, come to me first. She's less than useless in a crisis."

"Like I told your mum," Ripley said. "I'm not here to cause any trouble."

"Well, I think your friend's done more than enough of that for the both of you," he said. "I'm surprised he wants to come back here after the warning he got last time."

Ripley would have to ask Ian about that warning when she saw him.

"He thinks he has something to prove," she said.

"He'll have a job proving anything against that lot," Gareth said.

"The truth has a way of coming out," Ripley replied.

He looked at her quizzically for a moment and then smiled a lopsided grin.

"Right, well, I'd better get going. Call me if you need anything, will you?"

He scribbled down his number and handed it to her with another mixed smile.

"And look, just watch out for that Hewitt bloke, will you? He's got problems, that one."

He flinched as his phone rang, and stepped away to answer it, waving an apologetic goodbye. She watched him slope off, wondering if she may have judged him too harshly. He seemed genuine enough in his assessment of his mother's opinion of herself. Ripley was beginning to understand that Bron was the kind of woman who loved a drama, no matter how friendly she appeared.

As she walked back to her car, Ripley was surprised to see the same black Range Rover in the far corner of the car park. There was no sign of the beautiful young man she'd met at the burial chamber, but she was sure it was the same car.

RIPLEY HAD TAKEN a couple of pizzas away from the pub with her. She wasn't about to start cooking a meal for herself and Ian when he arrived. True to his word, Detective Harding turned up at six with a contrite and sullen Ian Hewitt in tow.

"Are you going to go see her then? Megan, that is." Harding asked, while Ian installed himself in the doghouse. Harding shifted awkwardly from foot to foot, as though nervous of the potential confrontation.

"I said I'd help Ian, so I guess I owe it to him and to the Shields family, of course, to hear both sides of the story," she replied, keeping her voice calm and level.

"Tread carefully, that's all," he warned. It wasn't aggressive. He was just trying to keep the peace. "Anne Shields is a volatile woman at the best of times. She may look fancy but she's thrown enough punches in her time. And Megan's not been well recently. Beneath all that healing stuff, she's still a little girl and her mum is just looking out for her."

"But you believe her statement?" Ripley asked. "About Ian?"

"A complaint has been made," he replied. "And we have to follow it up. There were witnesses and he has a motive to harm her."

"True," said Ripley. "But nothing actually happened to the girl."

"Only because the intruder was interrupted," Harding said, his voice getting more tense. "Look, you said yourself that you don't really know him, and he's shown quite a nasty streak while he's been here so far. The best thing you can do for him is try to get him to drop all this and go home. I know he's angry, but an eye for an eye is not the way forward."

Ripley didn't respond.

"When you visit them, you'll see how vulnerable that girl is. Maybe you'll even see why her mother is so angry at the way he's behaved towards them. They've had enough upheaval in their lives."

"I can see how much Megan means to the whole community," Ripley said, "and I know you want to protect her, but Ian swears he didn't go back to their house. Perhaps Anne is mistaken."

Harding smiled sadly, a sideways tilt of the head. He looked tired.

"She's adamant it was him she saw," he said. "Why would she lie?"

"To stop him causing any more trouble," Ripley said. "He was due to meet a woman called Caroline Clifton at Anne's house that day, did he tell you that? Someone else with an axe to grind after her meeting with Megan didn't go as planned. They were going to go in together and tackle Anne head on, but when he got there Caroline was already being escorted from the premises. Did Anne tell you about that?"

"No," he said, looking baffled. "That's the first I've heard of it. But I'm not surprised he's found other unsatisfied customers."

He smiled at Ripley's confused expression.

"Just because I don't want the family harassed in their own home, doesn't mean I buy into all this healing stuff," he said. "It stands to reason that there'd be more people who'd felt cheated when it didn't work. There will always be angry people with something like this, where there is so much at stake, you know? I guess it's my job to make sure none of them take that frustration too far."

"And I'm sure you do it very well," Ripley said. "But I'm surprised Anne didn't mention the incident with Caroline Clifton when she was busy laying out her complaints against Ian."

"Perhaps she thought it would be wasting more of my time," he replied, slightly barbed.

Hmm. Or perhaps it didn't fit her narrative.

He stood for just a moment more, presumably waiting for her to agree. Whether he noticed the squaring of her shoulders or wasn't up for any conflict, Harding turned on his heel and walked away with a tense smile.

"Call me," he said again, over his shoulder, "if anything else comes up."

Ripley shut the door and turned to find Ian standing in the doorway.

"So I'm a dead man walking, then?" he asked morosely, holding his hands out in front of him in mock shackles. "Sounds like they've got the whole thing sewn up."

"They're only going on what little evidence they've got."

"The world according to Anne Shields," Ian huffed.

"You need to stay positive," Ripley said, walking back into the kitchen and flicking on the oven to warm the pizzas.

"I just wish I could remember what happened that night," Ian said.

"Maybe there isn't any more to remember."

He scraped back a chair beside the small kitchen table and sat down, elbows on the table, face cupped in one palm.

"This is very good of you, Dr. Ripley," he said.

"It's fine," she replied, sliding the pizzas into the oven. "And please call me Alex."

"Sorry," he said.

"It's fine," she said again. "I'm guessing we're going to spend quite a lot of time together in the next few days so we can dispense with the formalities. I agreed to help you when we first met, and I know I got sidetracked by work, but I'm here now, and I'm happy to help if I can."

He smiled sadly, and hung his head.

"But you don't even know me," he said quietly. "How do *you* know I'm not the kind of mad man who would break into a house and try to hurt a girl in a coma?"

She looked at him a moment, letting the question hang in the air as she dried her hands on a faded tea towel. She didn't think he had it in him to hurt anyone, but she wasn't going to tell him that.

"Well, are you?"

"No, of course not!"

"There you go then," she said, matter of fact.

In truth, she couldn't be sure that Ian hadn't done what he stood accused of, but it did seem out of character for the man she'd met on that Sunday morning debate show a few weeks ago, even if he'd lost himself in drink a little since then. She considered herself a good judge of character, and he didn't strike her as an eye for an eye kind of guy. She had no idea how she was going to help him, though.

"Why don't you go have a shower while I'll get these pizzas warmed up. I bet you're starving. If their coffee was anything to go by, I can't imagine the food in the Rhosfaelog nick was much to write home about."

"You're not wrong there," Ian said.

He hesitated by the door, holding on to the frame and looking as though he wanted to say something else. With a sigh and a small shake of the head, he turned away.

Ripley topped up her wine and set about laying the table. She had just taken their dinner out of the oven when Ian came back in, hair still damp and with a clean soapy smell following him.

"That's better," he said, sitting at the table as she put a glass of wine in front of him.

"You look like you could do with a drink," she said, kindly. "I promise to stop you before you get too drunk."

He looked like he might cry, but he buried it in a long swig of wine. Ripley was struck by the same feeling she'd had when she'd first met him: Here was a man lost in grief and desperately trying to find someone or something to blame for his loss, despite knowing that cancer was an indiscriminate killer. He looked small. Older than his years. Not in physical appearance, but in his eyes and the hunch of his shoulders. *Not the years, but the mileage* as Indiana Jones had once said.

Ripley wondered what he had been like when his wife was still alive, before her illness had been diagnosed. Had he always been quiet and contained, or had they danced wildly at parties into the small hours? Had they enjoyed good food and fine wine, opera and theatre, or a night in watching TV on the sofa? She got no sense of the man who had once lived in this shell and she guessed that, much like herself, he was trying to figure out how to rebuild without his spouse at his side.

She checked her phone, casually, for the umpteenth time today, to see if there was any news from Neil Wilcox, or better still, from John. Nothing.

She brought the pizzas to the table along with the rest of the bottle of wine. They both ate hungrily in a surprisingly companionable silence until Ripley realised that Ian had stopped eating, mid-slice and was looking at her with a whimsical smile.

"She would've loved this, you know?" he said. "Jane. She was always helping strange waifs and strays out with food or a bed or some well-timed advice. Nothing you can't fix with a good meal and a friendly ear, she always said. She was a much better person than me."

"How long were you together?" Ripley asked, encouraged that he was happy to talk about Jane.

"We met in school," Ian smiled. "But she was way out of my league. It wasn't until I got back from university and we bumped into each other again that I realised I might stand a chance. I even joined the church just so I could be closer to her. I suppose that was a little duplicitous, but I confessed in the end."

"Was she always religious then?" Ripley asked.

"Not as a child," he said. "Her father was a lay preacher. I think she rebelled against it for a while in her teens. She could be quite wild. That's why I thought she was out of my league. But by the time we met again in our twenties, she was a committed member of the local church. She lost her mum to cancer in her first year at Uni and dropped out halfway through her second, when it became clear that her father wasn't coping alone. I think, in the beginning the church gave them a bond, and a way to move through their grief together. But over time, she found her own strength in it."

"What about you?"

He took a bite of his pizza and washed it down with a swig of wine, thinking.

"I don't think I ever felt as passionately as Jane did. Not even in the beginning. I found a kind of calmness in the structure and routine of it all though, which I guess could be considered spiritual."

"But you don't believe in God?"

"The million dollar question. No, I don't suppose I do. I don't know."

He shrugged and sat back, pushing his empty plate away from him and picking up his glass. He peered at her over the top, gauging her reaction. Ripley said nothing, waiting for him to elaborate.

"I like the basic principles the church teaches. Kindness and goodwill to all. But it seems to come with so many conditions, you know what I mean? Like a hierarchy of who that kindness can be shown to. Anyway, I think I'm too much of a realist to believe in one divine being with some kind of roadmap for all of us. The only times Jane and I ever argued it was about her blind acceptance that everything that happened was part of some great big, unchangeable plan. It feels so defeatist, just holding your hands up and saying: 'Oh well, it must be God's plan.' Is that wrong of me?"

Ripley didn't reply. She could sense his frustration and she didn't want him to censor himself.

"When she was first diagnosed, she used that strong belief of hers to get through the treatments. She was sure it was all just a test of her faith. Don't get me wrong, she put her complete trust in the doctors. But she also coupled that with a lot of prayers. I don't know if you've seen anyone go through cancer, but it's a long and painful process. It's so hard to stay positive. And yet, through every knock back and every failed round of treatment, she hung on to this belief that her suffering was part of God's plan for her."

He emptied his glass and Ripley topped them both up, still not speaking. Her questions would come soon enough.

"By the time she met Reverend Rodwell, she'd all but accepted her terminal diagnosis. And then he told her about Megan. She was like a dog with a bone after that. She kept saying that she wouldn't have met the Reverend if she wasn't meant to visit Megan and be healed. Finally, I agreed to bring her. I didn't really think she had anything to lose. Shows what I know."

He took another swig of his wine and then, very deliberately, put the glass down on the table, as though conscious of not drinking too much too quickly.

"Her diagnosis *was* terminal though," Ripley began. "So you knew she didn't have long. But you said you blame Megan and her mother for her death. Why?"

"I don't blame them for her *death*," he clarified. "Of course I knew she would die. We'd both been living with that knowledge for a long time. When she died, I blamed them for making it happen quicker. The doctors had given her at least three months to live, see? And she died a week later. The day after visiting Megan."

He took a deep breath and Ripley noticed a small shudder of his shoulders when he let it out.

"You should have seen her when she walked— *walked*—out of that house. She was buzzing. She'd been wheelchair bound for over six months and all of a sudden she could just get up and walk out of there. As far as she was concerned, every ounce of belief she'd ever invested had just been justified. She was alive. Vital. Elated. She believed she'd been healed. The next day she was dead, and the doctors told me her rapid decline was due to all her activity the day before."

"But Jane believed she had been healed? As you said, she walked out of there on her own. How? If you're going to accuse these people of fraud, you need to have another explanation for what happened to her that day."

Ripley wasn't trying to wind him up, but she wanted to understand what had gone on. If Jane Hewitt had been stuck in a chair for over six months, how could she possibly have walked out of the house on her own after such a brief meeting?

"All I can think is that we were both caught up in the moment. I mean, you've got to give them credit, the whole experience is well choreographed. Perhaps she was hypnotised by the idea. I don't know. But she did walk! She could hold her own weight without me lifting her for the first time in months. She as good as danced out of there."

"Yet you have doctors who will testify that she was incapable of walking."

"Exactly," he said. "Look, I don't know what happened. What I do know, though, is that in the moments before she died, she finally realised there was nothing left to believe in. As we sat in that hospital room, and she drifted in and out of consciousness, she told me I was right. That I'd always been right. There was no plan. She said she felt like she had spent her life talking to a hollow sky. And that's what killed her. I know there's nothing I can do to prove it either way, but they lied to her. They gave her hope and when it failed, it stripped her of her faith, and a part of her soul. I'll never forgive them for that."

He hung his head, spent. Ripley saw his left hand tremble where it rested on his right arm. His hands were so thin, his wedding ring slid loose on his finger, moving closer to the knuckle. He pushed it back with his thumb.

He looked up at her with eyes so hollow and sad that she instinctively reached out across the table to take his hand. Catching herself, she picked up her wine glass instead.

"I understand," she said. "And I will try to help you get through this, but I don't want you to waste time or money on a court case if you have no evidence of fraud. Whatever happens, you'll only have one chance to bring a case, and without hard evidence that they deliberately misled you, you will almost certainly fail."

"I know," he said. "But I have to do something. They can't just make people believe that Megan's healing them and take their money. That's got to be criminal."

"Did they ever demand money for any part of the experience?"

"No," he said. "Not directly. Though the donation form was right in there with all the disclaimers we had to sign before and after the prayer meeting."

"Do you have copies of that paperwork?" Ripley asked.

"Yes," he replied. "Back at home. But it basically says they make no guarantees of healing and can't be held responsible for anything that happens after a meeting."

"And you both signed it?"

"We had to before they'd let Jane meet Megan. Like I said, I didn't think she'd have anything to lose."

"It's okay," Ripley said, gently. "It doesn't mean you don't have a case. I'll have to look at the wording, but if you're not bringing an actual complaint about the efficacy of the healing, then whatever you signed shouldn't have much bearing. It shows they're wary of being sued though, which may help."

"They'd have to be, wouldn't they?"

"Hmm," Ripley mused. "Tell me about this Caroline woman, then. You had hoped to build a case together? What's her story?"

Ian sat up straighter in his chair, seemingly happy to move away from his own experiences with Megan and Anne.

"Well," he said. "She called me just after that debate show you and I were on. She said she'd also been to visit Megan, and she understood why I was so angry."

"Why?"

"Her son was sick. Some kind of degenerative disease. Something genetic, I can't remember the name. Anyway, he'd got to the point where the doctors had said there was nothing more they could do and she'd done exactly what we had—started looking into other avenues, other possibilities. Hoping for a miracle."

"Did she say how she'd heard about Megan?"

"Caroline was part of some support group for kids with her son's condition. Apparently one of the other parents had seen something on a forum somewhere. They'd only told her about it because they knew she and her husband were regular church goers and they'd thought it might bring them some comfort."

Ripley nodded, finishing the last of her glass of wine and topping it up again.

"Anyway, she told me they'd discharged him from the hospital and had taken him across to see Megan."

"And?"

"And nothing. He'd shown no signs of improvement and he died a few days later. Two months before his tenth birthday."

"God, that's so sad," Ripley said.

"Anyway," Ian continued. "She said they had felt so stupid for believing in healing miracles in the first place, they'd said nothing to anyone about it. But then, when she saw me on that show, she knew they weren't alone. She said it was the first time she had even considered that perhaps Megan and moreover, Anne, were the ones to blame. Just as they were with Jane."

Ripley didn't want to start down the path of blame again.

"So what happened?" she asked.

"I suggested we should go there together and have it out with them. I thought we might get them to admit that they knew it was all fake if we both accused them. It would have been his tenth birthday that day. She told me that when I finally caught up with her in that lay-by. I think it was too much for her, really, to go back there on that day. I feel terrible for even suggesting it, but I thought we'd have a better chance together."

"And that was on Wednesday?" Ripley asked.

"Exactly," he said, looking down at his own empty glass and pushing it away.

"So what happened then? She drove home, and you went back to have it out with Anne alone?"

"Something like that," Ian said. "I left her parked up on the side of the road. I offered to drive her home, but she said she'd be fine. Granted, I probably wasn't thinking right, either. I was so angry. For her, and for me. I wanted them to know there were more of us gunning for the truth. And they wouldn't get away with their lies. I went back to the house. But when I got there, there were more cars in the driveway, so I parked outside for a while to wait for my moment."

He looked down again, ashamed.

"I had a bottle of whiskey in the car I had bought for later," he said, quietly. "I had a sip, you know, to give me courage."

"A sip?" Ripley questioned.

"All right," Ian snapped back. "I got drunk. I was working up the courage to go in. I remember standing outside their front door, shouting. I kicked a flower pot on the path and smashed it. I'm not proud of it."

"It's all right," Ripley said. "I'm not judging. What's done is done. What happened then?"

"Reverend Rodwell came out and told me to leave. He said he'd called the police."

"And you left?"

"Yes," he said, insistently. "I may have been drunk, but I was still fit enough to know I shouldn't drive, so I left my car there and walked back along the cliffs to the pub. I was going to stay there for the night. It took a while. When I got there, I ordered some food, and carried on drinking. I don't remember much after that."

"But you stayed in the pub, for the night?"

"No," he said, sounding glum. "I can't remember why not. They must have been full. I was wandering along the main road looking for a taxi when the police picked me up. Anne had already made her accusation by then, and they'd been out looking for me. It's not looking great, is it?"

"I'm sure we'll come up with something," Ripley said, trying to lift the mood.

"I'm sure *you* will," Ian replied pointedly. "That's why I agreed to be on that panel show in the first place. To meet you. I'm sorry it's turned out like this."

"Don't be," Ripley said. "You were right to get in touch. All we have to do now is prove that you were nowhere near Megan when her mother says you were. And if we can't do that, we have to figure out why they're trying to frame you for something you didn't do."

"Because I've been going around badmouthing them, perhaps?" Ian asked, sarcastically.

"Maybe, but that would see them accused of wasting police time, if we could prove they knew it wasn't you," said Ripley, standing up and taking both of their glasses over to the sink. "The best thing you can do right now is try to remember as many other details as you can from the night they say you broke in. Write everything down. No matter how small. Something will be in there that can help you, I'm sure."

3rd December

THE GREY MORNING light seeping through the thin curtains woke Ripley early. It took a moment for her to remember where she was—yet another strange bed away from home, trying to help someone she barely knew, all to keep her mind off her own troubles.

She reached for her phone on the bedside. A few emails had come in overnight about the book signings she was due to be doing next week, but nothing from Neil Wilcox. No news of John.

She lay in bed for a while, blankets tucked up under her chin, listening to the sea crashing onto the beach below the cliffs. Gulls screeched. A dog barked somewhere off in the distance. A strong gust of wind rattled the window in its frame. Odd sounds, outside her normal routine.

Downstairs, hair still damp from the shower, she cupped a mug of steaming coffee in both hands and blew on it. It smelled good. There was no sign of movement yet from the small annexe where Ian was sleeping. Hopefully, the smell of coffee wouldn't wake him. Last night's conversation had shown her quite how open his wounds still were and Ripley didn't particularly want him to know she was heading off to meet Megan this morning.

Finishing her coffee quickly, she decided to risk getting breakfast in that little cafe she'd passed on the way in. With coat and phone in hand, she winced as the front door creaked open noisily. There was no point lingering to see if the sound had woken him, but as she sat in the car waiting for the old heaters to clear the windscreen, his face appeared at the window in the kitchen. He waved, and she gestured that she would call him, before backing up and heading off down the long, potholed drive.

The car rattled along the rutted track towards the main road, dashboard squeaking and loose change jingling in the cup holder. In the field off to her left, a man strode towards the cliffs, bundled up against the wind in a long coat and a woollen hat, with his dog bounding along joyfully in front of him. A bracing Sunday walk. It was nearly nine, and the sky was still grey and dull. She doubted it would brighten much today.

She was grateful to hit the tarmac at the end of the drive and shift into a higher gear. The road was empty, though there were lights on in most of the houses. Early risers around these parts. She passed the church, quiet and still against the flat sky, and headed back out of the village.

Ripley was relieved to see the lights on in the café too. The windows were steamed up, but she could make out a figure at a table in the corner. Parking on the road outside, she headed in.

"Hello love," a round-bellied, bald-headed man called cheerfully as the bell over the door announced her entrance.

"Morning," Ripley replied, smiling.

"What can I get you?" he asked.

Ripley looked above him at the old-fashioned plastic letter board advertising a Full Welsh Breakfast for three pounds, among other combinations of toast, eggs, beans and bacon. She wasn't sure how it differed from the Full English, but she was willing to find out.

"I'll have the Full Welsh Breakfast, thanks," she said. "And a white coffee, please."

"Lovely," he replied. "Sit yourself down then. I'll just be a moment."

His accent was warm and lilting, emphasising the soft vowels in that sing-song way that always made Ripley smile. She chose a seat near the window, and nodded an acknowledgement at the young, dark-haired man sitting at the other table as he lowered the corner of his paper to look at her.

"Morning," he said.

His voice was deep but cheerful, and seemed to match his slender good looks. His hair was neatly combed in a side-parting that gave him an air of control and efficiency. He turned the page of his newspaper with deliberate, delicate fingers, aligning the edges.

"Good morning," she replied.

He didn't quite bring the paper back up fully again, instead watching her from behind it, eyes bright beneath hooded lids. He was handsome in a neat, precise way. Not her type, but she could see it. He looked as though he might be about to start a conversation, so she turned away, fixing her attention instead out the window at the row of cottages which stood opposite.

The one in the middle had some sort of gargoyle sticking out of the small porch roof above the front door. It was a strange-looking thing, grotesque and ancient, carved from stone but painted black, with a long red tongue protruding from its mouth. It was unlike anything Ripley had ever seen. More decoration than folklore, but pretty ugly nonetheless. More likely to ward off potential visitors rather than evil spirits.

Ripley noticed Bron bustling up the path of the next house along, carrying a basket in one hand and a small bag of wood in the other. She knocked on the door and Ripley heard her chatting merrily to the old woman who answered as she moved inside. Bron was obviously quite a figure in this community.

She glanced at the man at the next table, whose eyes darted guiltily back to his paper like some third rate spy from a 1960s movie. Ripley sighed.

"Here you are, love," the cafe owner said, delivering her breakfast to the table. "The best of Welsh there for you."

"Lovely," Ripley said, assessing the plate. Two fried eggs, bacon, sausage, beans as standard, but she also found cockles and some laverbread which were obviously the Welsh components. Her mouth watered at the thought of tucking in.

"And there's your coffee," he said, plonking down a large mug of milky beige liquid. "Enjoy."

"Thanks, it looks great."

"Best breakfast in Rhosfaelog," he beamed, turning to the man at the table.

"More tea there, Reverend?"

The young man shook his head and folded up his paper.

"No thanks, Owen," he said, in that resonant baritone. "I'd best go put the heating on. Can't have everyone catching cold during the service, can we?"

"I don't know," Owen smiled. "Might help 'em stay awake!"

Aha. So he was Reverend Rodwell. No wonder he was looking at her strangely. Bron had doubtless told most people who was staying in her cottage by now. Ripley should probably seize the initiative and introduce herself properly. Rodwell stood up, slipped his hat on and left the folded newspaper on the table.

"Will we be seeing you there this morning then, Owen?"

"I'd love to, Rev, I really would, but there's the business to think of."

"The Lord helps those who help themselves, Owen," Reverend Rodwell said, smiling.

"Exactly," said Owen. "I knew he'd understand."

Rodwell rolled his eyes in mock despair and Ripley couldn't help but smile as he caught her eye.

"And what about you, Dr Ripley?" he asked, stopping at her table, and grinning at the look of surprise she tried to hide.

So much for needing to introduce herself.

"You'll be joining us for this morning's service, won't you? We'd love to see you there."

"I'm afraid I'm busy today," she replied.

"Oh, that's a shame. Well, never mind. How long are you staying?" he asked, reaching into the inside pocket of his coat.

"Just a couple of days," Ripley said, vaguely.

"Wonderful," he beamed, leaning over to lay a glossy leaflet on the table. "We're holding a very special prayer service tomorrow. In the church hall. All welcome."

He tapped the leaflet. It was the same one she'd already seen. When she didn't reply he placed a hand on her shoulder. Hot and invasive. It was all she could do not to shrug him off.

"Please do come, Dr Ripley," he said. "I'd love you to see what we do first hand."

Ripley heard the challenge in his invitation. She nodded curtly and dropped her shoulder enough to make him move his hand.

"I'll do my best," she said.

"I'll look forward to seeing you there," he said confidently.

He knew he'd rattled her. She saw a flicker of satisfaction pass across his eyes. His smile already dropping as he turned to the door.

The bell over the door jangled as he opened it and side-stepped to let a woman through before he left. Ripley was sure she saw a look pass between them. A shake of the head from Rodwell, the tiniest frown from the woman. It was all over in a second. As the woman sashayed importantly past, Ripley felt the cold wind rush in from outside. She shuddered. The bell rang again as the door shut.

The woman shook her coat off and draped it over her arm, answering Owen's cheerful "Hello!" with a tight smile. She looked at Ripley impassively and wove her way through the tables towards the one that Reverend Rodwell had just been sitting at.

Her dark shoulder-length hair, neatly styled and framing a razor sharp fringe, gave her an austere, almost Teutonic look. Her large, slightly hooked nose reminded Ripley of her paternal aunts. Her father's three sisters all shared a sort of joking pride about their big noses, and always remarked on any they spotted of comparable status, greeting its owner as though there was some secret society of large-nosed ladies. Ripley had inherited her mother's features, fortunately.

The woman sat down at the table and arranged her coat on the chair beside her. Ripley noticed Owen watching her and looked up at him.

"Tries to get me down to that church every week, he does," Owen said, from behind the counter. "Never going to happen."

"Are you not into the church at all? Or just *his* church?" Ripley asked.

She watched the Reverend cross the road, his arm raised in a pleasant wave at that same blonde-haired young man she'd seen at the burial chamber. They stopped to chat, the smallest of touches between them—a squeeze of the arm and a warm smile which told Ripley they were close friends.

"Oh, no, it's nothing personal," Owen replied. "He's a lovely bloke, the Rev. Bit young and energetic for some of the old regulars, but nah, it's just not my thing. I'd rather spend an hour in the pub with a nice pint and a good friend than in a cold church talking to a God who's better off tending to those more deserving. Each to their own, though, eh?"

"Right," she agreed, watching the Reverend and the young man walk away together, deep in conversation.

The woman behind her opened the newspaper Reverend Rodwell had left and looked up surreptitiously. Ripley looked away as the woman's gaze fell on her. In the reflection in the window, Ripley saw her slip something from the folds of the newspaper and tuck it into her coat pocket. *What was that?*

"So what're you here for then?" Owen asked, bringing her attention back to their conversation. "You're staying over in Bron's cottage, aren't you? I make the bread she puts out for the guests."

Just as Ripley had assumed: There wouldn't be many places she could go in this village without people knowing who she was. She must be the only strange face in the village at the moment too. Apart from Ian, of course.

"I'm just doing a bit of research," she said. It was a handy catch all and rarely provoked too many follow-up questions.

"Research is it? Bron said you'd written a book. We get lots of writers down this way, you know? Must be the sea air. Well if you're going to write a book about us, you need look no further. I've got loads of stories for you. I'm sure you'll need a devilishly handsome leading man."

He winked conspiratorially, chortling at his own comment, but then caught himself and frowned.

"Hang on a second, though," he said, looking confused. "Didn't the Reverend just call you Doctor?"

"You got me," said Ripley, smiling. "I'm a doctor of theology, and I write books about the subject. I've just finished one about faith healers."

She saw no harm in telling him. He may not be the religious sort, but his business clearly benefitted from the local faith healing industry that had grown up around Megan. He may be a good person to talk to about their special girl and her mother.

"Theology, eh? Well, I don't know much about that. But you just give me the nod, love. For the price of a cup of tea, I can tell you things that have happened around here that'll make your hair curl."

He chuckled and set about drying the cup he'd just washed up.

"I'll bear that in mind," she said, finishing the last of her food and placing her knife and fork together. "So, what can you tell me for the price of a breakfast?"

"That all depends on what you want to know," he said, filling the cup with coffee and carrying it over to the woman at the other table. "Sordid affairs, mysterious deaths, missing cats... It all goes on around here."

Owen stopped at Ripley's table, picking up her plate and napkin and balancing the lot easily on his sturdy arm as he gave the table a cursory wipe with a grey cloth. "Really? It seems so peaceful."

"That's what they like you to think," he chuckled. "There's plenty of intrigue, believe you me."

"Well," she smiled. "I'd only just published a book about faith healing when someone told me about Megan Shields. Too late to go in the book, but I wish I'd heard about her sooner. She'd have been perfect to include."

She noticed him stiffen slightly, but she couldn't decide whether that was because she'd mentioned Megan, or because he realised he wouldn't get to share his collection of local gossip.

"In what way would she be perfect?" he asked, sounding wary.

"As a case study," she replied. "The book was an investigation into whether faith healing is a genuine thing. Whether there are actual miracles, or if there's always another more plausible explanation."

"And what was your verdict?"

"Inconclusive," she said, honestly, "Not including the scammers and the outright frauds, I guess I just found it hard to prove that any of the healings were an actual miracle."

"That what you're looking for then, is it? A miracle?"

"Proof of one, I suppose, yes," she replied. "But I kept finding other explanations. Medical errors, or treatment successes which had been played down in favour of claiming a healing miracle, placebo effects, claims of illness or injury where none existed in the first place. Nothing that could truly be defined as a miracle."

"But just because you can't explain something doesn't mean it has to be a miracle, does it? I mean, maybe it's just something you don't understand." And he went back to wiping down his surfaces.

"True," said Ripley. "The problem is that there are a lot of people out there making a lot of money by claiming to be healers, and preying on those too desperate or vulnerable to see through it."

"I hope you don't think that's what's going on here." He'd gone from wary to defensive.

"Not at all," Ripley said. "I'm just interested in the subject, and I was surprised, given how many people claim to have been helped by Megan, that I hadn't come across her earlier. That's all. I'm keen to meet her and see for myself."

"Got something wrong with you then, have you?"

"Not that I want to talk about," Ripley replied.

"Fair enough," he conceded. "Believe you me, I've not got a religious bone in my body, but there's something very special about that girl, and she's helped more people than I've served hot dinners. If anything was going to make me believe in God, then it would be seeing all the people whose lives she's changed. And all the while her own just life ticks by without her being able to enjoy any of it, poor scrap. I don't have to believe in God to know she makes people better. I've seen it with my own eyes."

"Then you should count yourself very lucky," Ripley said, her tone placatory, "to live so close to someone so special. It must really help the whole community."

"You're not wrong there," he said. "But I still wouldn't wish what's happened to her on my worst enemy. I can't think of anything worse than being locked in like that, body getting older, mind still working, but not being able to wake up. And she was a right little tearaway as a nipper, she was. Poor kid."

Ripley sensed that the conversation was over. And he was right. Megan was trapped in a coma, and even if her mother was laying bigger claims to her talents than perhaps existed, that was not something Megan had any say over. She was as much a victim in this as anyone else.

Ripley thanked Owen for her breakfast, left her change as a tip and bundled up again to head back out into the cold. Her conversation with him had convinced her that she would get more out of a face-to-face meeting with Anne Shields, and hopefully Megan, than she would out of talking to anyone else in the village.

IT DIDN'T TAKE Ripley long to find Megan Shields's house. The address Ian Hewitt had been accused of breaking into last week was on the outskirts of the town in a relatively new estate, and the Shields's bungalow was easy to distinguish by the minibus outside, with that now familiar *God's Gift* slogan painted on the side.

Ripley parked a little way off and waited in the car, watching the house for a while to get a sense of who might be there. Two other cars in the drive—both top of the range black Range Rovers—suggested there were other people in the house, though she could see no signs of life inside.

The bungalow itself looked like the show home for the whole estate. Uniform drapes hung in each of the front windows, with plain net curtains shielding the rooms inside from prying eyes. A white picket fence surrounded a manicured patch of lawn, with neat, functional flower beds filled with low-maintenance shrubs. Even the pair of gnomes on the edge of the lawn were bland and featureless, if that were possible. It looked new and characterless, as though still waiting to become a home.

After only a few minutes watching the place, she saw a sleek, dark red saloon car ease into the driveway. A bit flashy for these parts.

She was surprised to see Reverend Rodwell step out of the driver's side, smoothing his hair in the window as he shut the door. He leaned into the back seat and brought out a heavy looking metal briefcase, which he gripped in his left hand as he locked the car and strode to the front door. He used his own key to let himself in, passing a friendly greeting with someone just inside the door.

Bron's son, Gareth, wearing a dark suit and black rollneck pullover, leaned out of the door as the Reverend patted him on the shoulder. He checked the driveway and the road beyond. His gaze lingered on Ripley's car for a moment before the door swung shut again. His dark frame now masked the two narrow, opaque windows in the top half of the front door. Whatever he had been doing before, he was on door duty now that the Reverend was in the house.

Was he the doorman Ian had seen throwing Caroline out? From the brief chat she'd had with him outside the pub, he didn't seem like much of a hard man. Maybe they just relied on his size to intimidate any troublemakers. She was glad of a friendly face on the door, but still figured it would be better to wait until the Reverend left before she made her approach. He wouldn't be long; his morning service was starting soon.

As she waited, she typed out a text to Ian, arranging to meet him in the pub car park at lunchtime. He pinged a reply straight back. "See you there." He must be bored stiff. She'd be going crazy if she were stuck in that cottage all day.

She tucked the phone into her pocket and went back to watching the house. She could just about make out figures moving in the large room to the left of the driveway, but she couldn't see who or how many.

After only a few minutes, the Reverend walked back out of the front door, case still in hand, though it looked a lot lighter from the way he held it. Gareth walked him out to his car and the two of them exchanged a few words and nods before the Reverend slipped into the driver's seat and backed out of the drive, taking off at a fair speed. *Showing off in his fast car.*

Ripley sank back into her chair as he passed, hoping that he wouldn't look across and see her. She watched in her wing mirror as his car disappeared around the corner and only when he was out of sight did she breathe out, happy to have stayed under his radar. She was fairly sure he would want to supervise any visit she may have with Megan—he would want her to see them in the best light.

Waiting a moment to be sure he hadn't turned back, she stepped out of her car and walked quickly towards the house. The flagstones along the pavement here looked clean, almost unused compared to those near her home in Manchester, which were dirty and waxed with chewing gum and the stains of the thousands of lives lived on top of them.

She strode up the neat garden path and pressed the doorbell, listening to the soft melodic chimes echoing beyond the door. Gareth's bulky figure loomed up to the glass. When the door opened, he frowned fleetingly as he recognised her, and then smiled nervously.

"What are you doing here?" he asked, automatically pulling the door shut behind him, closing them both out of the house. His eyes darted up and down the street.

"You didn't tell me you worked for the family," Ripley said, smiling sweetly at him.

"Just filling in today," he replied. "Simon's usually the one out front."

"Keeping guard?"

"Welcoming the guests, I think they call it," he grinned. "Though, he's better suited to it than I am."

"Well, here I am," she smiled, using both hands to present herself. "You can welcome me. I was hoping to talk to Anne."

"Have you got an appointment then?"

He looked genuinely perplexed, as though he must have overlooked her name on the schedule.

"I didn't know I needed one," Ripley said. "How do I make one of those? Can I do it through you?"

"Who is it now, Gareth love?" Another lilting Welsh accent from further down the corridor. A woman's voice, smoker's hoarse.

"Just someone wanting to see you, Anne. I've told her she needs an appointment," he called over his shoulder, before whispering to Ripley, sounding more concerned than aggressive. "You shouldn't be here without the Reverend's say so."

"I just want to talk to her," Ripley said.

"He'll have my guts," he pleaded.

"Well, who is it?" Anne's harsh voice came closer to the door.

Ripley heard a tut and some muttering, and the door was pulled open and Gareth brushed aside by a tall, elegant woman in a smart, straight, deep red skirt set. Her hair was neatly styled in a short bob and her make up was professionally applied, though still cracking in the puckers on her top lip. Her brows knitted into a frown as she assessed Ripley.

"Oh, it's you. What do you want?"

Of course she'd recognised her—Ripley had been a guest on the same television show on which Ian Hewitt had publicly lambasted Anne and her daughter.

"I just wanted a quick chat."

"Francis warned me you were in town," Anne said, looking at her watch. "I've got ten minutes. Get out of the way, Gareth. Stop being so rude. Come in."

Gareth begrudgingly allowed Ripley to pass.

"But Anne, Simon said—" he protested.

"Hush yourself, or I'll let your mam know you still can't keep a civil tongue in your head."

"Come through," Anne said, "I'm sorry. He's not our usual man. Simon always insists people make an appointment. He likes to know exactly what's going on. But he's not here today and you've made the effort to come all the way over, so I'm not going to turn you away. Unless you start making trouble."

"I won't," Ripley reassured her. "But I'm staying in the village for a few days, so I can always come back another time, if now is inconvenient."

"Not at all," said Anne, shaking her head over her shoulder. "I was just about to have some tea. Won't you join me?"

Both her demeanour and her accent seemed forced—her airs and graces sitting uncomfortably on her, as though this was a costume she was still growing into.

"That would be great," Ripley said. "Thank you."

She followed Anne down the neat corridor. There were no personal touches on display out here. No photos of kids, no piles of shoes or bundles of coats. Ripley wondered if it was always this tidy, or if there was another part of the house where their daily life happened.

They passed another room, and through a half-open door Ripley caught a glimpse of two young children, a boy and a girl, wrestling with each other in a room strewn with brightly coloured plastic toys and open picture books. The girl was beating the boy over the head with an oversized teddy and he was squealing in delight. A TV in the corner was playing cartoons too loudly.

"Stop it you two," Anne snarled in at them, before smiling thinly and rolling her eyes at Ripley as she shut the door and drowned out the noise of their squealing.

"My youngest," she explained. "Twins. Double trouble. They're home-schooled. Better for them in the long run, what with all the attention Megan gets."

Ripley didn't think they looked like they were doing much schooling, but who was she to judge?

"Come on through," Anne continued.

Ripley followed her into a wide, white kitchen. Clean and glossy. Again Ripley was struck by the feeling that this was more like a show home than a real home.

Anne turned and looked at her, a fixed smile on her lips.

"So, what can I do for you then, Dr Ripley?" she asked, the challenge clear in the slight tilt of her head.

"Well," Ripley said, leaning against one of the kitchen counters. "I wanted to talk about Megan."

Anne froze for a moment, mugs in hand, smile wavering. It was the briefest hesitation, before her shoulders dropped slightly.

"Is this a personal visit?" Anne asked, still busy with the kettle. "Or are you just looking for more material for your book."

"Can it be both?"

"I don't think we want to feature in one of your books," Anne said, turning around with two mugs of tea. "No offence."

"None taken," Ripley said, accepting the drink.

Anne Shields sat down heavily at the table, and Ripley sensed her friendly demeanour faltering for a second. The woman took a deep breath and turned her sigh into a cooling blow across the top of her mug.

"Listen," Ripley said, sitting opposite her. "The book is published already. It's all out there. If I'd known about Megan beforehand, I might have approached you to feature her story, but now, I'm just an interested party. She seems to have a lot of supporters."

"I saw you," Anne said, levelling sad eyes at her. "On the telly with that awful man, Ian Hewitt."

Ripley dipped her own eyes. It must have been a painful watch for Anne, given Ian's scathing attack on her daughter. Ripley hoped that she'd come across as more of an objective voice, but she doubted it. Anne's guard would be up,

"They invited us too, you know?" Anne said, matter-of-fact. "To go on that show."

"You didn't want to do it?"

"Not really, no. I think people either believe or they don't. No point fighting about it. Did you know he broke in here? Tried to get to Megan? I had to call the police."

"I was told," Ripley said, noncommittally. She wasn't sure from Anne's comment whether the woman knew Ian had been released into Ripley's care, but she assumed that she may not be quite so friendly if she did.

"I feel sorry for the poor man really. You could tell he loved his wife. I don't blame him for being angry. But I won't have him badmouthing my Megan or trying to hurt her. And I can't have him turning up here drunk, shouting the odds in front of the neighbours and all. It does none of us any good."

"You're sure it was Ian who broke in?"

"I saw him with my own eyes," Anne said. "I know it was dark, and he shone his torch right in my face, but still, I've no doubt it was him. You should've heard the things he was saying about Megan before. And about me. I don't want her hearing that kind of language."

"I know it's no excuse," Ripley said. "But he is grieving."

"He needs help," Anne replied, harsh and bitter. "And I hope he finds it before someone else gets hurt."

"Someone else?" Ripley pounced on the comment. "Megan wasn't hurt, was she?"

"No," Anne stuttered, realising her mistake. "But that's not the point, is it? He was in our house, in the middle of the night. If I hadn't found him... Well, it doesn't bear thinking about."

"It must have been very frightening, finding someone in her room like that," Ripley said, aiming for a sympathetic tone.

"Not *someone*—Ian Hewitt," Anne snapped.

Anne took a sip of her tea and peered at Ripley over the rim of her cup, assessing her.

"That's why you're here, isn't it?" she asked. "He's your friend, and you're trying to protect him."

Ripley hesitated, wondering how best to frame her response so that she didn't get shut down immediately. Anne was clearly as shrewd as her appearance and demeanour suggested.

"Not protect him, no," said Ripley. "I want to help him through this, preferably with no further damage to either party. He feels like you tricked his wife. I just want to understand your side."

Anne straightened her back.

"Knowing what you do for a living," she said, coldly. "I don't have to justify anything to you."

"And I'm not asking you to. I just want to understand what happened with Jane."

"Of all the cases in your book, did you find one that you fully believed in?" Anne asked. "Because from what I read, it didn't seem that way. It looked like you were hell bent on making everyone out to be a fraud, and I won't have you coming in here and doing that to us."

Ripley was surprised by the criticism. She thought she'd been fair and balanced, especially in her opening chapters.

"There were *some* interesting examples," she said. *In amongst a lot of liars and charlatans.* "But I couldn't find anything that I thought was a miracle."

"Well," said Anne, standing up aggressively. "Maybe that's your problem. You're looking for the wrong definitions. Because I've watched countless people visit Megan and I understand her gift in a way a stranger never could, not even you."

"So explain it to me," Ripley said. "I genuinely want to know what you believe."

Anne sighed and leaned against the kitchen counter.

"Over the years it's become clear that Megan acts as a kind of amplifier of people's needs. It's as simple and as complicated as that. And before you ask, yes, I *do* think it's miraculous. I will swear to that on any Bible."

"What does that mean? An amplifier?"

"Well, in the beginning it was more difficult to see, because I assumed people were just visiting her to be nice. To keep her company. Maybe even to put their own problems into perspective, you know?"

She opened a drawer and took out an elegant-looking, metallic e-cigarette and took a few puffs, blowing the vapour out in a thin stream. She eyed Ripley suspiciously, waiting for the challenge. It wasn't forthcoming.

Do what you want to your own body.

"Anyway," she continued. "As I watched people come and go, and listened to their prayers, I noticed a pattern. Megan doesn't heal them herself, she just helps the person in question to channel their own faith and energy towards whatever need they are expressing."

Ripley frowned, not understanding what Anne was saying. Anne took another puff of her vape and shoved it back in the drawer, coming back to the table and sitting down opposite Ripley.

"Basically," Anne continued, "she gives up her own energy, her life force, to help others. And whatever need they present her with, consciously or subconsciously, is what she addresses. So while Jane Hewitt may have believed she wanted to be healed, I don't think that's what Megan saw. I don't think that was the gift she gave her."

She looked up at Ripley with such a strange mixture of pride and sadness that Ripley felt she was finally seeing the real Anne Shields. Proud mother. Staunch defender.

"But Jane walked out unaided," Ripley said. "So what happened? She thought she'd been healed."

"Only because she didn't properly understand what she'd asked for," Anne said, her brow furrowing. "She knew when she came here that she was near the end of her path. What she really wanted was one more day to be herself. To be normal. To be happy. To hold her husband. To dance barefoot. Those were her words. That's what she asked for. And that's exactly what she got."

How convenient.

"But she believed she'd been healed," Ripley said again. "You let her leave here believing it. And when it all ended, she felt her faith had been unfounded. She felt, and Ian does too, that she'd lost the thing she held so dear: Her trust in God."

Anne sighed heavily. More in sadness than frustration.

"I am truly sorry that she felt that way, but it's not our fault she didn't understand properly. Without God's love, Megan would not have been able to help her. It was precisely Jane's strength of faith that made her particular miracle possible."

Ripley watched Anne carefully as she spoke, assessing her body language. The woman clearly believed in her daughter's ability completely. Unless she was one of the best liars that Ripley had ever encountered.

"Do you describe Megan's gift this way to your visitors before they meet her?"

"No. It would put too much pressure on them. They would over think their need. It just wouldn't work. It has to be organic."

As explanations for healing miracles went, this kind of made sense, but Ripley couldn't help feeling that it was a convenient rationalisation of what had happened during Jane's visit that Anne had concocted after Jane's death to explain away the perceived failure. If only Jane had heard Anne's definition of Megan's gift, she may not have felt so betrayed by God in the end.

"Would it be possible for me to meet Megan? Not necessarily now, but at some point while I'm here?"

"Do you have something you would like her to help with?" Anne asked, the hint of scepticism in her voice. "An illness, perhaps?"

Ripley hesitated again. She could make something up, but given what she'd just heard she didn't think it would help. How was she supposed to investigate their claims if there was nothing tangible for Megan to help her with?

"You'll forgive me for being suspicious," Anne continued, taking another sip of her tea. "I don't want to waste Megan's time or energy. She'd happily help anyone with anything, but she hasn't been well lately and, in the light of recent events, I have to protect her. Do you see?"

"Of course," said Ripley.

"If there *is* genuinely something that Megan can help you with, then I'm sure we can find time for you to sit with her. I would love you to experience her gift first hand. But if you just want to observe her for your research, then you're better off joining the rest of them at this group prayer meeting tomorrow."

She said it with such distaste that Ripley frowned. How Anne could put Megan through something so public had been playing on Ripley's mind since she first read about the group meeting. Now that Anne had brought it up herself, Ripley had to ask the question.

"How does that work then? The group meeting? Do you really take Megan out into the crowds?"

She had failed to disguise her tone enough and Anne visibly bristled.

"Don't presume to judge me, Dr Ripley."

Ripley began to protest but Anne spoke over her.

"Megan's gift is a complex and powerful one, and we want her to share it with as many people as possible. She is under the best care at all times. I would never do anything to hurt my daughter."

Her anger had quickly dissipated and, by the end of her sentence, even she didn't sound too convinced by her own protests.

"I'm sure you wouldn't. And I didn't mean to suggest it. I just find it hard to imagine, given her condition."

"She has full time care and state-of-the-art equipment. Which means she's a lot more mobile than you'd think. I know that the group meetings tire her more, but she is a strong girl. And we don't do them often."

Ripley didn't know what to say without sounding even more judgemental, so she held her tongue.

"As I said," Anne filled the silence. "You can see it for yourself tomorrow. So unless there's really something you personally need, there will be no point in you seeing her today. She doesn't need gawkers."

"Well, there is something," Ripley said, hesitantly. "But I'm not sure it's enough..."

Anne sat forward, head tilted, looking into Ripley's eyes.

"What is it?"

The only thing that Ripley could think of was her lungs. She was still struggling with her breathing if she got above a slow walk, but, it had only been a couple of weeks since her near drowning, and it was far too early to tell what the long-term effect would be. Was it disingenuous to use it as an excuse to get a meeting with Megan. How else would she get to meet her? She was going to the group meeting, anyway, but it would be impossible to get a true sense of Megan's so-called gift in a crowd.

"I had an accident," she began, eyes downcast. "A few weeks ago. I was trying to save someone from drowning in a lake and I ended up nearly drowning myself. I haven't been well since. The doctors say my lungs may never fully recover."

She looked up in time to see a flicker of interest cross Anne's eyes. Megan's condition was the result of a near-drowning, so Ripley had guessed it would strike a chord. She knew she was laying it on a little thick, but she told Anne about the girls in the lake, and how they all thought they'd seen an angel. She wanted to make sure that Anne saw her as someone who had tried to help. It would ease some of her suspicions.

When she'd finished her tale, Anne stood up without responding and turned her back. It took Ripley a moment to realise that Anne was flicking through an appointment book on the counter.

"You're in luck," she said, turning brightly. "Megan has a little time this morning."

What a coincidence.

"I just need to go through some paperwork before we go in. If you agree, then we would be happy to help."

"Sure," said Ripley. "Fire away."

Another peal of screams and bickering carried down the corridor from the twins.

"Let's go somewhere more conducive to a quiet chat," Anne said, gathering up the appointment book and a pen. "Follow me."

Ripley drained the last of her tea and followed Anne back out into the corridor and through to a waiting room. A small coffee table, littered with leaflets, squatted in front of a narrow, uncomfortable looking sofa. On the other side of the room was a large wooden desk with two hard chairs in front, and a large padded chair behind. Anne took the big chair and indicated for Ripley to sit opposite.

Ripley sat with her hands folded in her lap, waiting for Anne to finish gathering papers. On the wall behind the desk were a handful of framed photographs featuring small groups of people, all in matching God's Gift branded T-shirts, standing in lines, beaming at the camera as Anne stood out front in each, clutching a series of oversized cheques. *The fundraisers.* Ripley studied the faces as Anne continued to rifle through her paperwork.

"We didn't do any of this in the beginning, but it's become a necessary evil these days. That Ian Hewitt isn't the only one who's tried to cause trouble because things didn't work out how they wanted. So now, I'm afraid we have to make sure we go through everything beforehand. Managing expectations, Simon calls it. I hope that's okay?"

The hard, patronising tone of her voice made Ripley uneasy. It felt like a warning: *People like you, coming in here and stirring up trouble.*

"Absolutely fine."

She noticed that Reverend Rodwell was in each of the fundraiser photographs, usually in the centre of frame, close to Anne. And that same, angelic-looking young man Ripley had seen around a few times cropped up in most of the more recent photos. His neat blonde curls and blue eyes were unmistakable. His expression was always the same—neutral, disinterested, distant. He was also the only one not wearing a branded T-shirt. Too cool for school.

"Who is that?" Ripley asked, pointing him out. "Standing between you and the Reverend?"

Anne looked up to check.

"Oh, that is Simon," she said, with almost maternal pride. "He is amazing. Only been with us for a year, but he's turned the place around. He's so organised. Basically runs everything now. I don't know what we'd do without him. Why do you ask?"

"Oh, no reason," Ripley said. "I've just bumped into him a couple of times since I've been here."

Anne frowned thoughtfully.

"Funny. I thought he'd gone away for the weekend," she said. "Probably just didn't want me to know he was still in town on his days off. I try not to call on him, but I can hardly manage without him. He works so hard."

She looked at Ripley, papers neatly arranged in front of her.

"Before we start," Anne said, cautiously. "I want to ask you about your own faith. Obviously, I heard them describe you as a Miracle Detective on that telly programme. What does that mean, exactly?"

Here we go.

"Well, firstly I'd like to point out that it's not a description I like to use myself, but basically it means that I investigate claims of miracles to see if there is any truth in them, or whether there could be another explanation."

"Who's that for then?"

"Sorry?"

"What I mean is, who exactly is it that asks for you to investigate these miracles? Or is it just something you do for your own entertainment?"

"No, not at all. All sorts of people ask for my help. The police, courts, doctors. I've even done some work for the Vatican."

"Really?" Anne sounded both incredulous and impressed. "Why on earth would they ask for *your* help?"

Charming.

"Well," replied Ripley, "in order to make someone a saint, a certain number of miracles need to be attributed to them, and those claims must be properly investigated to make sure that they're true."

"So you've confirmed miracles before then? For the Vatican."

Ripley saw Anne's demeanour change instantly, subtly shifting from suspicious to keen. On the surface, she was trying to remain businesslike, but Ripley had seen this same shift in others before—the moment when the penny drops that, if they play their cards right, Ripley could be exactly the person they need to validate their claim of a miracle. She was not about to admit to things she'd never done, but she could see that familiar chink in Anne's armour.

"I was asked to investigate for them, yes."

She'd been hired to play the Devil's Advocate on that occasion, and it had been her job to debunk the miracle claims as rationally and thoroughly as possible. The beatification in question had gone ahead anyway, despite her protests. Enough others had claimed and confirmed the miracles for it to count.

"Well, that *is* interesting," Anne said, sitting back. "So you do, ultimately, believe in the possibility of miracles? I'd got the impression from your introduction on that programme and from your book that you were a non-believer."

"No, I'm not a non-believer at all. I just demand more physical proof than most. Believe me, I'd like nothing better than to have a definitive answer on the miracle question."

"But you've yet to find it?"

Ripley nodded.

"And if you did? Would you be happy to share it? Or would that ruin your reputation?"

"I'm only interested in the truth," Ripley said. "Honestly."

"Ah, well, isn't that always the problem with matters of faith," Anne said, leaning back again. "Your idea of truth versus mine."

"I like to think I'm objective enough to see both."

"That would make you a pretty special woman, Dr Ripley."

Ripley didn't detect the slightest hint of criticism in Anne's comment and it took her off guard. Anne turned the two pieces of paper around to face Ripley and placed the pen on top.

"These are our two disclaimers," she said. "We require everyone to sign them before entering Megan's room. You'll see that the first reminds you that you are meeting my daughter for a private prayer session, and you acknowledge that any reaction you may experience as a result is entirely unpredictable and a positive resolution to whatever ails you cannot be guaranteed. We are happy if your experience is positive, and sorry if it is not, but there are no guarantees either way."

She delivered the well-practiced disclaimer as rote. Ripley took the pen and tapped it against her thumb as she looked over the documents. There was something so cold and commercial about these typed pages, with their logo at the top that felt at odds with Anne's view of her daughter's role in life.

Once again, Ripley got the feeling that Anne was not altogether comfortable with the business side of this venture, noticing how she fidgeted with her fingernails, as though itching to just get the signing done and let Ripley experience things for herself.

"So how does it work then?" Ripley asked.

"What? The meeting?"

"No, the business side," she said, waving her pen over the pages in front of her. "All this."

"How do you mean?"

"Well, I assume you get paid for this service, but it says nothing here about rates or payment methods. So how does it work?"

Anne laughed awkwardly, wrinkling her nose in distaste at the mention of money.

"Oh no," Anne protested. "There's no charge."

"Wow. Okay. But how do you survive?" Ripley asked. "I mean, what about Megan's care? It can't be cheap to keep everything running."

"No, it's not," Anne huffed. "We are very lucky that the church supports us. Reverend Francis helped us to set up a charity, and he's a very active fundraiser. Of course, many of Megan's visitors leave us a donation, and some of them are very generous. But really, every penny counts. The whole village is very good about helping where they can. It's very reassuring."

"I see," Ripley said. She was sure the whole village was fully supportive—from what she'd seen so far, apart from some spectacular coastal walks and the abundance of ancient monuments, visiting Megan was the only other reason to come to such an isolated spot.

"But nothing is obligatory," Anne said, almost defensively. "We make that clear to our visitors. It's all in the documents there."

Anne tapped the pages on the desk and Ripley smiled tightly. Taking the hint, she spent a moment reading through the rest of the document. It was a straightforward disclaimer, exactly as Anne had explained. No harm in signing it. She turned to the second page.

"That one basically says that you can't sue us if you're unhappy with the outcome of your meeting," Anne said, sounding dismissive. "It's a new one we've had to start using, since..."

Ripley nodded, reading again. There were two grammatical errors in the opening paragraph. She doubted that a signature on this piece of paper would stand up in court against a well-evidenced argument, so she signed it and handed them both back.

"Well, Dr Ripley," Anne said. "If the Vatican trusts you, so do I. And if you can look me in the eye and promise me that you won't do anything to harm my daughter, then you are welcome to sit with us."

Ripley looked into Anne's eyes, and saw a woman who was desperately hoping that Ripley would see in Megan what so many others had, and use her status to spread their message. But she also saw something else—a mother, still trying to justify to herself why this was happening to her little girl. She saw pride and defiance in Anne's eyes but, beneath that she saw her fear that Ripley would walk away without witnessing what made her daughter so special.

"I won't deliberately do anything to harm your family," Ripley said, fixing Anne's gaze.

Of course she meant it. She never *deliberately* set out to hurt anyone. But if, along the way, she found that people were using faith to trick others, she'd take them to task, and if that harmed their business, so be it.

"Good," said Anne.

"As I said," Ripley continued, feeling it was important to add a disclaimer of her own. "I'm only interested in the truth."

"And I'm sure you will find it here," Anne said, smiling. "Wait here a moment, please."

She headed off through a set of double doors into a room beyond. Ripley heard the beep of machines and was reminded of her brief stay in hospital recently. She had been lucky not to sustain any lasting damage from her time in the lake. Lucky to have been pulled out of the water in time. But had it really been just luck? The question would always haunt her.

Some piped choral music began playing through speakers mounted in the ceiling above her, and Ripley caught a whiff of a newly struck match, followed by the unmistakable smell of incense. Anne was setting the scene.

While waiting, she checked her phone again. Still nothing from Neil Wilcox. She wondered if Neil and his team were any closer to finding John in Afghanistan. She hated not knowing, but she understood that they wouldn't be able to tell her anything until they had a definite answer either way.

What would John make of all this? If anything, he was even more cynical than Ripley herself. Perhaps because he'd seen first hand some of the destruction caused in the name of religion. Especially to the children. Even though they'd never had kids of their own, John had always been hugely protective of children's welfare. He'd be appalled at how Megan was being used as a commodity here, and he wouldn't want to listen to any talk of healing miracles as an excuse for her exploitation. Ripley missed him so much.

She turned in her chair as Anne swung the double doors open triumphantly.

"Come on through," she said. "Megan's ready for you now."

MEGAN'S ROOM LOOKED younger than Ripley had been expecting, decorated as it was in the bright colours and designs of a child rather than a young teenager. Of course, Megan would have had no say in the decoration and Ripley wondered whether in part the room was designed to remind visitors of the childhood their young host had lost.

The hi-tech bed dominated, but they'd gone to a lot of effort to make it feel like a home rather than a hospital room. The bed frame was bright red, rather than the typical clinical grey, and the bedcovers had a line of parading cartoon elephants marching across the bottom, each holding the tail of the one before it.

Megan was propped up, surrounded by pillows and cushions in shades of pink and red, and even the tubes and lines that supported her life were colourful and patterned. The whole image felt desperately sad—a forced jollity that did little to mask the tragedy of this young life on pause.

"Megan, darling," Anne said in a sweet, sing-song tone. "This is Dr Alex Ripley, my love. She's a very important guest, and she's going to sit with us for a while. Okay?"

Anne smiled at Ripley, nodding as though Megan had somehow communicated her consent. Ripley bristled, uncomfortable with being described as 'very important'. Anne smoothed the covers over Megan's chest and indicated where Ripley was to sit—a neat chair beside the bed, upholstered in red with white buttons sewn into the back.

As Ripley sat, Anne stood by Megan's side and took her hand, reaching across the bed to take Ripley's hand too. Ripley hesitated just long enough to prompt a small, encouraging nod from Anne. She closed the circle, taking Megan's hand cautiously, fearful of disturbing her, but reminding herself that Megan would be used to this, given how many visitors she must receive. Once again, Ripley felt a pang of sympathy for this young girl who had no say in how her life was playing out.

The whole scene was perfectly set, from the peaceful choral music playing at just the right volume to be uplifting but not intrusive, to the low, gentle lighting, the hint of incense in the air. Instead of filling Ripley with a sense of being closer to God, it simply reminded her that this was a business, with everything designed to play on her emotions and make her believe in the healing power of faith.

She tried to push her cynicism aside as Anne began to pray in a soft voice, but she found it almost impossible to do so. Anne's tone sounded forced, like one of those awful relaxation soundtracks—a soft near-whispering monotone which made Ripley's skin crawl. She tried to zone it out, focussing instead on Megan.

She was a pretty girl even though the pallor of sickness hung on her like a cloak. The pale waxiness of her skin suggested she had been indoors for too long. Ripley noticed that someone, most likely Anne, had applied a little rouge to Megan's cheeks and some natural-toned colour to her lips. If anything, the make-up made her appear even more deathlike, but Ripley could understand why Anne would want her little girl to have some colour in her cheeks.

Trying to rise above Anne's monotonous prayer, Ripley concentrated on the connection with Megan's hand, feeling it growing warmer. She could feel a pulse there, but couldn't determine whether it was her own or Megan's. Even Megan's face looked more peaceful than it had just a moment ago. Perhaps the girl felt their presence and was glad of the company. Or maybe Ripley had just acclimatised to the sight of her.

Ripley had read several studies about brain function in long term coma patients, and the idea of them being present, yet slightly removed, fascinated her. Anne clearly believed that her daughter could hear and comprehend everything she said, and Ripley wondered what kind of neurological studies they had conducted on the young girl's brain function after her accident. It reminded her again just how lucky she had been with her own near-drowning. She could have ended up like this. Or worse.

Perhaps because she was thinking about her lungs, or maybe thanks to the faintly chemical smell that hung in the air, Ripley felt a sudden burning in her chest, constricting her throat.

She coughed, instinctively taking her right hand out of Anne's to cover her mouth. Anne frowned, stopping her prayer to allow Ripley's hacking to subside.

"Sorry," Ripley whispered, when she could pull in a breath without coughing. There was a faint rattle as the air struggled into her lungs, but she swallowed the desire to cough again. She didn't replace her hand in Anne's.

As Anne was about to resume her prayer, the door burst open, ruining the peace. Anne twisted around, jumping up almost guiltily as the young, blonde-haired man Ripley now knew to be Simon hurried in. Ripley dropped Megan's hand, but stopped short of standing up herself.

"Sorry to interrupt," he said in a library whisper. "Anne, I need a quick word."

Anne looked back apologetically at Ripley, but allowed herself to be guided from the room by Simon's hand on her elbow. He looked back over his shoulder at Ripley, but she couldn't read his expression before he turned away. Suspicion, most likely.

She couldn't quite make out what he was saying as he closed the door, but she was sure she heard him ask: "What on earth do you think..." The rest was lost as the door clicked shut. She turned her attention back to Megan, suddenly feeling quite overwhelmed by the situation this child was in.

"Just you and me now, kid," she whispered.

She took the young girl's hands and held them firmly, hoping that if Megan did have any consciousness at all, she would feel this. Leaning in closer, Ripley spoke to her.

"Megan, I'm sorry for what happened to you. For what is still happening. You don't have to do any of this, you know. You don't have to let them use you like this. It may not feel like it, but you do have a choice. You can choose to come back, or you can choose to go. But you have to make the choice yourself. Do you understand?"

She didn't know what she was expecting, but Ripley was a little disappointed that there was no response. Maybe Megan really didn't have any choice. Ripley continued to hold her hands as she studied the tubes that were feeding her and keeping her functioning in this state. *What am I doing here?* It was all so distressingly callous—to let all and sundry traipse in and invade this poor girl's peace. Even if it paid for everything the family could want or need.

Ripley thought of John again. What would he do if he saw this? Call social services, no doubt. He always plumped for the official channels.

She felt a sudden increase in the heat generating between their clasped hands. It was uncomfortable—clammy and wet. Small beads of sweat glistened on Megan's brow. Perhaps her body temperature was yet another thing the poor girl had no control of.

Ripley shivered, torn between letting go of Megan's hands or comforting her. A low level, insistent beeping began from one of the machines monitoring her. What was happening? Should she call Anne?

She was still holding Megan's hand when the door opened again and Anne walked in, looking flushed. Embarrassed? Or chastised?

"I'm afraid I have to ask you to go, Dr Ripley," she said, her voice wobbling slightly. "Megan needs her rest."

Simon remained in the waiting area, arms folded smugly over his chest. What had he just said to her? Ripley let go of Megan's hand, placing it gently back on the bed and standing up.

Anne froze as she noticed the urgent beeping—a momentary pause before she leapt into action, pulling an alarm cord beside Megan's bed and checking her temperature and pulse with shaking hands.

"What happened?" she demanded, her voice full of accusation. "What did you do to her?"

Before Ripley could answer, a young man in a medical smock ran in.

"Clear the room," he ordered.

"Get out!" Anne shouted at Ripley.

Ripley grabbed her things and headed for the door.

"I'm sorry," she said. But no one was listening. Even Simon didn't give her another glance as she passed. He had a strange look on his face. Concern, definitely, but Ripley also saw annoyance there. She left the room in chaos, heading back out to the quiet of the corridor.

Anne's younger daughter stood in the doorway to their lounge room, watching impassively as Ripley hurried out. She stuck a tiny finger up one of her nostrils as Ripley passed her, inspecting the treasure she found there with a keener interest than the debacle in her sister's bedroom.

Gareth stood in the open front door, his face the picture of concern.

"What's going on?" he asked.

"Megan's had some kind of turn," Ripley said.

"What happened?"

"I don't know. She—"

"I'd better go help," he cut across her, looking unsure of what to do.

She nodded and left. It was only as he closed the door that she realised it must have been Gareth who called Simon in. Was he that scared of her being alone with Anne and Megan? What did they think she would do?

"Dr Ripley!"

She looked around to find Simon hurrying down the path after her. Ripley turned her back on him and continued to walk back towards her car. She wasn't in the mood for any further confrontation.

"Dr Ripley! Sorry, can I have a quick word?"

Ripley slowed, surprised by his polite tone, but didn't turn round yet. He caught up with her and fell in stride alongside, breathing heavily. *Maybe my lungs aren't that bad after all,* she thought. *Or maybe he's just really unfit.*

"Hang on a second, will you?" he said, grabbing her elbow to get her to slow down. "I just want to talk to you. Please."

Ripley stopped, shaking her elbow free of his grasp.

"What?"

"You should have told me you wanted a private meeting with Megan. These things need to be carefully managed."

I bet they do. Carefully stage managed, more like.

"I was there in good faith, thank you," Ripley said, turning to face him. She had no doubt he intended to stop her getting any further with Megan. Why else would he have come in on his day off?

"Of course you were," he said. "It's just that your reputation does somewhat precede you."

He smiled as he saw the frustration flicker over her face. It wasn't a kind smile.

"Yes, I suppose it does," Ripley said. "But Anne knows who I am and what I do, and she seemed happy for me to meet Megan. Keen even. Until you turned up."

"Yes, well. She doesn't always know what's best in the long term," he said, his lips trying to hold on to the smile, though his eyes shone fiercely.

"And I suppose you do?"

"Yes, I do," he snapped. "And I was clearly right in this situation too, given Megan's condition after being with you for just a few moments."

"Is she all right?"

"I don't know," he said, tersely. "What happened in there?"

"Nothing," she said. "I was holding her hands, and I felt her begin to get really hot and then the beeping started. I didn't do anything. I swear."

He ran a hand through his hair, growing frustrated.

"She's a very sensitive girl," he said. "You shouldn't have been with her. She will have picked up on all that toxic negativity you spout. Anne was stupid to let you in. Especially when we have such a big day tomorrow."

Aha. So that's it. She saw exactly what he was about now. The group meeting might now be at risk and Simon was doubtless worried about all those donations they would lose out on if they had to cancel.

"She's worth more than this, you know," she snapped, turning on her heel and stalking away.

He caught up with her, grabbing her arm again and pulling her close. "That family have gone through more than enough in the last few years. They're not doing anything wrong here. Now, I know you're some kind of hotshot about all things religious, but I'll tell you this for free: I've seen with my own eyes the good that girl does. I can't tell you how or why it happens, but I've seen it and I believe in her. I know you make your living debunking this kind of thing, but I'll save you some time here. She's completely legit."

Ripley shook her head and set off again, unwilling to rise to a response. She was aware that he'd stopped, obviously feeling that his piece had been said.

"Just go home!" he called after her. "There's no story for you here."

She stopped dead, reeling back round on him. She was sick of being told to back off.

"I'll be the judge of that," she shouted, gratified to see him take a small step backwards. He started towards her again though, threateningly, and she turned on her heel and stalked back to her car. Her heart was thumping, but if she'd ever had any doubts about seeing this case through, Simon had just made damn sure she would stick around.

THE DARK CAME flooding back in and the beeping faded away. The voices were all swallowed up by the rushing water, blood, whatever it was that filled her ears. There had been a deep pain there. A different kind of pain. It had felt strange far away and closed off. *I can't reach it. It's locked away too deep.*

There had been something else, an annoying little thing, which had felt much closer, but it disappeared almost as soon as she touched it. And that's when she felt the real pain. Pain hidden behind a wall that Megan couldn't get around. She'd tried to call it to her, as she had done before, but it was a strange shape— one she didn't recognise and couldn't hold on to.

I called it, but it didn't listen. It wouldn't move. She had tried so hard, pushing at that wall with all her strength, but it hadn't been enough. And then the link had been broken, and now she was drowning in this bleak sadness. There was nothing she could do.

Or was there? Through the darkness, she realised that she could still see the outline of the wall. Maybe she could try again. When she'd had a little rest.

RIPLEY WAS STILL seething when she pulled into the pub car park. Ian was already there, sitting on the wall, and he hopped down as she climbed out of the car.

"Good morning?" he asked.

"Interesting," she replied. "You?"

"I guess," he said. "I'd been going through my notes and trying to write down anything I remember that might help."

He flashed a small black notepad at her before tucking it back into his jacket pocket.

"How did that go?"

"Slow," he smiled ruefully. "The demon booze seems to have made swiss cheese of my memory."

"I know what you mean," she said. Ripley had lost enough memories of nights out after overdoing it. Most of them probably embarrassing enough to want to forget, anyway.

"I came up with something though," he said, hopefully. "I was going through my phone and I did make a few calls to Caroline Clifton around the time Anne says I was in their house."

"Right," Ripley said, not sure how it would help.

"Well, I was calling her from here. Outside the pub."

Ian clearly had a point, but Ripley was struggling to see it. He noticed her blank expression.

"Well, I left her a message, see? Because she wasn't answering. That's what I remembered. I was leaning against the wall here. So you'd be able to hear stuff, wouldn't you? Gulls and the sea? Would that be enough?"

He was grasping at straws, but he sounded more positive than he had since Ripley'd met him. Perhaps there was something in it.

"If you called from here, then the police would be able to triangulate your call with the phone company, but I doubt it would place you far enough away from their house to count. But, if Caroline kept the message and there are any distinctive sounds in the background, that might help corroborate your story. Have you tried calling her again?"

"Yeah, I've tried a couple of times today, but her phone just goes straight to voicemail."

"Never mind," Ripley said. "We'll try her again after lunch. It's good for you if there are others who also have an axe to grind. We shouldn't let the fact that they've accused you of breaking in distract us from your own case against them. Come on."

She smiled at him and opened the door to the pub, following him in. The bar was relatively quiet, with just two tables occupied. The same barmaid was polishing glasses behind the bar. Her smile dropped as she saw them.

"You're barred," the barmaid snarled at Ian, slamming the glass down and leaning forward with both hands firmly planted on the bar.

"He's with me," Ripley said.

"I don't care, love. He's not welcome in here, and I told him that the last time I chucked him out."

Ripley looked across at Ian, who shrugged.

"I don't remember," he whispered, already turning apologetically back towards the door.

"Fine," Ripley said, shaking her head.

She followed him out into the car park but was suddenly struck by a thought.

"Wait here a second," she said, dashing back into the pub. The barmaid looked up again, annoyed.

"Sorry, can I just ask a quick question?" Ripley asked.

The barmaid sighed.

"If it's quick. I've got customers to deal with."

"You say you barred him? When was that?"

The barmaid frowned.

"Oh I dunno, a week or so ago," she said, noncommittally.

"Can you be more specific?"

"No, love, I can't."

"Why did you bar him? What was he doing?"

"He was drunk, he was shouting his mouth off. We had a family in for a fiftieth anniversary dinner, and he was bothering them. Carrying on like that. Especially in front of the kiddies."

"Did they book?"

"What's that now?"

"The family group. Did they reserve a table?"

The barmaid rolled her eyes.

"Yes," she said sullenly. She knew what was coming and reached across for the reservations book.

She licked her finger and flicked backwards through the pages, a day at a time. Finally, she tapped a page.

"Here you go," she said, turning the book round to face Ripley. "Last Wednesday."

"Can you remember what time you chucked him out?"

"Oh God, love, really?"

"It's important," Ripley insisted.

"It was early," the barmaid huffed. "Too early to be that drunk, anyway. Let's see. They'd booked for seven-thirty and they ordered pretty quickly on account of the kids. They were in the middle of their main course, I think. Yes, that's right. Must have been just after eight. Eight-fifteen at the latest."

"Thanks," Ripley said, turning back to the door with a small frown.

"I wouldn't go wasting too much time on him though love," the barmaid called after her. "He's a nasty piece of work."

"Don't worry about me," Ripley said, smiling over her shoulder. "I'm tougher than I look. Thanks for your help."

She hesitated at the door, puzzled by the timeline of Ian's evening last Wednesday. If he'd been kicked out of the pub as early as a quarter past eight, he'd have had plenty of time to reach Megan's house on foot before nine. He said he'd phoned Caroline after nine, and Anne had logged the break in at five-to-nine exactly. So had Ian gone back there? Had he called Caroline after he'd been caught and run away, hoping that it would give him an alibi? Ripley was reminded just how little she knew him. The barmaid's description of him was harsh, but perhaps Ripley just hadn't seen that side of him yet. He seemed fairly harmless, but she was smart enough to know that still waters run deep. It would really help to talk to Caroline Clifton. If only they could get the woman to answer her phone.

When Ripley emerged from the warmth of the pub, Ian was leaning on the side of her car, looking down at his phone. He tucked it away as she approached.

"Still nothing," he said, shrugging.

"Come on then, Trouble," Ripley said brightly. "We'll have to find somewhere else for our lunch."

It was probably a better idea for them to get further afield for a while. Ian was clearly unpopular among the locals and had obviously been making a nuisance of himself in the village. Their animosity was understandable given their protectiveness of Megan, and Ripley needed to keep all of her avenues of investigation open right now. After all, she was perfectly capable of offending people in her own right.

Ian was silent for the first part of the drive, staring out of the window as they drove along the main road, past the church, past the cafe, past the turning for Megan's road. She couldn't help craning her neck too as they passed. She slowed as she saw an estate car in ambulance livery parked at an angle across Megan's driveway.

"What's going on there?" Ian asked.

Ripley shrugged. She didn't want to get in to what had happened when she'd visited Megan earlier, but she hoped the girl was okay.

"I bet they've hurt someone else," Ian said bitterly.

Ripley tutted, Ian was becoming a bit like a broken record. Anne Shields may be in the business of over-exaggerating her daughter's talents, but she was no villain. Ian and Jane had gone there of their own volition and had believed in Megan's gift while it suited them. What happened to Jane afterwards was tragic, and while Ripley agreed that Anne could be accused of robbing her of her faith, she couldn't believe that they had deliberately set out to hurt Jane. What would be the point?

Still, Ripley was worried about Megan now. What if the girl had heard her advice? What if she *had* chosen to give up? Ripley swung the car in a wide turn across the road and pulled into the cul-de-sac.

"What are you doing?" Ian asked, nervously.

"Get down," Ripley said, and Ian flipped the lever to lay his seat back.

"I'm not supposed to go anywhere near them, remember?"

"I'm just looking," she replied, through a ventriloquist's grimace. "You stay down and don't make a sound."

Megan's house squatted at the top of the turning circle, the two Range Rovers nestled side by side in the drive beside Reverend Rodwell's flashy saloon. The car skewed across the drive was an emergency vehicle from a private clinic, dressed in the familiar green and yellow of the Ambulance Service, but clearly marked private across the bonnet.

Ripley slowed to a crawl as they pulled in to the turning circle. Ian craned his neck to see and quickly ducked back in his seat as the front door opened. Ripley pulled to a stop opposite the drive as two uniformed paramedics left the house, each one received a pat on the shoulder from Reverend Rodwell.

With serious nods and glances exchanged, the paramedics were on their way. Rodwell stood in the doorway watching them all the way to their car. Only as they pulled away did he notice Ripley. She waved brightly and lowered the window, leaning across Ian's reclined body to see him better.

"Everything okay?" she called. "Do you need any help?"

She saw Rodwell force his grimace into a smile.

"Ah, Doctor Ripley," he called, his voice tight. "Back so soon?"

"I was just on my way out for a drive up the coast and saw the ambulance," she said, the picture of naïve innocence. "I couldn't just drive on by without seeing if there was anything I could do. Is Megan okay?"

"Jesus," muttered Ian. "You are something else."

"Fine," Rodwell called back sternly. "We're all fine."

"Well, if you're sure..."

"Goodbye Dr Ripley," he said firmly, hand on the front door ready to close it. "Be careful on that coast road. It's got some dangerous stretches."

"I'll take it slowly," she called. "See you tomorrow then."

His pained smile dropped before the door was properly closed.

"Arsehole," Ripley said as she pulled away, raising the window again.

"See you tomorrow?" Ian questioned, starting to sit up.

"Stay down until we've gone round the corner," Ripley snapped.

Ian lay back in the seat again.

"What's going on tomorrow?"

"There's a group prayer meeting in the church, with Megan. Rodwell invited me. Though I'm not sure I'll still be welcome."

"You're not really going are you?"

"Of course," she said. "How else am I supposed to see how their operation works? Everything is far too controlled in that house. They can engineer everything to create the perfect atmosphere for a spiritual encounter. I want to see what happens when Megan is brought out into a less controlled group environment."

She turned out onto the main road and accelerated away.

"Okay, you can come up now," she said.

Ian wound his seat back up and watched her for a moment in silence.

"Don't you think it's sick that she'd do that to her own daughter? Wheel her out in front of a group like some performing monkey. Doesn't that strike you as cruel?"

Ripley sighed. It was a difficult one to understand when you looked at it rationally, but when Anne had explained it to her, it had made sense.

"Maybe, but if even one person feels a benefit, Anne feels it's worth it. As far as she's concerned, this is what Megan was put on earth to do and if she doesn't allow it, she's denying God's gift."

Ian snorted, shaking his head.

"You think there's something in it, don't you?"

Ripley frowned, not saying anything. He loosened his seatbelt enough to swivel to face her, an incredulous look creeping across his tired features.

"You do. You believe her. I can understand why you would. I was fooled myself when we first met her. That Anne is a canny saleswoman."

She could hear the anger bubbling in his voice already.

"No, Ian," she said calmly. "I don't *believe* anything. I haven't seen enough to convince me either way. I'm just saying that I understand why Anne feels justified in parading her daughter in front of all those strangers. I want to go tomorrow so that I can see it for myself. I'm not inclined to make any kind of judgement before that."

"But you met her today, right? You sat with Megan?"

"Yes, briefly, but we were interrupted."

"And? Did you feel something *special?*"

He snarled the last word.

"I can't say. The whole experience is quite surreal, isn't it? I think if I had something that needed healing and I already had a strong faith, it would be hard not to be swept along in the moment."

"Like we were," Ian said.

"I guess, but there's a difference between being swept along and what you described happening to Jane. She got up and walked out of there, pain free. That's what you told me. And she travelled home, pain free. And she spent the evening with you, pain free."

"What are you saying? That she *was* healed?"

"No," she replied quickly, sensing him becoming more agitated. "There's no way of ever saying that, is there? There are no medical records of her transformation, only your description. But you were there. You saw it. What do you think happened to her?"

He sat quietly for a moment, shaping his answer.

"I think she wanted to believe so much that she willed herself better," he said. "She was so caught up in the idea that her faith had been rewarded that she simply transcended the pain for a while. But they led her on. They made her believe that she could feel things she couldn't. She was ecstatic. But once the euphoria wore off, her body had nothing more to give. She'd used up the last dregs of her energy believing their lies. And they'd used up the last of her faith."

"Maybe she got exactly what she asked for," Ripley said, knowing he wouldn't want to hear it. "Maybe what she really wanted, deep down, was one last night of normality. One more night with you. Perhaps she used the last of her energy, and her faith, to have that. Maybe you both misunderstood the gift."

He was already shaking his head.

"They said she was healed. But if she had been, she wouldn't have died would she? She would have stayed healed and we would have had the life they'd supposedly given us back."

His voice cracked as he finished his rant. His shoulders sagged and his head dropped. It was all still so raw for him.

"I can't imagine how hard it is for you to accept," she began. "I know you want to blame them for Jane's death, but perhaps you should focus on those few hours of pain free joy you had together and not on this vendetta. You should try to get rid of this anger before it consumes you."

"I can't," he said. "Every time I remember how happy she was that day, all I can think is how they cheated her. Her faith was so pure. It made her so happy. They had no right to take it from her."

"I know," Ripley said. "But as far as Anne's concerned, you both just misunderstood the gift Megan gave you."

"Why are you defending them?"

"I'm not, Ian. I'm playing Devil's Advocate."

Of course," he muttered. "You're good at that."

Ripley almost stopped the car and kicked him out. He'd asked for her help, but he just wouldn't listen.

Even accounting for his grief, she was tired of his petulance.

"Listen," she snapped, "you asked me to come down here and check things out. You asked for my help. If it's revenge you want, you're barking up the wrong tree. And if you're naïve enough to think that anything I've just said won't be levelled at you during a court case, then you're even more stupid than you're acting. They can pull a hundred witnesses out of a hat to testify to Megan's good works for every one you find to cry foul. And they have the perfect fallback position: There are no guarantees when it comes to God's will."

"I thought you believed me," he said, sulkily.

"I believe that you feel everything you've told me about your experience there, I'd be a fool not to. But I don't like being told what to think by anyone. If you want my help, you've got it, but just let me do my job without behaving like a petulant child."

She accelerated again, a little of her own childishness rising up. Ian sat in silence for a moment, his face still hard, his lips pouted. Perhaps she'd been too harsh, but he wasn't making any of this easy for either of them.

"I'm sorry," he said, finally. "You're right. I shouldn't be taking any of this out on you."

"It's okay," she said. "I just think you need to be realistic about what's going on here. If there's any way you are going to bring a case you have to put your emotions aside and deal in facts. That means first we have to clear you of their charges and second, we have to find at least one other witness who will testify to feeling coerced and deceived. And that means getting hold of Caroline."

He nodded, contrite.

"Okay."

Ripley turned off the road into the car park of an average looking pub. One other car in the pot-holed car park, empty window boxes, and a faded sign promising quality food. It would have to do.

"Right," she said, more brightly than necessary. "Let's get a pint and some stodgy food and make a plan then, shall we?"

REVEREND RODWELL CLOSED the door and pressed his head against it. That Ripley woman was beginning to annoy him. Perhaps it had been foolhardy to invite her to the group meeting tomorrow, but Simon had agreed it was safer for Megan if they kept Ripley firmly in their sights and managed any future meetings themselves.

Simon had been so pleased with himself for interrupting her session with Megan. What had Anne been thinking? She was too naïve—that was the problem. She couldn't be trusted alone with a woman like Ripley.

It was so frustrating that Megan had gone downhill again. Anne was nervous enough about the group meeting as it was, without Megan getting sick now.

Perhaps they *should* cancel the group meeting. Megan's health had been in a slump for a while, and though the paramedics were confident it was just a blip, perhaps he could use it as an excuse to stop Dr Ripley getting too close. He didn't want her picking through their business. There were a few loose ends that would need tidying up before the charity came under much more scrutiny. He was damned if he would let a busybody like Alex Ripley ruin this for him.

Simon was right to be cautious, but he'd finally agreed to Rodwell's plan to invite Dr Ripley along to the group session where they could control her better. If they played their cards right, they may even get her to endorse Megan's gift. *Now wouldn't that be a turn up for the books?* He could see the headlines now. "Alex Ripley, Miracle Detective, confirms divine intervention in sleepy Rhosfaelog." He'd be covered in glory.

"Have the doctors gone, then?"

He looked up to see Anne standing in the corridor, hands wringing her skirt nervously. *God, she's such a worrier.* He smiled and walked towards her, reaching his hand out to take hers.

"They're gone," he said soothingly. "Everything's fine."

"They were in with her for ages," she said.

"Come on," he deflected. "Let's have a nice cup of tea, eh? You heard them, she's fine. They were just being thorough. That's what we pay them for."

What we pay them far too much for.

She smiled at him, watery eyed.

"She's fine, Anne. Just a little tired, is all. It's been a busy time for her recently. Takes a lot of her energy doesn't it. And she's probably picking up on your worries too. What with all this break-in business."

"But, what if she did something to her, Francis? What if she came here to do what her friend couldn't?"

"Shush," he said, placing a finger gently on her lips. It made him shudder inside. "You were silly to let her in, Anne. You can't trust everyone. Especially not someone like her."

"I know. I just thought that if the Vatican trusts her enough to pay for her opinion, it would be perfect if she could see Megan's gift for herself."

She's such a fool.

"Megan's just tired. She'll be right as rain tomorrow."

"But.."

"No. That's enough," he said, more harshly this time. "Now you need to calm down and stop worrying. It's a mild infection, that's all. They've given her some medicine and she will be fine."

"Do you think we're pushing her too hard?" Anne asked, flicking the kettle on and gathering some teacups.

"Not at all. She is in God's hands, remember? We're just helping her to share his love. The Lord has entrusted her with a great gift, and it's only natural that she must travel a difficult road. But we can travel with her and give her our strength and our faith. Through good and bad. We are her rock and her anchor. We'll never let her come to any harm."

His voice had risen almost evangelically over the growing sound of the boiling kettle and as it suddenly clicked off and fell silent, he moderated his tone again.

"She is an exceptional girl, Anne. You know that. You know how strong she is. Trust in her, and trust in God's plan for her. Everything will be just fine."

Anne nodded, almost convinced. She poured the water into the teapot and brought the tray of cups, the teapot and milk over to the table. She busied herself for a moment, stirring and then pouring out the tea. Weak and pale, just how he hated it.

"I don't think she should do this group meeting tomorrow," she blurted out.

He had known this was coming. Anne was like an open book. She always had a wobble before the group meetings. She'd already got him to agree to only doing one a month. He wasn't about to drop this one. Despite his earlier consideration for Megan, she would have to do it. It was the surest way of getting customers in for one-to-one sessions for the rest of the month. The group healings were their shop window.

"It's too late to cancel it now," he said. "People are coming from all over. The pub and the B&B are both chock-a-block. There are even people staying out in the caravan park for this one. Ron opened up special."

"But she's not well," Anne insisted.

"She's fine," he snapped and then softened immediately. "By morning she'll be right as rain again. Now, drink your tea and calm down. You shouldn't get so worked up. She'll feel it."

"You're right," she said.

He watched her slurp her tea over the brim of her cup, lips puckered and wrinkled from years of smoking. It was all he could do to keep the smile fixed on his face. She looked at him, eyes twinkling hopefully.

"I've been thinking, anyhow," she said.

Oh God. What now?

"Oh yes?" he queried.

"Well, maybe it's time we have a break for a little while," she said, slurping again. She smiled at the surprised look that had obviously crossed his face.

"Don't worry," she laughed. "I don't mean a break from us. I mean a holiday. Perhaps a week away together. As a family."

Oh joy.

"After the group session, perhaps," she ploughed on. "I thought we could head down to Swansea. There's a beautiful place on the Mumbles we could stay in. Even just for a few days. The kids would love it. And Megan could get some rest in the hospice."

"You've been looking into it, then?"

He didn't mean to sound so accusatory, but she'd caught him off guard. He should never have started the relationship with her, but it had been the easiest way to get her to trust him. And it helped to cover any suspicion about his real relationship with Simon. The idea of going on a holiday with Anne and those bloody twins was anathema to him. If he was going to spend any money on a holiday, it would be somewhere warm, far away from all this, and with Simon, not Anne.

"Well, that would be just lovely," he said, ignoring the look of hope and excitement that flashed across her face. "But don't forget we've got this hearing about the break-in, and we've also got a full appointment book."

Her face sank again, and he felt just the slightest mean-spirited flush of pleasure.

"Oh yes," she said, sounding glum.

"Maybe we can sort something out after Easter," he said.

He should feel bad, giving her hope like this, but it was the only way to keep her happy and shut her up. Besides, he always found the right excuses to put off any of her little ideas when she sprung them on him.

"Let's concentrate on this hearing. And getting Ian Hewitt out of our lives for good."

"Do you think it will work?"

"Of course," he said. "You should trust me more, you know?"

"I do. But I feel bad for him."

"Well, you shouldn't," he snapped. "He's a chancer."

She didn't look convinced.

"He just needs to be encouraged to leave us alone and stop bothering Megan. We agreed, didn't we? Okay?"

"Okay," she smiled, weakly.

"Good girl," he said, patting her arm.

Such a frustrating woman.

IAN ORDERED HIMSELF a second pint as their sandwiches arrived. Ripley chose water. She'd never been much of a beer drinker and the ale she'd just finished was already sitting heavy. As she'd expected the menu was full of pub basics—battered, fried and stodgy. The barman had looked at her askance when she'd asked him to substitute her chips for a salad. Sadly, when it arrived, she realised salad here meant a plappy lettuce leaf, a slice of watery tomato, and half a raw onion. She wished she hadn't bothered.

They had put aside the tension of their discussion in the car, and Ian had talked fondly about his early days with Jane and how he'd joined her church especially to get closer to her, and how she'd pretended to be cross when he'd finally confessed that fact.

"Do you still go?" Ripley asked.

"Not since she died," he said, taking a sip of his pint.

"You should."

He raised an eyebrow as though surprised she would recommend the church.

"You've been going for a long time, you know people there," she explained. "People who also knew and loved Jane. I'm sure you'd find support among friends."

"Maybe I would," he said. "But I'm not sure it's what I want right now. I tried, in those first few weeks after she passed, but I couldn't get myself to go through the doors."

Ripley nodded sympathetically. The church had been a big part of Ian and Jane's lives, and he would find a lot of support there, when he was ready to go back. Now was not the time. He needed to lay this anger to rest before he could move forward, and she'd already told him as much in the car. There was no point going over it again. She changed tack.

"Right," Ripley said. "Now, I don't want you to take this the wrong way and I know your memory is hazy, but I need to question your timings last Wednesday."

Ian frowned.

"When I went back in to the pub and asked that barmaid, she said she'd kicked you out around eight fifteen."

Ian's frown deepened, a confused look spreading over his face.

"Really?"

"And you think you called Caroline Clifton at nine?"

"Just after," Ian said. "My phone logged the call."

He pulled his phone out and found the call list, turning the screen to show Ripley. Sure enough, there was a 29 second call logged at three minutes past nine.

"And this was when you left her the voicemail?"

"Yes, ever since then her phone's been off."

"So," said Ripley. "We have at least forty-eight minutes unaccounted for between you getting kicked out of the pub and your call to Caroline, which could have been enough time for you to get back to Megan's house. Anne reported the break in just before nine."

"The state I was in, it would have taken much longer than that the get back along the cliffs. I would just have likely pitched right over into the sea."

"But it would have been half the time on the road," Ripley countered.

Ian was about to snap again but his face softened into a sad smile.

"Devil's advocate?"

"Someone's got to ask," Ripley agreed.

Ian sighed and drained his pint.

"I'm sure I would remember walking back there, though," he protested. I left the pub and sat on the bench by the car park for a while to gather my thoughts. Then I called Caroline. I must have sat there for longer than I thought. I'm sure I was still outside the pub when I called her."

"Okay," said Ripley. "Let's try calling Caroline now. See if she can tell us anything."

Ian picked up his phone and dialled, holding the handset between them so that Ripley could also hear Caroline's voice apologising for not being able to take the call.

"It's been like that for days now," he said, putting the phone down.

"And you have no other details for her? A home number?"

"No," he said. "All I know is that she lives in Cardiff. But that hardly narrows it down, does it?"

Ripley picked up her own phone and opened the browser, typing in a quick Google search for *Caroline Clifton Cardiff*. The screen refreshed with several results, but it was the top one that caught her attention: A link to an online news article from yesterday's South Wales Echo.

Husband's plea for wife to come home. *A Cardiff man has issued a desperate plea for his wife to come* home. *Caroline Clifton has been missing for three days now, and her husband, Gavin...*

"Ian," Ripley said, a nervous flicker hitching her stomach. "Look at this."

She laid the phone between them, leaning forward as she clicked the link to expand the rest of the story.

Husband's plea for wife to come home. *A Cardiff man has issued a desperate plea for his wife to come back home. Caroline Clifton has been missing for three days now, and her husband, Gavin, is worried about her state of mind. Caroline had become depressed after all attempts to find a cure for their terminally ill son had failed. She went missing on Wednesday, which would have been their son's tenth birthday. "I feel like I've lost everything," Gavin Clifton told us. "I can't keep going without her. She is my rock. I'm so worried about her. Just come home, love. We can get through this together." Gavin Clifton has offered a reward for any information that leads to his wife's safe return.*

"Oh my God," Ian muttered, pulling the phone closer to him. "Missing for three days from yesterday? That was Wednesday. The day I saw her in Rhosfaelog."

"So she didn't go home after you left her," Ripley said.

"What does this mean?" Ian asked.

"I don't know," Ripley replied, pulling the phone back towards her and returning to the original search results. There were a couple of repeated versions of the same story from different news outlets, but no new detail.

There were other articles about Caroline and Gavin's struggle to find help for their son, and a fundraising page to help with his care that gave more details of his illness, and the sad announcement of his death. She would come back to them later. Another thought struck her.

"More worrying," she said. "It means you may have been one of the last people to talk to her before she went missing."

"You don't think I—"

"Oh God, no," Ripley replied quickly. "Not at all. I'm sure it's just a horrible coincidence. You said yourself how upset she was. But we need to tell someone. It might help them find her."

But Ripley never bought into coincidences. Caroline Clifton had gone missing on the same day she'd visited Anne Shields and told them she would expose them as frauds. The day Ian was arrested for a break-in he swears didn't happen. How far would Anne and her people go to protect their business? The hairs on the back of Ripley's neck stood up. *What happened to Caroline Clifton after Ian left her in that lay-by?*

IAN COOKED THEM both a simple meal, while Ripley trawled the Internet looking for any more details about Caroline Clifton. She came up blank, apart a home number which she called, leaving a message for

Caroline's husband, trying to explain who they were without worrying him unnecessarily. She also left a message with the Cardiff police team who were leading the search for Caroline, telling them what she knew and leaving Ian's details. She was told that an officer would call back.

Nothing she'd found had given her any more to go on than that first article, apart from a little more detail about Caroline's son's illness and the number of routes the family had tried to ensure his survival before finally visiting Megan.

Halfway through eating, Ian's phone rang.

"It's a Cardiff number," he said excitedly, showing her the phone before answering it.

"Hello?"

His face fell almost immediately.

"Yes, that's me."

He came back to the table and sat down.

"Oh yes. Hello Mr Clifton. Thanks for calling back."

Ripley signalled for him to let her hear.

"I'm just going to pop you on speaker," Ian said," so that my colleague can hear us too, if that's okay? No we're not police. No, definitely not press. We just want to talk to you about Caroline."

He laid the phone on the table, on speakerphone, in time for Ripley to hear the man's reply.

"Where is she?"

"No, Mr Clifton—" Ian began, but Ripley put a hand up to stop him from speaking for a moment.

"Mr Clifton," she said calmly. "My name's Dr Alex Ripley. I'm afraid we're not calling with news. We wanted to ask you some questions, if that's okay?"

"I've answered all the questions I can," he said, sounding weary. "If you don't have information, I'd rather you weren't clogging up the line."

"Please," Ripley said. "Just a few minutes. It's important."

He sighed.

"You're the ones from that TV show, aren't you?" he asked. "I recognise your names."

Ripley and Ian exchanged a surprised glance across the table.

"Yes," Ripley said, hiding her own sigh.

"This is all your fault, you know?"

The surprise turned to confusion.

"She would never have run off if she hadn't seen that show. It drove her mad, that. Thinking those people had tricked us too. That she could have done something different, maybe. That she'd wasted our last chance to save him. She wouldn't have thought any of that if she hadn't seen you on that show. And she wouldn't be blaming herself like she is now."

Ian held his hands out in a "what now?" gesture and Ripley shrugged, lifting a cautionary finger.

"I'm sorry you feel that way, Mr Clifton," she said, keeping her tone as neutral as possible. "And I'm very sorry for the loss of your son."

"Thank you," he said, automatically.

There was another silence. Ian blinked slowly, frowning. He tilted his head. Sensing what he was about to say, Ripley shook hers, but he said it anyway.

"I saw your wife the day she went missing," Ian blurted out.

Silence greeted his revelation.

"Mr Clifton?"

"Yes," he said quietly. "I'm still here, sorry. You were with her?"

"We had arranged to meet."

"What are you saying? Were you...? Was she...?"

"No," Ian said quickly, not wanting the poor man to be even more confused. "We agreed to meet at Anne Shields's house. We wanted to have it out with her, and if she wouldn't admit the whole thing was a scam, then we were going to go to the papers."

"She went back there?"

"We were supposed to go in together," Ian said, sounding a little more defensive. "But Caroline got there early."

"I begged her not to go back," Gavin Clifton said. "I told her it would only hurt her. Why did you encourage her?"

"She called *me*," Ian protested. "She said she understood how I felt."

"She did, did she?" Gavin spat. "Well that's good. Because she doesn't seem to have a clue how I'm feeling."

"I didn't want to cause any trouble," Ian said. "She contacted me after the show. She said she understood.

She said she blamed them for your son's death, like I blamed them for my wife's."

"Our son died," Gavin said flatly. "There was nothing more anyone could have done. He was tired. He'd finished fighting. The sooner Caroline accepts that, the sooner she can begin healing. That's why I made her promise not to go back. I begged her not to go there in the first place, but she'd been convinced that he could be healed. She should never have taken him."

"Did you not consent?"

"It wasn't a matter of consent," Gavin said. "I could see he only had days, maybe even hours to live. How could I stop his own mother from trying everything she could to save him. Once he was gone, though, I just wanted her to stop. Stop blaming the world. Stop shouting at God. Just stop struggling, like Tom had. He knew it was time to go. If anyone was to blame, it was us. It was our blood that made him. That unique combination of her and me that made him sick. That's what we need to deal with. But we need to do it together."

Neither Ian nor Ripley knew quite how to respond.

"I'm sorry," Ian said.

"So what happened there?" Gavin asked. "Where is she? Is she with you now?"

He sounded tired. Worn out. As though he'd been offered a ray of hope like this too many times in the last few days.

"No. We don't know where she is, that's why we're calling," Ian said. "I saw her outside their house last

Wednesday. They were throwing her out. She was upset, so I went after her, but she wouldn't tell me what had happened."

"She told me she was going across to Abergavenny to see a friend. But her friend said she knew nothing about the visit," Gavin said. "I've been going mad trying to find her. It didn't cross my mind she would go all the way back over there. She promised she would drop all this."

"What exactly happened when you took your son to see Megan?" Ripley asked.

"I told Caroline it would be a con, but she insisted we go. Said her friend in the group here had sworn by them. And Caroline, well she couldn't accept that there was nothing more to be done. She was sure we would find something to fix Tom. She's that kind of woman, see? Every problem has a solution. Sometimes you have to throw energy at it, sometimes money, most often both. She wouldn't let it go. I didn't like the idea of it—Tommy seeing this poor girl in a coma. But Caroline was desperate, and that woman, Anne, said all the right things, you know? She promised they could help. She gave us hope. Well, I guess we were both sucked in. We just wanted him to get better."

Ian nodded in silence.

"So you took him to see Megan?" Ripley prompted.

"We did," he said, sounding almost guilty. "It didn't do any good, of course. It was just wishful thinking, wasn't it? I told her that. When he died, it was as though the defeat was worse for Caroline than the fact that our boy was gone. She'd fought hard to find a cure and now she thinks she's failed him. Underneath it, she misses him as much as I do, but she's looking for answers where there are none. She wants to know why this happened to our boy. To us."

"I'm so sorry," Ripley said, hearing his pain across the line.

"But the problem is," Gavin continued, "once she saw that debate show you two were on, she decided that those people were to blame. I told her she was being ridiculous—it was just the hand we'd been dealt. Tom's cards were marked from the day he was born, and if anyone has to shoulder the blame, it's us. But Caroline insisted they'd lied to us. Wasted our time. They'd taken our money when they knew nothing would change for Tom. Money that everyone had given to the Tommy Fund, to help with his treatment. I told her not to give them anything, but she said that's what the money was for. She's like that, a bit, you know? She thinks you can pay for solutions, and then gets angry when it doesn't work."

He stopped for breath. They said nothing.

"I know I sound harsh," he continued. "But I've lost my son too. And surely it's better to work through this together. I just don't understand why she's gone off on her own. She's not quite right at the moment. I'm worried she might do something to herself. And now you're telling me she's been back to that place and got into another argument with them on the same day she disappeared. So where is she?"

"That's what we're trying to figure out," Ripley said. "Is this kind of thing in character for your wife? Has she gone off before?"

"No, never," he replied. "She's always been a homebody, you know? She likes quiet weekends together doing stuff in the garden or watching a movie all bundled up on the sofa. She's never really been one for going away travelling, even before Tom got sick. She's quiet. Timid, even."

Ian raised an eyebrow incredulously, indicating that this was not how he would have described the woman he'd met outside Megan's house.

"And there's nowhere else you can think of that she might have gone? Family? An old friend?" Ripley continued.

"I've tried them all," he replied. "Besides, why wouldn't she just tell me she needed a bit of time on her own? She knows I'd be worried half to death. She wouldn't do that to me."

"Did you have any further contact with the Shields family? After she first complained?"

"No," he said. "Well, there were a couple of phone calls from that guy from the church charity. The Reverend fellow. He offered to return the money she'd given them. He was very pleasant about it all. Very sympathetic. Caroline told him to stuff it."

"She didn't want your money back?"

"She says they're trying to pay her off to keep quiet. I've told her she's being irrational. It's not like they gave us any guarantees he would get better. How could they? They made it very clear we were just going to sit with that poor girl and pray. It was just the most awful thing, seeing those two poor kids together. Megan and Tom. It's not fair, is it? Life. Anyway, Caroline kept going on about how they'd lied and I got quite cross with her, actually. It's the first time I've ever shouted at her. But it's only because I'm hurting too, and she's wasting so much energy being angry with that family. I told her she had to drop it, and she promised. I really thought that was the end of it. I can't believe she went back there again. Without telling me."

"Perhaps she just didn't want to worry you," Ripley said.

"Didn't want me to know, more like," he said, sounding disappointed. "And now she's probably scared I'll find out. I just wish she'd come home. Or even call to let me know she's okay. I mean, why wouldn't she just call?"

Ripley knew that feeling all too well: Life on hold, waiting for news. Dreading each knock on the door or ring of the phone in case it's the news you've convinced yourself you'll never hear. Not knowing whether to grieve the loss of your spouse, or keep hoping that this will be the day they walk back through the door.

"I'm sure she'll come home soon," Ripley said. "Grief can make us do strange things."

"I hope so," he said, sadly. "Are you still there, then? In that village. What was it called?"

"Rhosfaelog," Ian said. "Yes, we're here."

"Maybe I should come. To look for her."

Ripley shook her head vigorously.

"When I saw her last," Ian said quickly, "she was leaving town. She said she was driving back to Cardiff."

"I just don't know what to do," Gavin said.

"Well," Ripley said. "You can let the police know that she was last seen leaving here. You said you'd thought she was in Abergavenny before, so they would have been looking in the wrong place. This may be exactly the lead they need."

"Thanks," Gavin said. "To be honest, the police don't seem too bothered. They think she's just gone off upset and she'll come back in her own time. I don't get the sense they're following any leads. Not that there have been any. Until now."

"Why don't you give me the details of her car," Ripley said. "I've got some friends on the force who owe me a few favours. I'm sure I can get someone to run a check on the roads out of here last Wednesday and see how far she got. I'm not promising anything, but it might help you figure out where she's gone."

Ripley knew it would technically be treading on the feet of the force looking into Caroline's disappearance, but she also knew how difficult it was to get the police to take a missing person case seriously enough to dedicate proper resources to it. Unless it was a child, or the circumstances were suspicious, they treated most cases as a relatively low priority.

She took down the make, model and licence number of the car and promised Gavin she'd call him back as soon as she found anything out either way, and he agreed to phone them if he heard from Caroline.

When they hung up, Ian just looked at Ripley across the table. Neither of them wanted to say it first.

"You don't think—" Ian began.

"What? That her disappearance has something to do with her threat to go to the papers about Megan?" Ripley asked. "I bloody hope not."

"But it *is* suspicious, isn't it?"

Ripley got up, clearing away their plates. Of course it was suspicious. There was every likelihood that Caroline had holed up somewhere to lick her wounds and try to reset her mind. It was the kind of thing Ripley might do herself in the same circumstances. And yet, this was a coincidence too far. On the same day, two people had made it clear they were planning to bring a case against Anne and Megan Shields. One had been silenced by false criminal accusations, and the other was missing. Exactly the kind of coincidence Ripley hated.

"Let's not jump to any wild conclusions," she said, stacking the plates in the sink. "I'll get hold of my friend and see if we can trace Caroline's car. I'm sure she's just taking a bit of time to heal."

"Or they've made sure she can't talk to anyone."

"It's one thing accusing them of fraud, but to suggest they've had a hand in Caroline's disappearance is a different story altogether. Especially without any evidence. I know you don't trust them, but we need to keep some perspective here."

She picked up her phone and left him to deal with the dishes, heading off to call Emma Drysdale—the forensic investigator she'd been working with up in the Lake District, and an old and trusted friend.

She pulled on her coat and headed out into the cold, feeling the need for a little privacy to make the call. Her niggling doubts about Ian's version of events on the night of the break-in meant she didn't quite trust him. He was almost certainly a good guy, but something was telling Ripley to play her cards close to her chest for now.

She crunched across the gravel driveway and leaned against the side of the cottage, out of the wind.

"Alex," Emma Drysdale said, sounding pleased to hear from her. "How are you? Have you recovered from your lakeside misadventure yet?"

"Not quite," Ripley said, feeling instantly comforted to hear her friend's voice. "But I'm getting there."

A gull squawked and wheeled above her, battling the winds.

"Where the hell are you? Sounds like a scene from The Birds!"

"I'm on the coast in North Wales, over on Holy Island, Anglesey."

"Blimey," Emma laughed. "Wouldn't you be better off taking your holidays somewhere warm?"

"I wish," Ripley replied. "But this is no holiday."

"You're not working again already, are you? You must be a glutton for punishment."

"Not working, really. Just trying to help someone out. Can I ask a favour?"

"Aha," Emma said. "And here I was thinking you'd called for a chat. Ask away."

They had been friends long enough for them to not beat about the bush. Their friendship had grown out of a respect for each other's work, and they had helped each other out numerous times over the years, both professionally and personally.

Ripley paced along the narrow path past the back wall of the cottage as she explained the situation with Ian, Caroline and the Shields family. Apart from a few exclamations, Emma listened in silence until Ripley told her what she was calling for.

"I can run her number plate through the ANPR database and see if they've picked her up on any of the cameras," Emma said.

Ripley knew the acronym well, Automatic Number Plate Recognition, or ANPR, was a network of cameras placed at strategic points around the country to help police identify cars known to be associated with some kind of crime, or to link cars to known crimes after the event. They could monitor everything from counter-terrorism and organised crime to uninsured vehicles using this system, and Emma agreeing to check it was what Ripley had been hoping for.

"Thank you," she said, feeling a wave of relief that they may come up with something to help Gavin Clifton find his wife.

"Obviously, I'll have to think of a clever excuse if anyone asks why I'm using it to trace Caroline Clifton's movements, but that shouldn't be too much of a problem. Leave it with me."

"You're a star," Ripley said.

"I know," Emma replied in a mock weary voice. "But listen, if you honestly believe these people have hurt her, report it. We don't want you going off all gung-ho again, do we?"

"I will," Ripley assured her. "As soon as we come up with anything that constitutes evidence. As it stands, the police assume she's just holed up somewhere trying to get over the loss of her son. I'd love to believe that's true. But if I find out otherwise, I'll go straight to the police."

"Make sure you do," Emma said, serious now.

"Yes mum!" Ripley teased. "Anyway, I've got to go in, I'm freezing my face off out here."

She hung up as she rounded the corner and was knocked back by an icy blast of wind. Even for December, it felt brutally cold. She was surprised to see two people on the cliffs in the distance, walking away from the ancient burial chamber towards the pub. It was amazing the awful weather tourists would suffer to get a glimpse of these ancient sites. She still hadn't had a chance to look up the full history of the place. *So much for a little break by the sea.*

By the time she got back inside, Ian had finished the washing up and was off in the annexe. Ripley could hear the shower running. She poured herself a glass of wine and stood in front of the kitchen window, watching the light fade until all she could see was her own reflection in the glass.

Ian's shower had finished, and all had gone quiet in his annexe. Ripley realised she'd been staring out of the window for almost half an hour, slowly sipping her wine, lost in a reverie about Megan and their strange meeting, about Anne's reasons for keeping her daughter in the spotlight as she was, and about Caroline's disappearance.

She snapped out of it as Ian opened the door and filled the room with old, yellow light.

"Alex," he asked tentatively. "Are you okay?"

"Hmm," she turned, stretching her neck and back. "Lost in thought."

"Did you get hold of your friend?" he asked. "Can he help?"

"She," Ripley corrected automatically. "And yes, she's going to run Caroline's number plates and see where the car has been in the last few days."

"That's amazing," Ian said.

He got himself a glass of wine and topped hers up at the same time. As he put the bottle down, he smiled at Ripley.

"I can't thank you enough for helping me like this," he said. "I'm sorry I've been so argumentative. I just—"

"It's okay, Ian," she said, holding her glass towards his. "I do understand what you're going through. Now, cheers! Here's to finding Caroline, getting you an alibi, and putting a case together to help you both."

He clinked glasses with her, but didn't smile. Ripley pulled back a chair from the table, and had only just sat down when the huge kitchen window behind her came crashing inwards, shattered glass spraying across the stone floor. They both screamed. A rock skittered to a stop on the tiled floor, a piece of paper wrapped around it.

"What the hell?" Ian asked, rushing towards the shattered window.

"Stay back!" Ripley said, sprinting to the front door and out into the driveway.

She could hear footsteps running away and instinctively headed after them, shouting at the perpetrator to at least show their face. The footsteps left the gravel and by the time Ripley reached the gap in the hedge, whoever had hurled that rock was at least halfway across the field, heading towards the cliffs and the pub. Young, fast feet, fleeing.

There was not enough light to see anything more than the shape of the attacker. Tall, slight and athletic. Head and face covered by the hood of their coat, back straight as they ran at full tilt. Ian arrived by her side.

"Did you see who it was?"

"No," Ripley said. "Too dark."

She turned back towards the house, ushering Ian with her. She was pretty sure that any message delivered so violently was meant for him.

"Come on, let's get back inside and call the police."

She bolted the front door once they were inside, her heart still thumping. Ian stood still in the corridor, staring at the rough rock that lay on the floor in front of the broken window, wrapped in paper. He seemed frozen.

"Wait here," Ripley said, crossing to the window. Her feet crunched on the glass which had scattered all the way across the kitchen floor. She peered out through the gaping hole where the single sheet of glass had been punched through by the flying rock. The pane had cracked diagonally into the corners. The smallest tap would bring the lot crashing down.

Whoever she'd seen sprinting away was long gone, but she couldn't help feeling they were still being watched. She shivered. She wasn't usually easily intimidated, but they were totally isolated out here, and somebody obviously wanted to scare them. Ripley didn't like it one bit.

She drew the curtains tight, though they billowed open again with another icy blast of wind. Crouching down, she prodded the rock, which squatted menacingly on the floor among thousands of tiny glass splinters, the paper still wrapped around it.

Ripley reached into her coat pocket and pulled out her woollen gloves. If there were any prints on the rock or the paper, she didn't want to do anything to disturb them. Gloves on, she picked up the whole package and carefully unwrapped it, teasing the paper open. Three words, scrawled in thick capitals in black marker pen: *LEAVE HER ALONE.*

"What does it say?" Ian asked, stepping forward into the kitchen.

Ripley held it up for him to see.

"Charming," Ian said.

Ripley laid the paper on the kitchen table and put the rock on top. She'd received plenty of warnings, veiled and blatant, in her time, but this was childish in its bluntness, both in content and delivery. Who would resort to such basic intimidation methods? Surely not Anne Shields? Perhaps one of the locals had got wind that Ian was staying at the cottage and had tried to scare him off. Somehow, though, she felt sure she was now included in the threat.

"We should tell Detective Harding," Ian said. "They can't get away with this kind of intimidation."

"I'll do it," Ripley said pulling out her phone. It would be better coming from her.

Perhaps due in part to the sound laughter and revelry in the pub in the background of the call, Detective Harding had initially seemed reluctant to come all the way over to the cottage for something as trivial as a broken window.

"It's probably just kids messing around," he assured her.

"It feels an awful lot like intimidation," Ripley replied. "Which could easily end up with their case against Ian being thrown out of court."

There was silence on the other end of the line for a moment, and then a heavy sigh.

"Stay where you are, and don't touch anything," he said. "I'll be there as soon as I can."

RIPLEY WAS NOT great at sitting still in times of stress. It had already been half an hour since she'd called Detective Harding, and she had been pacing impatiently ever since. They had moved into the lounge for warmth, closing the kitchen door and shoving some blankets up against the bottom to keep out some of the wind that was still whistling in through the broken window.

Ripley paced as she tried Bron's number for the third time that hour. Her mind raced as she listened to the monotonous rings. *Had this really been intended to run them out of town? Is this what they'd done to Caroline too? Threatened her into silence?*

Ian sat in an armchair, hands folded in his lap, fingers drumming each other repetitively. He'd barely said anything since they'd come into the lounge. Ripley was about to hang up in frustration when the ringing cut out.

"Bronwyn Williams," her cheerful voice chirped in answer, as though it was a perfectly normal time of day to be getting a call.

"Oh, hi Bron, it's Alex Ripley here," she said.

"Oh right, hiya love," Bron's demeanour seemed to change when she heard who was on the line. "Is everything all right? Is there a problem? It's not the bloody boiler, is it?"

Someone's trying to run us out of town. Hardly the opening gambit she should go for.

"Someone's put a rock through the kitchen window."

"Oh bloody hell," Bron said, sounding annoyed. "Why?"

Her response caught Ripley off guard, she had been expecting concern but Bron just sounded angry.

"Well, I don't know," she replied defensively. "I ran out to see but they'd already legged it. It had a note wrapped round it telling us to leave her alone."

"Oh, right," Bron said, as though everything suddenly made sense. "Sorry love, I thought you meant one of you two'd done it. So someone *else* has put a rock through the kitchen window have they?"

"Yes."

Isn't that what I just said?

"Oh dear. Are you all right? Are you hurt?" Bron asked, finally sounding concerned.

"Not hurt, no," Ripley said. "Just a little shocked."

"Oh, I'm sure you are, love," Bron said sympathetically. "Listen, don't you worry. I'm sure it's nothing. It's not the first time we've had kids chucking things through those windows, and I'll bet it won't be the last. As long as you're not hurt. That's the main thing."

"This wasn't a kid," Ripley said indignantly. "Someone is trying to warn us off!"

"Warn you off what exactly, love?" Bron laughed.

"Being here? Me helping Ian? Visiting Megan?"

"Sounds a bit over-dramatic, if you ask me," Bron said, flatly. "People aren't like that around here."

"Right," said Ripley, thinking of her altercation with Simon outside the house earlier. "Of course not."

"At worst, it'll just be someone a bit worse for wear on their way back from the pub having a laugh at your expense," Bron said. She made it sound perfectly natural, as though this sort of thing went on all the time around here.

"I called Detective Harding, but he hasn't got here yet."

"Oh, you didn't need to have troubled him," Bron laughed again, as though Ripley was some naïve child. "You should have called me first, I told Gareth to tell you that. Didn't he tell you?"

I tried three times in the last hour!

"I tried," Ripley edited herself, not wanting to sound accusatory.

"Oh, sorry love, I've been out," said Bron. "Listen, I can hear you're worried. We'll get this sorted, all right? You sit tight, and I'll bring one of my boys over now to get that window boarded up, okay? Make sure you feel safe in there. All right?"

"Great, thanks," Ripley replied, not quite sure what she'd been hoping for. She felt both patronised and belittled by Bron's offhand response. This was a threat, after all. No one could deny that. And Ripley didn't believe for one minute it was some local kid trying to put the scares on the tourists. Unless they'd been told to do it.

Ian was looking at her, waiting for her to tell him what had been said.

"Well?"

"She said it was probably just someone messing around," Ripley explained.

"This is bullshit!" Ian shouted, standing up and grabbing his coat.

Ripley tried to get between him and the front door before he could get there, but he was too fast. His fingers scrabbled angrily on the stiff bolts, finally yanking them back.

"Where are you going?" she asked.

"I'm not going to be intimidated by a woman like Anne Shields," he snapped. "She may think she's got everyone in this town fooled, but I've seen through her, and she's not going to scare me off like she did to Caroline. I'm going over there."

"I wouldn't do that if I were you," Detective Harding said gruffly, stepping through the door that Ian had just flung open.

He put his hand on Ian's chest and moved him back into the small hallway before shutting the door. Ian turned, began to protest, but obviously thought better of it. Harding propelled him past Ripley and towards the lounge, leading him towards the armchair he'd just left.

"Now, why don't you take a seat while I talk to your friend here about this incident," Harding said.

He clearly didn't have any time for Ian. *So much for innocent until proven guilty.* Perhaps he'd just had enough of responding to emergency calls that involved this stranger harassing members of his community.

"Get your hands off me," Ian railed, turning away from him. "I'm not the one in the wrong. She thinks she can just play with people's lives and if anyone complains, then she can intimidate them into silence. I'm not having it."

"Sit down," Harding shouted. "Or I will be forced to arrest you again."

Ian did as he was told. Ripley bristled. There was no need to treat him like a criminal. They were the victims here.

"Right. Thank you," Harding said, turning to Ripley. "Now, where's this window then?"

Ripley threw a glance at Ian, who scowled back but nodded.

"In the kitchen," Ripley said, leading the way to the door and moving the blankets so they could open it.

The room was ice cold now. The curtains billowed, kept aloft by the almost constant blast of wind coming off the sea. Ripley shivered. The corner of the note fluttered, still held in place by the heavy rock.

Harding crossed to the window and pulled the curtains back, stooping to look at the hole. He wiggled the glass and another huge shard dropped to the floor and smashed. He turned back to Ripley, nodding.

"Right then," he said, getting his notebook out of his pocket. "What time did this happen?"

"Not long before I called you," she replied. "About nine o'clock."

"And you didn't see anyone?"

"No, I *did* see someone," she said, exasperated. She'd already told him this on the phone. "I saw someone running away, but I couldn't see who it was."

"Can you describe them?"

"No," Ripley replied. "It was dark, and they were already half way across the field by the time I got to the gap in the hedge."

"I see," he said, snapping his notebook shut again. "So nothing then."

Ripley couldn't help rolling her eyes.

"He was about six foot," she began.

"He?" Harding asked, opening his notepad again and inexplicably licking the end of his pen. "So the perpetrator was a male?"

He spoke slowly as he wrote the single word in his notebook. Ripley got the sense he was being deliberately officious but she couldn't quite figure out why he would waste all of their time like this. Because she'd pulled him out of the pub? Or because he wanted to wind her up?

"Yes, male, about six foot," Ripley confirmed with barely contained frustration. "He was wearing a black hooded coat or a sweatshirt."

"You're sure about all of that?" he asked, hesitating to write it down.

"Yes, of course. Well, as much as I can be. I mean, obviously it was dark, but it looked like a man. Broad shoulders, athletic, fast runner."

"Huh," he said, questioningly. "It's just that, when I arrived, I clearly heard Ian accusing Anne Shields of doing this. He was heading over there to have it out with her, wasn't he? So I'm a bit confused now that you're saying it was a man you saw running away."

Is he being deliberately dense?

"I'm sure even Ian wouldn't imagine that Anne Shields would come all the way over here *herself* and chuck a rock through the window."

"Oh, I see," he said, nodding slowly and smiling as though everything now made sense. "So you think she got one of her 'heavies' to come round and scare you both off?"

He chortled.

"Don't make it sound so ridiculous," Ripley finally snapped. "She has a vested interest in both Ian and I going home and leaving her to get on with her business."

He snapped his notebook shut, put it away and took a step towards her, squaring his shoulders. *What is his problem?*

"So why don't you then?" he asked.

"I'm sorry, what?"

Ripley couldn't quite believe what she was hearing. Was he in their pockets too?

"What I mean is, why don't you both find somewhere that isn't this village to wait for the hearing. I mean, I get that you booked the place before you knew he'd be released into your custody, but given how people around here feel about him, why stay and wind everybody up?"

"Are you serious?" she asked, incredulously. "Your official response to someone throwing a rock through my window with a menacing threat attached to it, is that I should heed the bloody warning and leave?"

She wasn't able to hide her anger. He stammered slightly, but she wasn't about to wait around for his justification.

"Someone came all the way out here, after dark, to deliberately intimidate us, and your answer is that I should just do what they say?"

"Now come on, calm down," he said. "That's not what I meant at all. All I'm saying is, perhaps given the fright you've had and the fact that someone is obviously riled up about him being here, and you both poking your noses in, I can't see why you wouldn't want to take yourself out of harm's way."

"Because," said Ripley, defiantly. "I don't respond to threats."

He crossed to the table, noticing the paper fluttering beneath the rock. Ripley winced as he picked up the rock and moved it aside, holding the paper aloft in both hands, getting his own fingerprints all over it. He held it up to the light.

"Not much of a threat, really, is it?" he said, casually.

Christ, this guy was something else.

"Are you kidding?" she spluttered, pointing at the shattered window.

"No, I don't mean the way it was delivered," he said. "That was definitely threatening. What I mean is, they haven't given you an 'or else' have they. 'Leave her alone, or else.' You see?"

"I took the rock and the smashed window to be the or else," Ripley said. "A hint of the danger to come if we don't leave her alone."

She watched in despair as he folded the piece of paper up and tucked it into his pocket.

"I thought you might have been able to get some prints from it," she said, sounding more plaintive than she'd meant to.

He laughed. A sarcastic little chuckle.

"Oh yeah," he said, still chuckling. "I'll get my best men right on it. You're not in the city now, love."

Ripley's temper rose again.

"Look, I'm sure you think you have more important things to deal with, but the least you could do is take this seriously."

"I *am* taking it seriously," he said. "There's just not very much I can do about it. And I think you'd both be better off out of the village until his hearing is over and this is all done with. It'll only cause more trouble, you staying. I'm just trying to keep the peace here."

Ripley could have slapped him. He just wanted an easy life.

"You were the one who asked me to look after him. And all you asked me to do was make sure that he didn't go near them. And I've done that. Now, he swears he never broke in that night and we think he has an alibi to back him up, but you're all so certain that Anne is right and he's just some drunken crank, that nobody will stop to consider that Anne might actually be trying to set him up with this whole break-in story, just to stop him from destroying their business with his fraud case."

"That's a pretty serious allegation," he said.

"So is breaking and entering," Ripley retorted. "And yet you believe her. You've got the evidence right there in front of you. Someone has just aggressively warned us both to stay away from Megan, and you're happy to pass it off as some kind of prank. What the hell is wrong with you?"

"I'll tell you what's wrong with me," he said, rounding on her angrily. "Ian Hewitt has been stirring up shit around here for weeks now, so I'm not surprised people want him gone. And while you might have got a fright, neither of you was injured so, apart from damage to the window, there's nothing much to investigate. My recommendation is that you remove yourselves from harm's way, since neither of you actually needs to be here, and your presence is causing so much trouble."

Even as he spoke he moderated his anger.

"Look," he said, when he saw she wasn't buying his argument. "This is a small village, and it doesn't take much to wind them up. Aside from a halfway decent pub, a nice cliff walk and some old stones, Megan is the only thing that keeps people coming here and spending their money. Now, I'm not saying there's some kind of racket going on, like you're suggesting. But people are naturally protective of their own. That's all."

"Is that what happened to Caroline Clifton, then?"

Ripley had pulled the name out with no warning and was watching his face for a reaction. All she saw was blank confusion.

"Who?"

"Caroline Clifton," she repeated. "She went missing last week after visiting Megan and Anne."

He looked genuinely stumped.

"What?" he asked. "I've never heard of a Caroline Clifton. Who is she?"

As Ripley filled him in on what she knew about Caroline, her son, the meeting that Ian had arranged, and his brief conversation with her before she disappeared, she saw his expression turn from surprise to bewilderment. If there was any kind of conspiracy, she was pretty sure this was the first he was hearing of it. She doubted he'd be a good enough actor to fake otherwise.

"You're sure about this?" he asked when she'd finished outlining what she knew.

"Well, we know she came here and we also know she's been missing ever since," said Ripley. "Draw your own conclusions."

"And that was the day I arrested Ian Hewitt?"

"Correct."

Harding pulled a chair out from beneath the kitchen table and sat down heavily. A man with too much to take in suddenly.

"And who was she, again?" he asked.

Maybe he's just not that bright, Ripley thought.

"She had brought her son to meet Megan, and when he died, she accused them of deception. She was last seen leaving their house…"

"In fact," said Ian, arriving in the doorway of the kitchen. "She was last seen being thrown out of their house. They said they'd called the police. That would be you, wouldn't it?"

His combative stance was understandable, but it was unlikely to help get Detective Harding on side. Sure enough, Harding had stood up again as soon as Ian appeared.

"Hmm," he said, shoulders set. "I didn't get any call like that. Maybe, after she left, they figured there was no need to bother me."

"Or maybe they didn't want you asking any questions about where she'd gone," Ian huffed.

The news of Caroline's mysterious disappearance had obviously unsettled Harding. She threw Ian a look which she hoped told him to back off and let her handle it. It didn't stop him coming in and sitting down. It was an uncharacteristically confident gesture from him, Ripley thought, given that both she and Harding were still standing. Looking closer she realised that Ian's hands were shaking. Conflict did not come naturally to him.

"Well, she's been gone since Wednesday," Ripley said. "We've told her husband. Apparently she'd told him she was visiting friends in Abergavenny on Wednesday so, when she didn't come home, they focussed the search around there. I'm sure you'll be getting a call from the Cardiff police in the morning about it."

"Great," Harding said, running his hands through his hair. He took the seat opposite Ian at the table and looked at him for a moment. Ripley got the sense that it was the first time he'd looked at Ian as anything other than a public nuisance.

"So, she was a friend of yours then, was she?"

"No, not at all," Ian frowned. "She called me after… well, after that debate show on the television. She told me her story. How she felt that Anne Shields had lied to her. We agreed to meet. To have it out with them."

Ripley saw the young policeman bristle again. *Wrong choice of words, Ian.*

"So, let me get this straight," Harding said, leaning forward, elbows on knees. "You both brought your terminally ill loved ones to sit beside a young girl who's been in a coma for years, and when they didn't miraculously get better after a half-hour visit, you cooked up a plan to come back here and discredit them. Stir up some shit. What were you hoping to get out of that, huh? Money? A miracle? To bring them back from the bloody dead?"

Ripley took an instinctive step forward. Obviously Detective Harding was frustrated, but Ian's grief was raw enough that this might provoke him to violence. The last thing he needed to add to his rap sheet was assaulting a police officer.

"Putting all that aside for a moment," she said, calmly placing herself between the two men. "Caroline Clifton is definitely missing, and her husband is beside himself."

"And you're convinced Anne has something to do with it?" he asked, not angry anymore, but still struggling to understand.

"I think she has the most to lose from any fraud charges," Ripley said.

"Oh God," Harding said, looking down at his hands. "This is mental. You're seriously telling me you think Anne's done something to this woman?"

"Or someone else in the business," Ripley nodded.

"Well, I'll need to follow that up. That's a serious thing."

Ripley couldn't help feeling that the idea of a 'serious thing' overwhelmed the young officer. There was a big difference between a break-in and what she and Ian were suggesting now. *What were they suggesting?* Intimidation? Kidnapping? Worse?

Perhaps Harding was right: If someone was willing to make Caroline disappear for causing a fuss, maybe she and Ian *would* be better off getting out of the village. But that was just ridiculous. Megan may earn them all a good deal of money, but Ripley had seen the look in Anne's eyes when she'd talked about her daughter. Anne believed wholeheartedly in Megan's gift and she had the faith to defend it. She didn't need to resort to this kind of intimidation.

"We know nothing about Caroline, really," Ripley said. "Only what her husband's told us. Perhaps you should talk to the officers looking into her disappearance. They may have a different angle."

Harding stood up again, straightening his jacket distractedly.

"Yes," he said in a quiet, pensive voice. "I'll do that."

"What's going on here then?" Bron's sing-song, gravelly voice carried through the door before she came into the room. She stopped in her tracks, eyes wide in mock consternation. "What the hell have you done to the place? Oh, hiya Dylan love. You didn't need to come all the way out here on your night off. I can deal with this."

"Oh, hiya Bron," said Harding, hovering in the doorway as she bustled past.

"Are you all right, darling? You look a bit peaky," Bron said, cupping Harding's cheek in her hand.

"I'm all right, Bron. Got a lot on, just now, that's all."

"You get yourself off then," Bron said. "We'll clean up here. I've got Gareth with me."

"Right," Harding said.

He looked at Ripley.

"I'll get back to you as soon as I know anything," he said.

Bron frowned. Ripley nodded. Harding left.

"Did you see anyone then, love?" Bron asked, turning to Ripley. "I'm minded to get them to pay for the bloody window."

"Yes. I saw someone running away, but it was too dark to make them out," Ripley replied.

"Hmm," said Bron, thoughtfully. "Could've been anyone, then?"

She shrugged and bustled back outside and bellowed:

"Gareth! Go get some of that board out the shed there, will you? We've got a window needs covering up."

She came back in, kicking the shards of glass with the toe of her boot.

"What a mess," she said, looking up at Ripley and giving her a broad smile. "You're lucky I don't take this out of your deposit, love."

"What?" Ripley said, not sure if she was joking. "This was an attack aimed at us. We didn't do it."

Bron thumped her playfully on the arm.

"Bloody joking," she said. "Right. Come on. Let's get on with it."

She ushered them all into the kitchen doorway as she gathered up a broom from the corner.

"Why don't you two get your things together while I clean this lot up?"

Ripley stopped in the doorway.

"What?"

"Gather your things, love," Bron explained. "You won't want to be staying here any more, will you?"

Ripley frowned.

"Are you not frightened?" Bron asked, broom hovering over the glass.

"You think they'll come back?"

"Well, you can't be too careful, can you? Besides, I would rather there wasn't any more damage to my property."

Charming.

"I thought you said it was probably kids."

Bron said nothing, sweeping angrily. She didn't like being challenged, that much was clear. But Ripley didn't like being told what to do, either.

"We'll leave in the morning, as planned," Ripley said. "I only booked for two nights, anyway."

Bron humphed as she crouched down to sweep the pile of shards into a dustpan.

"Suit yourself," she said, huffily, depositing the shards in the kitchen bin.

Outside, Gareth was roughly fitting a square of chipboard over the broken window, dislodging the loose glass inside but finally stopping the flow of cold wind.

They all jumped as another few large shards of glass shattered on the floor behind them.

"Oh for God's sake, Gareth," Bron snapped. "I've just swept that."

"Sorry Mam," he said, lowering the board again.

He didn't look sorry, scowling at his mother's back as she bent to sweep up the new glass. He put the board down on the ground and pulled a hammer from his belt, staring at Ripley with baleful eyes. Any earlier friendliness was gone.

Ripley held his gaze until he turned away from her and lifted the board over the window. Slim, tall and athletic. *Was it him she'd seen running away from the cottage?* Surely not. Why on earth would he have thrown a brick through his own mother's window?

Bron wiped her hands on her jacket and looked at Ripley, sizing her up.

"Right then," she said. "If you're sure you're staying, I'm away to my bed. I'll be by in the morning to get the keys, but if you want to go before I get here, drop them in with Owen in the cafe. And try not to break anything else."

Ripley and Ian stood in silence, flinching as the front door slammed and the hammering began behind the window.

"She's a piece of work," Ian muttered, between bangs.

"Incredible," Ripley agreed.

"Perhaps we should just go," he suggested.

"Maybe. But not tonight. We'll find somewhere out of town in the morning."

"We could always go back to my house," Ian suggested.

"How far is it?"

"Couple of hours east," he said.

She shook her head.

"We'll find something closer, I've got a feeling things are about to get interesting."

"Do you think we can trust him?"

"Who, Detective Harding?" Ripley asked. "Yes, I do."

4th December

"YOU'RE UP EARLY," Ripley said, answering her phone as soon as she realised it was Emma Drysdale calling.

"Catching worms and all that," Emma replied. "I've got a day of meetings, so I thought I'd get a head start on your car search."

"You're amazing," Ripley smiled.

"Well, I'm not so sure," Emma said. "See what you think of this. I've got records of Caroline's car leaving Cardiff, and we can track her on and off all the way over the bridge towards Holyhead."

"Great," Ripley said, hopefully.

"Hmm," Emma replied. "So she crossed the bridge onto the island at ten past eleven in the morning. And beyond that, there's nothing."

"No cameras any further down the road?" Ripley asked.

"No," Emma replied. "But also no return journey. I've checked the database up until last night. Caroline Clifton's car never left Holy Island."

"You're sure?"

"Positive," Emma replied. "Unless she swapped cars or number plates, she's still there."

So there it is. That all too familiar uneasy tingling rose in her belly. Why would Caroline stay on the island but not meet up with Ian or come back to the village unless something awful had happened to her?

Ripley thanked Drysdale and hung up, heading back to the kitchen—now oppressively dark thanks to the boarded-up window. She made herself a coffee and leaned against the counter to drink it. The house was still quiet, with no sign of Ian and she wondered whether to wake him up and tell him what Emma had said.

As the first sips of coffee kicked in, she decided to leave him sleeping for now. She still wanted to go to the group prayer session that morning, and she didn't want to discuss it with Ian again. She rinsed out her empty mug and put it on the shelf, jumping as she heard his voice in the doorway behind her.

"You're still going, then?" he asked. There was a hint of accusation in his voice.

"I feel like I have to see it," Ripley replied.

"What about us getting out of here?"

"I'll only be gone an hour or so," she said. "Maybe you can find a hotel somewhere on the island and book us a couple of rooms. I'm all packed, so we can get going as soon as I get back."

"Okay."

He plucked a mug from the cupboard and loaded it with coffee.

"Are you going to be all right here on your own?" she asked.

He rolled his eyes.

"I'm a big boy," he said, smiling half-heartedly.

"Well, stay away from any windows," she said. "And keep the door locked. I'll let you know when I'm on my way back from the church."

"Okay."

"But call me if anything happens before then."

"I'll be fine," he said, getting flustered by her fussing. "Just go."

RIPLEY TOOK THE cliff path towards the village. It was a crisp morning and the cold, salty air prickled her cheeks. She checked her watch and slowed her pace. Too early, and she'd risk a confrontation, too late, and she'd make a scene by arriving when everyone was already inside. She imagined that neither Anne nor Reverend Rodwell would be too pleased to see her, but they could hardly throw her out in front of a crowd. Providing, of course, there was a crowd.

Ripley passed the burial chamber, smiling at the eerie wailing sound of the sea as the waves crashed into the bottom of the open chimney. Amazing to think, looking at the sea so far below, that the water could flood the chamber at high tide.

From her vantage point up here on the cliffs, she saw the branded minibus moving up the road towards the church, flanked front and rear by the two black

Range Rovers, like a presidential convoy. She stopped to watch them. Such an odd procession—the two heavy, black vehicles, surrounding the brightly coloured, cheerful bus. The young girl in a coma trapped inside, about to be paraded in front of a group of strangers searching for a miracle in exchange for a cash donation. Ripley felt the snarl twitch on her lip. *Perhaps I shouldn't go.*

But there was no other way of seeing the operation in full flow—the one-on-one meetings were too choreographed. She needed to see the full spectacle with her own eyes to see how they all played their part and get a sense of who was really calling the shots.

She reached the small path up from the coast to the church with five minutes to spare. Perfect. Walking slowly towards the church, she was relieved to see the small car park was already full and a number of cars lined the road either side of the church. It was a good crowd. People milled about beside their cars, filing slowly towards the front of the building, chatting to one another cheerfully.

Ripley hung back a moment, assessing the congregation. Gareth was standing sentry at the door, nodding politely to people as they passed. Was he always at these meetings? Or had he been brought in specifically to watch for her arrival?

Reverend Rodwell was on the other side of the open door, beaming at people and shaking their hands warmly as they arrived. He seemed relaxed—in his element. She saw Simon step out of the church and whisper something into Rodwell's ear. Rodwell leaned towards him, cupping his hand to shield the message, his fingers brushing the young man's cheek. An innately personal moment of contact, fleeting and subtle. Rodwell's hand lingered at his own ear for a moment after Simon stepped away, before he swung his gaze to the car park.

The branded minibus crunched its way up the side of the church, rolling to a stop just beside a side door which Ripley assumed led to the vestry. *Tradesman's entrance.*

A flurry of activity involving porters and paramedics saw Megan unloaded and transported inside. Slick and rehearsed—this was not their first rodeo. Still no sign of Anne, though.

Ripley scanned the rest of the faces in the gathering crowd, but saw no one she recognised, apart from Colin—the man from the coffee morning—who was one of a group of volunteers standing at the church gate greeting people and shaking collection tins, branded t-shirts pulled over their outdoor clothes. She knew it all went to help the charity that supported Megan, but Ripley couldn't help feel sickened by the cynicism of taking donations on the way into the service. No doubt they'd take even more inside once the miracles began to flow.

She reached up and pulled her woollen hat further down around her ears and lifted her thick scarf up over her chin. She hoped it would cover enough of her face to allow her to pass inconspicuously. It was cold enough outside that she wouldn't stand out too much in all those layers.

She jumped as her phone rang, and quickly pulled it out of her pocket and flipped it on to silent. It was Ian calling, but if she answered now, she'd only draw more attention to herself.

She looked up as Anne finally appeared by Rodwell's side at the church door. She looked stressed and harassed, leaning in to talk to him with close urgency. Rodwell snapped a reply, unable to conceal his frustration with her. He immediately tried to cover it with a smile as another of the faithful greeted him. As they moved on he turned back to Anne, face like thunder and sent her away, his hands emphasising his words in short, sharp gestures.

She may not have been able to hear him, but Ripley could have sworn she saw his lips form a stream of swearwords as Anne scuttled away looking cowed and upset. Interestingly, Anne didn't go back into the church, instead walking through the crowd and heading to their branded minibus at the top of the car park, not far from where Ripley was standing. Anne climbed into the passenger seat and sat there for a moment before she collapsed, crying. A private, raging fit of tears.

Ripley's phone buzzed again. Ian had left a long voicemail. Staying close to the wall she pressed the phone to her ear, just in case it was urgent. After a second or so of silence, she heard a scuffling sound and some muffled grunting. A pocket call. God knows what he was doing, though. She hung up long before the message had ended and tucked the phone away again.

While there was still a big enough group mingling outside the church, Ripley dipped her head and walked purposefully towards the gathering. She managed to slip in between a couple who were chatting to the Reverend, and a tall man who had stopped to talk to Gareth. She kept her eyes down, moved with the flow and got inside the church without either man stopping her. She didn't dare to look back.

The majority of the guests had filled the front pews, getting as close as they could to the action. Megan was already in the church, propped up in a bigger bed than the one she had at home. She looked so small and alone. Why was Anne not here with her? Probably still pulling herself together after her altercation with Rodwell.

Something about seeing the young girl so isolated and exposed made Ripley feel strangely protective, and again she was struck by that question: *How can Anne do this to her own daughter?* She must genuinely believe in Megan's gift, or she wouldn't put her through this.

Ripley's urge to go to Megan's side was partly relieved by seeing one of the young private medics step back up to the bed and check the tubes and pumps connected to her. They were all neatly tucked away, concealed as best they could be but still present enough to remind the audience of Megan's condition.

Ripley slid into a pew on her own, one row back from the nearest fully occupied one and placed herself on the far end, away from the aisle, and out of the central line of sight. She too her colourful hat off, but left her scarf on, head bent, pretending to read the leaflet she'd found on her seat giving full details of all the ways she could donate to the God's Gift charity. There was also a space to fill in her own details and write a short summary of her healing need, which Megan could 'attend to'. Ripley folded the leaflet up and tucked it into her pocket.

There was an excited thrum to the murmur of voices in the church, though it had the distinct feel of a gathering of strangers. Ripley overheard people introducing themselves to their neighbours, speaking in hushed, anticipatory whispers about the forthcoming meeting. Some shared details of their illnesses while others nodded sympathetically. All seemed universally accepting of the spectacular that was to follow.

A hush fell as the door to the church thudded shut. A tinny, warbling synthesiser organ started playing and Ripley raised her head to see a woman who looked for all the world like a white-haired version of Bron, hunched over an electric keyboard in the far corner of the church.

Ripley tucked her chin back into her scarf as Reverend Rodwell hurried down the aisle towards the front, only stealing a glance after he'd passed. He was no longer paying any attention to the congregation. It was time for business.

She felt her spine go rigid as Simon slipped into the seat behind her. He leaned forward, close to her ear.

"You shouldn't have come today," he whispered. "You'll only upset her again."

She could smell mint on his breath. His voice was soft, almost gentle, but the threat was palpable.

"Reverend Rodwell invited me, personally," she replied, not even turning to look at him.

She heard him suck on his teeth in distaste.

"I'm watching you," he said, sitting back on his pew, arms crossed.

Ripley shifted forward, feeling his eyes boring into the back of her neck. She looked up and smiled gratefully as a couple sidled into the pew beside her, bringing the cold of the outside in with them in their hurry.

The man beside her smiled back politely, clutching his wife's hand. She saw the look that passed between the two of them: full of excitement and hope. The woman looked gaunt. Paper thin skin stretched taut across her prominent cheek bones. Her hand tiny and skeletal in her husband's solid, gentle grip. Ripley caught her eye and smiled sympathetically, immediately checking herself again. The last thing the woman needed was her sympathy, though Ripley was already sure it was about the only honest thing she would find here today.

She half-turned to see if Simon was still scowling at her, but he had gone. There was no sign of him anywhere in the church. *Good.* She didn't respond well to being told what to do.

Reverend Rodwell paused beside Megan's bed, as though administering some kind of blessing. Anne had still not re-appeared, and Ripley wondered if she had been told to go and sit in the bus. What kind of hold did Reverend Rodwell have over them that he was able to exclude Anne like this?

The small, portable ventilator wheezed and popped, echoing in the open room as the burble of conversation subsided. The organ introduction began again, startling and odd. Pitched far too loud over the tinny speakers.

Ripley found herself staring intently at Megan's face. Was she searching for some sign of life? Some signal that Megan needed to be saved from this awful situation? Or was Ripley just as bad as the others in the room? Transfixed by the spectacle of a girl in a coma at the front of a church about to perform amazing feats of healing from her bed. But, looking around at her fellow audience members' rapt expressions, she seemed to be the only one finding any of this uncomfortable.

Reverend Rodwell moved across to the pulpit and, as the organ music faded, he began by welcoming them all to the gathering, and reminding them this special service was for everyone. He told them, beaming, that he was delighted to see so many new faces. Ripley kept her head down.

Rodwell's tone was upbeat as he explained the kind of things they could expect from this unique experience, citing wonderful healings that had occurred in the past. Miracles, no less. He was certainly passionate. Not quite reaching the euphoria of those American television evangelists, but more exuberant than the majority of vicars Ripley had ever heard preach.

After leading them all in a short prayer together, calling on God to attend with them, Reverend Rodwell began to invite volunteers to come forward.

"This is not a test of your faith," he reassured them. "God sees you. He has given Megan the gift to be able to help you. Come on now, don't be shy. We all need something. Who's coming up?"

A couple of tentative hands were raised around the church. Ripley sunk lower into her pew as Rodwell's eyes scanned the crowd, looking for a likely candidate. Strange that people were being so reticent. Isn't this what they'd come here for? No one ever wanted to be the first.

Ripley glanced across at the couple beside her. They were clearly here to find help for whatever was eating away at the woman, and yet they weren't putting themselves forward. She saw the tiniest shake of the man's head in response to his wife's querying look. *What are they waiting for?*

Ripley felt the thrum of excitement ripple through the room as the organ struck up again and Rodwell left the pulpit. He came down into the body of the church, microphone in hand, whipping the audience into more of a frenzy by getting them to shout out their needs. Other hands began to raise, more confident now.

As the congregation got behind Rodwell's demands for a volunteer, the noise level grew—harsh and jarring in front of this silent girl. It felt so selfish, all these grown adults shouting 'Me! Me!' with the desperation of kindergarten kids being offered free sweets.

Ripley glanced across at the couple next to her as the man rose from his seat, alternately waving his hand to the Reverend or clasping both hands together and holding them to the sky in prayer. He was shouting too. Ripley couldn't make out the words he was saying but the gist was clear. They were there for a cure for whatever was ailing his wife, and he wasn't going to leave without her being seen.

Ripley bowed her head again, focussing her attention on Megan at the front, trying to send her calming thoughts. She felt her own heart rate increase a little. A small, warm flash ran up her spine. For just a moment, it felt as though someone was squeezing her hand, but when she looked down, she realised she was clenching her fist in a tight knot. She relaxed her hand, rolling her wedding ring forward from where it had pressed into the skin of her knuckle.

Rodwell was heading up the aisle towards her now, reassuring everyone that there would be time for them all. He had locked on to someone three rows in front of Ripley. A blonde woman, tall and statuesque, sitting quietly with her long-fingered hand resting on the silver knob of a walking cane. She was one of the few not screaming for his attention—staring resolutely forwards, as though willing him to pass her by. But Reverend Rodwell had spotted something he liked. He stood beside her for a moment, smiling like the cat who'd got the cream, his tongue flicking across his thin lips in anticipation.

The woman jumped noticeably as Rodwell laid a hand on her shoulder, holding his other hand up to his face, index finger pressed against his lips, with the microphone clasped casually below, hissing a quiet, reassuring "shh" until the crowd fell silent amid disappointed murmurs. The organist slowed her tune to a soft, gentle one—nondescript and bland.

Rodwell's smile was superior and knowing enough to make Ripley's skin crawl. Whether there was any truth to Megan's gift or not, this man was playing for gains today. His smile turned serious as he dropped down into a crouch beside the woman. She continued to stare ahead, clearly embarrassed to be chosen. Ripley saw her fist clench tighter around the handle of her cane as Rodwell spoke to her.

"What's your name, child?" he asked, his tone somewhere between preacher and talk show host. Ripley guessed he had to ramp up the performance for an event like this if he was going to sell it. He was surprisingly good at it too.

"Georgia," the woman said timidly. "Georgia Boland."

"Georgia!" he shouted out excitedly for everyone to hear. A small cheer rose in response, but Ripley could already feel their needles of resentment that she had been chosen over them.

"Don't be shy, Georgia," he said, smiling expansively at his eager audience. "We're all here for you. What ails you?"

"Oh," she said, her free hand waving him away. "It's not really worthy of..."

"Nonsense!" he exclaimed, to the excited support of the crowd. "You are here, aren't you? You came to feel God's gift?"

She nodded, a little more confidently. He stood, hand still resting on her shoulder and turned to face the crowd again.

"Shall we start small, ladies and gentlemen?" he called out. "This woman, the beautiful Georgia, believes her problem is too small for us to worry about. What do we say to that?"

The crowd began a chant, led by a couple of clear regulars and the team of volunteers at the front of the church.

"Heal her! Heal her!"

Slowly, they all picked up the chant, getting more and more excited as the woman rose unsteadily from her seat, leaning heavily on her cane. *Collective euphoria,* thought Ripley. *The first step to believing anything.*

It felt like a Saturday evening game show. After all of Anne's peaceful murmurings at their home, this was a different scene entirely. Was that why Anne had stayed outside? How could she leave her daughter to face this alone?

When Georgia was finally on her feet, Reverend Rodwell held the microphone out towards her again.

"Tell us, in your own words, what it is that troubles you," he said, his voice gentle but commanding.

"I have this chronic pain in my leg," she said, sounding nervous and embarrassed. "My right leg. Sometimes I can't even get out of bed it's so bad. I'm trapped in the house most of the time."

The crowd had quietened again at Rodwell's bidding, listening to the woman's story as she explained that she'd had the condition for a number of years, and how it was stopping her from living a full life. Her partner had left her, she'd lost her job—the full works. The doctors had tried everything, but nothing helped. She'd all but given up hope of ever taking a walk in the country again, which was all she wanted to do. This brought baying from the crowd. No way should she give up hope! More cries of "Heal her!" and "Take her up!" echoed through the room.

Ripley noticed the door on the side of the church open a crack. She saw Anne peeping through the gap, her face a strange mix of sadness, worry and anger. She stared at her daughter through the small opening as though willing her to get up and walk out of there, away from this crowd of strangers baying for a miracle. Her hand gripped the edge of the door and for just a moment Ripley saw her struggling to keep herself away. The door closed again without anyone else noticing.

Rodwell waved his hand imperiously and Ripley saw Gareth hurry forward from the back on the hall with an empty wheelchair, ready to escort the woman down the aisle. After the smallest fuss, she was whisked to the front of the room and the promise of instant relief from her terrible pain.

Ripley watched, head still held low, as the woman was arranged by Rodwell so that she stood beside the bed, facing the crowd. At Rodwell's bidding, she took hold of Megan's hand. Reverend Rodwell called for silence and took Georgia's free hand in one of his and Megan's in the other.

The circle complete, he began a passionate, evangelical prayer calling on God, through Megan, to help Georgia. Almost as one, the assembled onlookers dropped their heads, hands clasped in prayer. In their muttered, free-form incantation, Ripley could hear snatches: *Megan. Gift. God. Heal.*

A hush fell among them as Rodwell left Megan's side and began circling the bed, now muttering his prayer under his breath like a man possessed. The performance was perfectly orchestrated to whip up the crowd, sweeping them along in the moment.

Ripley jumped as the man beside her grasped her hand, nodding at her reassuringly, as though she too needed his support. She withdrew her hand with a firm nod. *Don't worry about me, I'm just fine.*

Suddenly, a loud, exultant cry erupted from the front and all eyes shot up to see Georgia Boland stand up straight and cast her cane aside with a triumphant flourish. It clattered to the stone floor to a cheer of delight from the crowd.

Georgia clasped her hands to her face, her blonde hair trapped between her fingers, mouth open in amazement. She took a tentative step forward with Reverend Rodwell beside her, his arms dramatically poised and ready to catch her if she fell, but being sure to let everyone see that she was doing this all on her own.

And she didn't fall. Cautiously, focussing on her feet as she placed one in front of the other, she began to walk unaided, arms held out to the sides like a circus tightrope walker. The hushed awe turned to quiet exclamations of excitement and then cries of jubilation. She was walking! Shouts of 'Miracle!' and 'She's healed!' rang out among the crowd as she began to walk back down the aisle, gaining confidence with each step. 'Praise the Lord!'

Georgia quickly gained confidence, moving through the crowd, shaking people's hands, accepting high fives and hugs as she made her way up the body of the church. It was only as Georgia drew level that Ripley got a good look at the woman's face.

Despite the exuberant smile and the shock of blonde hair, she recognised her instantly. Under that blonde wig, and the fake stoop of the back and the fake limp, she was the same woman that Ripley had seen in the cafe yesterday morning. *What had she taken out of that newspaper? Payment for her performance today?*

The woman was a plant to make sure that everyone bought into Megan's healing abilities. And this captive audience had lapped up the whole sick performance. Did Anne know they were doing this? If so, Ripley had just lost any last vestige of sympathy for her. She glanced back at the small side door, but there was no sign of her now.

Ripley found herself staring aghast at the woman as she passed, still celebrating her so-called miracle. *How many of these stooges did they have?* Ian was right, this was out-and-out fraud. She wasn't sure she could stand to watch any more of this sham. If she lingered any longer, she would shout out the truth: *This woman is a fraud! That man is a liar! This child is being abused and you're all playing a part in it!* And it wasn't the time for that, yet.

Ripley stood up as the celebrations passed, just as Reverend Rodwell looked in her direction. His smile dropped for just a moment. There was a flicker of something there. Panic, perhaps? Anger, certainly. Her skin prickled. It was time to go.

She squeezed her way out past the couple beside her. The man blocked her briefly, clearly unimpressed that she wasn't joining in with their celebration. She shoved past him a little harder than was necessary and arrived in the aisle just behind the allegedly healed woman and her exuberant entourage.

Rodwell was already calling for a new volunteer to come forward and be healed as Ripley cast a quick final glance over her shoulder, and slipped through the side door she'd seen Anne at, into the small, dark room beyond.

RIPLEY LEANED BACK against the door, shutting out the cacophony beyond. She felt sick. Her heart was beating harder than it should be and she could feel her blood pulsing in her neck and temples. Her breath felt short, and her lungs were struggling to fill. *Am I having some sort of panic attack?*

"You?"

Ripley opened her eyes and saw Anne stand up from her chair in the corner, taking a few angry strides forwards before she stopped herself.

"What are you doing here?" she asked accusingly. "Haven't you done enough damage?"

"Reverend Rodwell invited me," Ripley replied, coughing harshly to try clearing her lungs. It didn't work. Her breathing was becoming laboured and raspy. Anne frowned.

"Are you okay?" she asked, as Ripley bent forward trying to ease the burning.

Ripley held up a hand to let her know she would be fine and coughed again, feeling her lungs opening up. She stayed bent over, pulling in increasingly deeper breaths.

"Sit down," Anne offered.

"No, I'm fine," Ripley replied. "I'm not staying."

The attacks, when they came, were painful and worrying, but they seemed to pass almost as quickly as they came on. Ripley could still feel a faint tickling burn in her lungs, but at least she could breathe again freely.

"Enough spying for one day," Anne sniped.

"I've seen more than enough, thanks," Ripley replied.

She moved past Anne towards the door leading out of the building, but stopped. She couldn't let this pass.

"Why are you hiding back here?" she asked, reeling back to face Anne. "Rather than supporting your daughter through that sham. You know what he's doing out there, don't you?"

Anne stepped backwards, retreating from the conflict.

"You don't understand," she muttered.

"I think I do," Ripley said. She kept her voice low, stepping closer to Anne again. "You told me she was special. You said she had a genuine gift."

"She does," Anne said, more forcefully. "She is exceptional."

"But you're happy to wheel her out there with that charlatan, letting fakers pretend she's healed them to con money out of people?"

Anne's slap came out of nowhere and stung like hell. Both women stood in shocked silence for a moment, staring at each other before Anne's shoulders slumped and she gripped the back of the chair in the corner, slowly easing herself down until she was sitting, head bent. Her sigh was deep and juddering.

"You don't understand," she repeated.

"Shall I tell you what I do understand?" Ripley asked angrily. "The woman Megan supposedly just healed was in the cafe up the road yesterday morning, accepting a package from your Reverend friend, presumably cash to compensate her for the fantastic performance she's just delivered."

Anne's eyes flashed. Anger, or panic? Ripley couldn't tell.

"He wouldn't do that," Anne snapped.

"I saw it with my own eyes," Ripley said, turning to go. She'd had enough of their lies.

"Wait," Anne said, standing up and getting between Ripley and the exit. "I know it's hard for you to understand, but Francis is a good man. He's dedicated himself to helping Megan do God's work. We couldn't do any of this without him."

Francis. Ripley had a flash of clarity. The way Anne's voice softened when she spoke about him. That slight tremble. It was fear. Not fear of upsetting him, but fear of losing him. Ripley had read it wrong.

"How long have you been together?" Ripley asked, cutting straight to the chase.

"What?"

"You and Reverend Rodwell. You're in a relationship, right?"

"Oh, no," she demurred. "No, it's not like that."

Ripley could see from the flush creeping up Anne's cheeks that it was exactly like that. She stared at her, letting the silence hang, and in it, a demand for an explanation.

"He's a very good friend to me, to us," Anne said, the blush rising. "He's helped me through everything with Megan, and he has done it all totally selflessly."

Yeah, right. Ripley thought of the flashy sports car, the nice coat, the good shoes. Not the average fare for a local vicar. But then, this was not your average church, thanks to Megan.

"So you let him do this to pay him back? That donation box must fill up nicely after people have witnessed a few so-called miracles."

"Will you report him?" Anne asked, stiffening.

"I have to," Ripley said.

"Because you don't think we should put Megan through this?"

"Because I don't like anyone preying on people's weaknesses or abusing their faith."

Anne laughed. A rueful snort of a laugh.

"I'm doing neither of those things," she said. "We give them hope."

"Without a care for the consequences," Ripley replied. "Is that what you gave Ian's wife? Hope?"

"She got what she wanted. What she asked for." Anne half-shouted.

"And she died too soon," Ripley countered. "And what about Caroline Clifton? She brought her son to see Megan in good faith. You gave her hope too, I suppose. Do you know how cruel that is? To give a parent hope when there isn't any?"

"Yes," Anne spat. "I know only too well."

"So why keep doing it?"

"I've seen so many sick children defy the odds to recover after sitting with Megan. She *is* special."

"Oh, you keep telling yourself that," Ripley snarled.

"The problem was with the boy himself," Anne said, her tone patiently explanatory. "He didn't want healing. He didn't want to be there. He was already gone."

"What do you mean?"

"He was barely alive when they brought him to us. Did she tell you that? He didn't even know where he was. He had given up. Megan is an amplifier, remember? It doesn't matter how badly his parents wanted him healed, if he wanted to die, that's what she would have heard, isn't it?"

"But you let them think she would help him."

"She did," Anne said. "She helped him die."

Anne was so convinced by Megan's gift that she would always find a way to justify everything they did. Ripley had heard enough. What they were doing in the church was pure deception. How many other visitors in that room had been planted there by Reverend Rodwell to trick those with genuine problems desperate enough to believe? It made her sick.

She could understand Anne's deep desire for there to be some deeper reason for Megan's condition. It was clear how they could have ended up where they were now, but the lie had run away with itself, led on by Rodwell's greed. Whatever gift Megan had, it had nothing to do with the cabaret going on inside the church right now.

"You can't let him keep doing this, Anne," Ripley said, eventually. "It's abuse. I know you have faith in Megan's gift, but what's happening out there is different. That has nothing to do with Megan and you know it. If you promise to put a stop to it, I won't report you."

Anne nodded, forlornly. She knew.

"And I want you to think seriously about these accusations you've made about Ian Hewitt, because if you're just lying to silence his complaints, you must drop the charges. Enough lies."

Before Anne could reply, Gareth burst into the room, his face ashen.

"Anne," he said, urgently. "Come quickly! It's Megan."

Ripley saw the confusion flicker across Anne's face. A mix of panic and hope.

"What's happening?" Anne asked.

"Just come, quickly!" Gareth repeated.

THE CHURCH WAS bustling with panicked activity. Medics swarmed around Megan as alarms filled the air, their sinister message clear for all to hear—Megan was struggling.

Reverend Rodwell was trying to clear the room, reassuring concerned punters that Megan would be fine. That this happened from time to time as the power of the Lord became too much for her.

"She's overwhelmed by the love in the room," he said to one visitor. "She'll be just fine in a day or so."

Anne bent over Megan as the medic worked around her, clasping her daughter's hand and whispering intently to her, mouth close to her ear. Some of the crowd lingered to watch, faces etched with concern tinged with voyeurism. These people had come for a show, and though this may not have been what they were hoping for, it was exciting nonetheless.

Ripley was sickened to see Rodwell cajoling one of the t-shirt wearing volunteers into position by the door to collect any donations on the way out. She hadn't seen him cast so much as a glance towards Megan since she'd been watching him. He was more worried about seeing all his profit walking out of the room.

"Get off her!" Anne shouted suddenly, and everyone in the church turned to see her shoving the medic to one side as he tried to administer to Megan. He moved round to the other side of the bed, intent on doing his work. There was a dull murmur from those few faithful who remained inside, and Rodwell signalled Gareth to shepherd the rest out as he hurried over to deal with Anne.

The ambulance siren was already audible in the distance. They would be here soon. Ripley moved close enough to hear the hushed, angry conversation going on between Anne and Reverend Rodwell.

"I told you she was too sick for this. We shouldn't have brought her."

"Calm down, Anne. Don't make a scene."

He turned her away from the room, guiding her by the arm. She winced at the pressure of his grip. Ripley couldn't hear the terse exchange that followed, but she could see from Anne's face how it hurt her. She felt compelled to intervene.

"Everything all right here?" Ripley asked, striding up behind Rodwell. "Do you need any help, Anne?"

Rodwell spun around, the angry look slipping from his face just too late to be hidden. Ripley smiled a crooked, knowing smile. *I wasn't talking to you.*

"Not from you," Rodwell spat. He cocked his head as he heard the sirens outside. "Sounds like the cavalry has arrived. If you really want to help, keep her out of the way so they can do their job."

The way he inclined his head angrily towards Anne, as though she was a nuisance, made Ripley seethe. Anne was back at Megan's side in a flash, clinging on to her daughter, crying and whispering to her. Ripley's heart went out to the poor woman. Rodwell clearly had an emotional hold over her that was strong enough to cloud her better judgement. Ripley took Anne's hand and patted it.

"The ambulance is here now," she said.

"I shouldn't have let her come," Anne muttered, tears streaking her make-up.

By the time Megan was loaded into the ambulance with the medic still at her side, Anne had been cajoled into the passenger seat of the branded minibus and, with Gareth driving, they set off in convoy, carving through the on-looking crowd. Ripley watched from the door of the church as the sorry procession sped off towards the main road. Reverend Rodwell appeared at her side.

"Well, that was an unfortunate turn of events," he said, his emotionless tone telling Ripley just how little he cared.

"Hmm. Just as things were getting interesting too," Ripley replied, with enough sarcasm to mark her hostility.

"It seems you're not destined to see a full service with Megan, Dr Ripley. Perhaps you're a bad omen."

"Don't worry, I've seen more than enough," Ripley said, turning to face him.

"Let me drop you back," he said, smiling.

Ripley didn't trust him.

"I'll be fine."

"Come on, I just want a quick word, and I know you didn't drive here."

He saw her reluctance and laughed.

"Oh come on, Dr Ripley, I only want to talk. In private. What do you think I'm going to do?"

Ripley could think of several things she wouldn't put past him, but she conceded to the lift. He was a pretty boy—not built for fighting.

On the way to his car, they weaved through the thinning crowd, Rodwell still trying to reassure many of them.

"Make sure you pass your details to the volunteers," he repeated, shaking hands, patting shoulders. "We'll get in touch shortly and arrange a private meeting once Megan's strength is restored."

Ripley spotted the couple she'd been sitting beside earlier. The man was easing his frail wife into the passenger seat of their rusty old car. She had a horrible feeling this had been their last hope. Something in the tender way he closed the door, or the brief moment he gave himself to sigh and collect his thoughts before resetting his brave face and climbing into the car beside his wife.

"You see that couple?" Ripley asked as they reached Rodwell's car. "In that old car there, just pulling away now?"

Rodwell nodded dismissively as he opened the driver's door and got in.

"That was it for them," she said, closing her own door as she sat beside him. "This was their last chance. They won't be coming back for a private meeting. Well, she won't anyway."

"We can't help everyone, Dr Ripley," he replied tersely, firing the engine and slowly reversing, still smiling and waving at the final stragglers.

"How much did you pay her then?" she asked, wanting to get her own accusation in before he started talking.

"I'm sorry?" he questioned, frowning at the road ahead.

"The blonde lady with the leg pain who, only yesterday, appeared to be a dark-haired lady who walked perfectly well without the cane."

"I'm sorry?" he asked again, incredulous now.

"So you should be," Ripley said, knowing he hadn't meant it like that. "I saw her sit down at the table in the cafe and take whatever you had left for her in that newspaper."

Rodwell's jaw tensed, but he still wouldn't look at her.

"I don't know what you're talking about," he said.

"Really? Because Owen seemed to recognise her, so I'm guessing she's been in before. I bet he'd be able to tell me if he'd seen you with her. It's a small enough village. I'm sure if I did a little digging..."

"What do you want?" he snapped.

"I want you to stop lying to people. And I want you to stop using that poor girl to further your own ends."

"You don't understand," he said, bitterly.

"So everyone keeps telling me," Ripley replied. "But I think I do."

"Megan *is* special. I know that what you've seen today has made you doubt us, but I promise you that there is a truth in there, beneath all the spectacle."

"You can dress it up however you like," she said. "From where I stand, what you're doing is fraud. And it has to stop."

"I know," he said, surprising her. "I think it may have run its course, anyway."

"That's a little callous, don't you think?"

"Maybe you're right," he said. "But perhaps, in all the excitement, we've lost sight of the child at the heart of it. She isn't well. I think she may not be with us for much longer. We've had a lot of failures recently. A few complaints. It's bad for business."

She couldn't think of a dignified response. He was clearly only in this for the money, and just as it was starting to fail, he was looking for a way to extricate himself. *Poor Anne.* If Megan *was* losing her battle, Anne would need all the emotional support she could get. And yet, here was her partner already planning his exit.

"So was Caroline Clifton bad for business, too?" she asked, voice sharp and angry.

She noticed his knuckles going white as he squeezed the wheel, a small twitch in his jaw as his anger bristled. *Now or never.*

"What did you have to do to make her shut up and go away?" Ripley asked.

His fingers drummed quickly on the wheel but he stared resolutely ahead. A vein pulsed in his temple, and his neck and cheeks flushed red.

"It's not what you think," he began, but Ripley was in no mood for his lies.

"Ian saw you throwing her out of Anne's house last Wednesday. She was visibly upset. And she hasn't been seen since."

"What are you talking about?"

He slowed the car almost to a halt and turned to look at her, confusion and surprise vying for space. A car hooted behind them, and he slowly looked back at the road, shifting into gear and pulling away. He waved a conciliatory hand over his shoulder.

"We paid her to go away," he said. Direct. Matter of fact. No hint of a lie. "She turned up at the house, shouting and screaming about her son. We can't keep having that kind of disruption outside. So I repeated our offer to return her donation if she would leave us alone. She took the money, but she refused to leave quietly because bloody Anne went and told her it had been her son's choice to die, and that Megan had helped him do that. She became violent, so I threw her out and told her we would call the police."

"And did you?"

"No," he said, frowning. "There was no need. She got in her car and drove away. I thought that was the end of it. I just assumed she'd come to her senses."

There was something he was hiding. They had already passed the pub and were rapidly approaching the driveway towards the cottage. She was running out of time to get the truth out of him.

"And you haven't seen or heard from her since?"

"No, thank God. Vile woman."

"So you didn't follow her? Make sure she stayed quiet?"

"What? No!" he replied, incredulously.

He stopped the car at the top of the driveway, switching the engine off and turning in his seat to face her. He sighed theatrically, leaning closer to her, suddenly conspiratorial. His aftershave was strong and sweet. His eyes glinted, his face far too close.

"Look, I know you want answers," he said. "And I don't want you jumping to these wild conclusions, so I will tell you my little secret. Even though I'm not proud of it."

He looked pained and frustrated. Was she getting to the truth here?

"Like I said, Megan hasn't been well recently and there have been more complaints than successes. We can't afford any more negative publicity. So, when I offered Caroline the money, and she turned it down...

well, I got the sense that there was something troubling her. So I upped the offer. I asked exactly how much she would need to disappear. To keep quiet. Anyway, when I asked her like that, Caroline opened up. About her broken marriage. About all the fights. I could see how much pain she was in. Please don't tell Anne this, but I agreed to give her more money. Enough to disappear, to leave her husband and start a new life without everything that haunted her. I promised not to say anything to anyone. She just wanted to vanish."

Ripley looked at him, searching his face for the truth. He seemed so contrite. So genuine. Was that all he was hiding?

"I had the money right there in the safe," he continued. "She left with a huge amount of cash in her bag, and she didn't look back. I'll bet she's somewhere nice and warm now, somewhere far away from all this. Mending her heart. At least, I hope she is."

Ripley stared at him. Was this true?

"You paid her off? And she went, just like that?"

"I gave her thirty thousand pounds," he said. "That was her price. I'm assuming that's why she didn't feel she could tell anyone. She felt guilty for taking the money."

Ripley shook her head, trying to rejig her understanding of the situation.

"Look," he said. "I'm just trying to protect Megan. Her care costs a lot of money. As you saw today, she may not have much longer. I'm trying to make sure that she and Anne are all right."

Ripley snorted.

"What about you and Anne?" she asked.

"Oh, I know you think I'm in this for myself, Dr Ripley. And you're entitled to believe it. I have done well out of being involved with them, I admit. I know Anne will be devastated when I leave them, but I have long felt that something else is calling me. Away from this place."

I'll bet.

She didn't like him, and she didn't trust him, but his explanation for Caroline's disappearance was the most plausible she'd heard yet.

"I'll walk from here," she said, opening the door.

As she stepped out of the car, he leaned across the passenger seat and called after her.

"If we agree to drop the complaints against Ian Hewitt, would that do it? Would that be enough to stop him going after Megan?"

"I shouldn't think so," Ripley said. "This all has to stop. That's the only way you will get him to back down. He doesn't want you to con anyone else. And neither do I."

She closed the door without slamming it, but her heart was thumping as she marched away. She was sure she would hear the engine fire up again, and the crunch of gravel as he followed her. Had Caroline really taken his bribe and gone to ground somewhere to start a new life without Gavin, without her memories of the awful legacy they'd jointly given their son? It would crush Ian's hopes for his own case if she had.

The wind was howling across the cliffs, trying to buffet her back up the driveway. Ripley bent into it, feeling it strengthen as she reached the end of the hedge and got the full force. She was grateful to step into the shelter of the cottage doorway.

Ripley finally heard the crunch of tyres at the top of the drive followed by a small wheel spin as Reverend Rodwell turned and sped off back towards the centre of the village. She breathed a sigh of relief that he hadn't followed her up to the cottage, but then he knew he'd be outnumbered with Ian there. Nonetheless she was pleased he'd gone. It was high time they left the village themselves.

She could hear his throaty engine gunning along the coast road, away from the house. Swearing at him under her breath, she wrestled with the old lock on the front door and pushed it open with her hip.

The cottage felt cold and the damp, salty smell hit her as she stepped through the doorway. *The joys of coastal living.* She shivered as she draped her coat over a hook and shut the door behind her. The house was quiet.

"Ian?" she called out. "You here?"

There was no response, but the door leading to the annexe was ajar and she heard a faint bang from within. Dropping her things in the living room, she pushed the door into Ian's annexe open and stepped in.

This part of the house was older than the section she was in and much damper. It felt colder through here than she'd remembered. Another thud drew her out towards the back of Ian's area, into the small rear porch with its rotting door which led out to the cliffs.

"Ian?" she shouted. "It's only me. Are you here?"

Again nothing. A chill blast of wind blew the back door open, banging heavily against the frame. So that's what the thudding was. No sign of Ian, though. Surely if he'd gone for a walk, he'd have closed the house up, especially after last night's incident.

She stepped out into the cold wind and shivered. The view out to sea along the cliffs was unobstructed, and Ian was nowhere to be seen. Another icy blast hurried her back inside. It was only as she tried to close the door that she realised the catch was broken— the old wood splintered around the rusty lock which had yesterday held it shut. She pulled it back into position enough that it held the door closed, but it wouldn't lock. She was damn sure it hadn't been like before.

Walking back through Ian's room, she was surprised to see his coat lying on the bed. He'd have to be mad to be out in that wind without a coat. Her stomach hitched. This wasn't right.

She lifted Ian's coat and found both his wallet and his phone lying beneath. The welcome screen of his phone showed the missed text from her as yet unopened. *Who goes out without a coat, phone or wallet?* He must be here somewhere.

She hurried out of his room back into the main house, checking the bathroom, lounge, and kitchen.

Even her own bedroom. All empty. There was no sign that he'd even had breakfast after she'd left.

She fished her phone out of her pocket and listened again to the voicemail from him she'd written off as a pocket call. This time she listened to it all the way through.

Now, the strange sounds took on a different significance. That initial grunt sounded painful, the scuffling, panicked. And in the quiet which followed, she could hear voices. Muffled shouting, what could have been a car pulling off on the gravel outside. And then absolute silence. A gull. A repeating thud which she now recognised as the door slamming against the frame. She listened to the message again, but couldn't make out any distinct words. None of it sounded friendly though.

She grabbed her coat and went to examine the broken door. The splintered wood was old and rotten, but it had definitely been forced.

Bundled up against the cold, she turned her attention to the path leading down to the cliff edge. The gate at the end was also open, but it always had been. She stood in the open gateway and looked left and right, scanning the cliff top for any sign of life.

In the distance off to the right she could see the pub, with only the standing stones and the gentle slope of the burial chamber between the cottage and the inn. To the left was nothing but open cliffs shrouded by a vast, grey sky.

Turning back to the house, she spotted two narrow, muddy furrows in the grass beside the path. Could they be scuff marks where something—someone—had been dragged down the path? *What had gone on here?*

She went back indoors and stood in Ian's room, casting around for answers. The bed was unmade, the indentation of his head still in the pillow. A water glass lay on its side on the floor beside the bed, and the carpet was still damp where it had fallen.

On the floor on the far side of the bed was his notepad. She reached over and picked it up. A small glint on the floor caught her eye. A single, cracked lens from a pair of glasses. The same shape as Ian's. She got down on her hands and knees to look for the frames, but there was no sign of them.

"Shit," she muttered, pressing her phone to her ear, already rehearsing what she would say when Detective Harding answered.

"Harding," he said in that slow-sounding drawl of his.

"This is Alex Ripley."

"Dr Ripley. What's up?"

"Something's happened to Ian Hewitt."

"What do you mean?"

"I've just come back to the cottage and the back door is hanging open. The lock is broken. Looks like it's been kicked in. He's nowhere to be seen."

"Oh for God's sake," he muttered. "When did you last see him?"

"First thing this morning, just before I left for the group prayer meeting at the church. He was going to find us a hotel somewhere out of the village to stay. We were planning to leave as soon as I got back."

"And you're sure he hasn't just gone out for a walk or something?"

"No," she replied. "His coat, phone and wallet are all still here."

"Right," he said. "Sit tight. I'm on my way over. Don't touch anything."

THE CONSTANT DRIPPING pierced his consciousness, breaking through the darkness, pressing down on his brain. Drip, drip, drip. Close to his face. Close enough that he could feel tiny splashes of water hitting his cheek with each drop. His mind swam in and out of focus, desperately trying to hang on to what was real— the sounds and smells that might explain where he was. Everything was dark. Everything hurt.

Too many mornings since Jane died, he had woken in a fog of drink and grief, struggling to swim back to the surface. But this was different. His pain was physical, and this darkness was all-consuming. He blinked, but nothing became any clearer. Was he blindfolded? No. There was nothing secured around his head. A flash of memory hit him: being dragged backwards through a door, hitting his head. A hand over his mouth, a cloth. A chemical smell stinging his eyes and lungs. Everything going dark. *He'd been abducted.*

He tried to lift his hands to his face but his arms were heavy and numb. His breath hitched, and a hot, tingling wave ran across the surface of his skin as the panic hit. He wriggled his fingers, willing the feeling back, trying to get the blood pumping up his arms. He shivered. So cold.

His breathing, short and panicked, bounced back off the walls close to him. Even in the dark he knew this was not a big space. Deep and damp. *Buried alive?* No—he could feel fresh air, with a salty tang. The smell of the sea. His panic rose again. He was trapped. And terrified.

Ian had never been good in tight spaces, and he knew that his panic could easily overwhelm him. He needed to focus on the little things to calm himself down enough to figure out what was happening. He lay as still as his trembling would allow, trying to slow his rapid breathing and focus on what he could sense around him.

His head throbbed—a great surging whoosh, in and out, as waves of pain pounded the inside of his skull. He concentrated on the sounds beyond the pulsing rush of his own blood. Was that a scream? Yes! No. There it was again. A gull. The same sound had woken him this morning. Gulls swooping over the cliffs outside the cottage.

Another memory popped into his head: Alex Ripley sitting in her car in the driveway. A small wave as she'd pulled away. A gull swooping in front of her car, crying out as she'd driven off, giving a voice to his own frustration at her going to that service.

Was that only this morning? He had no idea how long he'd been here. In this all-consuming darkness, there was no way of knowing.

Ian shivered as a cold blast of wind whistled around him, making a proper haunted house howl. The icy wind made him realise just how cold his legs were. Cautiously he tried to shift them and, to his relief, he found that they responded, though a surge of pins-and-needles raced through his muscles forcing him to stop moving temporarily. He lay still, tensing and relaxing his legs as the blood began to flow around his veins again. He'd obviously been lying in the same position for long enough that his legs had gone to sleep.

When the pain had subsided enough, he pulled his knees up to his chest, still lying on his side. His frozen joints ached as they bent for the first time in what must have been hours. He cried out as the sharp pain shot up his thighs. His knees had suffered in the cold for years, but he couldn't remember the last time he'd felt quite this frozen. He slowly stretched his legs again, repeating the action until the prickling subsided and feeling returned.

He was lying on a stone floor, cold and unforgiving. No time to wait. He pulled himself up into a seated position, feeling more stone barely an inch from the top of his head. The blood drained from his head instantly, sending it spinning. He felt himself swimming back towards unconsciousness. He breathed quickly and deeply, flooding his system with oxygen, head resting on his knees, hands down at his sides. *Hold it together. How the hell did I end up like this?*

He'd waved goodbye to Ripley, the gull swooping as she drove away, that niggling resentment that he would be trapped in the damp-smelling cottage all morning, consumed by hate and frustration for that awful Shields woman.

Coffee. He'd made coffee in a blue mug with a small chip in the handle.

Crunching gravel. Wheel spin. A car in the driveway, speeding towards the cottage. He'd ducked away from the window, rushing into his bedroom. Phone Ripley. He'd hidden the phone under his coat as the back door crashed open. They were already in the house. There was nowhere to run.

His attacker had come in fast and strong. Stronger than he looked. Hitting Ian in the face with some kind of bat, knocking his glasses flying. Could have been worse. Dragged out towards the cliff.

Panic. Were they going to throw him over? Was this what they'd done to Caroline Clifton? The last thing he remembered was the smell on the cloth. A second voice, one he recognised. And then nothing, until he came to in this stinking, dark hole.

He rested his head on his knees, willing his panic to subside. Listening for clues. It was cold and damp. Deep and solid. A whomping thud, muffled and ancient. *The sea.* Waves crashing onto stone. Distant, and yet he could clearly smell the salty tang. And something else. Urine. Had he done that? No. It smelled old and stale. Like the communal stairwell of the estate block he'd grown up in.

Pull yourself together. He breathed deeply again, smelling the sea salt, damp stone, stale urine and something else, again. *What is that?* Something rotten, mouldy. Putrid. Something had died in here recently enough for the smell to still linger.

Another muffled thud of a wave hitting the rocks, followed by a mournful wailing sound. An echo of nature, ancient and haunting. And Ian suddenly knew exactly where he was. In the burial chamber on the cliff. And the tide was rising.

He let out an involuntary sob. *Is this it? Is this how I'll die?* He didn't even try to hold back the tears. The waves thudding against the beach below drowned out his howls.

BY THE TIME Harding pulled up in front of the cottage, Ripley had gathered her few belongings and shoved them all in her car.

Harding looked flustered as he clambered out of his own car, his jacket tangling around his arm in a gust of wind. He flapped his arm to untangle it, swearing.

"He's not back yet then?"

"No," she said, shaking her head.

"Wishful thinking on my part," he shrugged.

Ripley led him through to Ian's room and out to the back door, standing to one side to let him see the broken lock.

"It was swinging open when I got back," she said. "I heard it banging. It looks like the lock's been kicked in."

He bent down and poked the shattered woodwork with the end of a plastic pen.

"It was pretty knackered already by the look of things," he mused. "You hadn't noticed any damage before?"

"We both checked the doors before we went to bed last night, what with the broken window. It was fine then."

"It doesn't look great, does it?"

"Then there's these," Ripley continued, leading him outside and pointing out the drag marks in the mud beside the path. "And the fact that his coat, phone and wallet are all here."

"Where are they?"

She directed him back inside and into Ian's bedroom. He slipped on a pair of nitrile gloves, handed another pair to Ripley, and carefully lifted Ian's phone from the bed. Realising that the screen was locked he looked up at her.

"I don't suppose you know the passcode?"

"No idea," she said.

"I also found this lens which looks like it could be from his glasses," Ripley said, picking it up from the bedside table. "And this beaker had been knocked over which suggests a struggle."

"Quite the detective, aren't you?" Harding muttered without malice, glancing briefly at the lens she was holding out to him, but picking up Ian's wallet and rifling through it.

"I was really hoping this wasn't a thing."

"A thing?"

"Something serious."

He ran his hands over his face, trying to steel himself for the action required. He pulled a handful of plastic zip-lock bags from his jacket pocket and slid Ian's phone and wallet into one, and the coat into a bigger, self-sealing one. He also took the lost lens, the tumbler, and Ian's notebook from the side table by his bed. It all felt very sinister, gathering his possessions as evidence. Evidence of something very wrong in this village.

"We should have gone last night, like you said."

Harding looked up at her, nodding his regret.

"Yep," he said. "Right then. Let's get this show on the road. Do you want me to organise you an escort off the island?"

"No, I'll be fine," she said. "I'm all packed and ready."

She had no intention of leaving the island while both Ian and Caroline were missing, but she thought it would only stress Harding out more if he knew that she was still nearby. She'd tell him later. Besides, she'd be out of the village, so hopefully everyone would assume she had got the message and gone home.

"What are you going to do?" she asked, as he ushered her towards the door.

"I'll get a search going for Ian," he said. "The guys are already out looking for Caroline Clifton."

"Did you get anywhere with talking to the officers in Cardiff who'd been searching for her?"

"Yeah, I spoke to them first thing, they've got nothing. It sounded like they thought the husband might have done something to her, to be honest."

"Always the husband, huh?" Ripley said.

"Usually," Harding replied. "Anyway, I've called him and spoken to him. The poor man sounds distraught."

Ripley had to agree.

"Strange thing though," Harding went on. "When I put in a request to track her car, it seems someone else was already looking for her. Totally unrelated. Forensics up in Cumbria. So I don't know what to make of it."

"It's not unrelated," Ripley said, shifting uncomfortably. "That was a friend of mine. I asked her to see if she could run a trace on the car to find out where she'd gone after visiting Megan."

"And you didn't think to tell me?"

"I'm sorry."

"And?" he asked. "What did this friend of yours discover? I'm still waiting for the results."

"That's the problem," Ripley said. "She can trace Caroline from her home in Cardiff all the way to crossing the bridge onto the island, but there's no sign of her leaving again."

"So the car's still here somewhere?"

"One would assume," Ripley agreed.

Oh shit," he said, shaking his head. "Right, well, I'd better tell the boys to keep an eye out for that, too. We've only got two extra officers on this as it is."

"I can help," Ripley offered.

"Yes. By getting out of the way. No offence, but I don't have the resources to protect you as well."

"None taken, I get it."

"Good," he said.

"Will you keep me posted?" Ripley asked. "Let me know as soon as you find him?"

"Of course," he said, pulling the heavy door closed behind them.

They both stopped dead on the doorstep, noticing Bron's battered old green Defender bouncing its way down the drive.

"Oh great," Harding said. "That's all we need."

Ripley felt exactly the same.

"Did you call her?"

"No," Ripley said. "I told her I'd drop the key in at the cafe on my way out."

"She's got her bloody nose in everything, that one," Harding muttered through clenched teeth, waving a friendly salute at the approaching vehicle. "Don't say anything about Ian."

Bron hopped out before Roger had even pulled the car to a complete stop.

"Hiya Dylan, love," she said in that familiar, cheery voice. "What are you doing here?"

"I just popped by to see that Dr Ripley was all right before she left."

"You are such a good boy," she said, patronisingly.

She turned her attention to Ripley.

"I thought you were going first thing," she said accusatorially.

"We were," Ripley said, suddenly aware that she had probably drawn attention to the fact that she was now leaving alone. "I'm just leaving."

Bron didn't seem to notice the change from we to I. She was already round the back of the Defender, opening the back door and hauling out a huge bag of clean, pressed laundry.

"Great," she said. "Just leave the key with Roger. My hands are a bit full. Useless lump has done something to his back, now, so he can't even help me with this lot."

Ripley and Harding stood aside as Bron bustled past them, somehow managing to open the heavy door with one hand, balancing the laundry on her hip. She was a lot stronger than she looked.

"Sorry for all your troubles," she called back to Ripley. "I hope it doesn't mean you'll leave us a bad review. Good reviews are our lifeblood."

"If you can't say something nice, then say nothing at all, my mother always told me," Ripley said, smiling falsely.

"Quite right," Bron said, disappearing inside. "Tara then, love."

"Well done," Harding muttered out of the side of his mouth. "The last thing I need is Bron getting involved."

He headed to his patrol car as Ripley dropped her bag into her own boot and crossed to the Defender to give Roger the key. Roger looked at her impassively as she approached, only lowering his window laboriously by hand when she tapped on it, holding the key up for him to see.

"Bron said to give you this," Ripley said.

Roger took the key and wound the window back up without a word. He looked at Ripley with the kind of distaste you would usually reserve for someone who'd insulted your mother. Strange man.

Ripley and Harding parted company at the top of the drive, with him turning towards the coast, and Ripley heading in the opposite direction, past the pub and out through the village.

DARK. LIGHT. DARK. Light. Dark. She felt like she was fading in and out. She was trying to concentrate. Trying to hear what the voices around her were saying, but everything just sounded far away. Like she was underwater. Always underwater. Apart from the beeping. That was loud. And always there. She hated the beeping. It stressed her out. Interrupted everything. It would never let her rest. Never let her sleep. She was tired. So tired.

She held on to the dark, letting it close around her like the water had all those years ago. Every day now it grew stronger, and she didn't know how much longer she could fight it. Or even if she wanted to fight it. She just wanted to sleep. To go. To stop it all.

She had been willing it on ever since that boy had visited. It had been so strong in him. Crystal clear, like a diamond, piercing through the dark. The deep, unwavering desire to just let go. She had tried to take it from him, to fill him with warmth again, but he pushed back. It was his. He wanted to keep it. And she'd envied him. She'd wanted it for herself.

It had stretched between them like an elastic band, dark black. Pain. Ink stain. And when it snapped, part of it stayed in her and part left with him. She had tucked it away and nursed it, and every time she had given the light to someone else, the dark had grown just that bit stronger. And right now it was closing its fingers around her insides and squeezing them in the tightest embrace. Just like when Mummy had cuddled her to sleep after one of her nightmares, back then. Before. When she would wake up screaming. When she could still wake up. Was she finally going to sleep forever? She hoped so.

The beeping started again, loud and long this time. It was too noisy in here. Everybody was shouting and nobody was listening.

Stop it! Just leave me alone! Please. Let me go!

But they weren't listening. Nobody ever listened to her. They were pulling her back again. Everything was getting further away again. Numb. The beeping slowed down again, becoming more regular. The dark grew distant. The world came closer. They'd won again. This time.

ANNE SHIELDS STEPPED out into the corridor and collapsed against the wall as the doors swung shut behind her. They had nearly lost her then. Megan's heart had stopped for just the briefest moment. Anne didn't care how brief the moment, it had stopped. And now Anne could hardly breathe, her own heart was pumping so hard.

Megan had been getting worse recently. More crashes. More difficulty staying stable. Was her gift fading? Is that why they'd had more complaints? Is that why that poor woman had died after they had all been so convinced that she'd been healed?

Anne sank into one of the plastic chairs lining the corridor. Doctors, nurses, orderlies and visitors bustled past. How many hours had she spent in hospital corridors over the years? Too many to count. But this was the first time she felt that she was actually losing her little girl. Megan was fading away and there was nothing Anne could do for her.

"How is she?"

Reverend Rodwell sat down beside her. Anne hadn't even noticed him arrive. He took her hand in his, patting it gently. She took it away. She didn't want him to touch her at the moment. He should have listened to her. Megan had been too ill to be put in front of all those people. She knew how those big group sessions exhausted her daughter, and yet she had still let him talk her into it. If anything happened to Megan now, Francis Rodwell would have to share the blame.

"Her heart stopped," she said, her voice still wavering between anger and fear.

"Oh my goodness," he said, grabbing her hand again and turning in his seat to face her. "What's happened?"

She stood up, not wanting him to touch her again. She could barely contain herself.

"We pushed her too hard, and she nearly died," she snapped at him.

"Nearly? Is she okay?"

"No!" she shouted. "She is not *okay*! She nearly died. Because we ignored her condition last night and forced her to go into that room with all those people. Knowing, mind you, how it always exhausts her. I should never have let you talk me into it."

"Now hang on," he said, standing up. "I couldn't have known this would happen. We talked about this, Anne. We decided together. Megan has great work to do."

"Which she can't do if she's dead," Anne snarled.

"But, if that is God's will," he began.

Her slap stopped him dead, spinning his head to the side.

"Don't you dare," she spat. Dr Ripley's words had been ringing in her ears since their conversation in the church. Where does God's will end and human greed begin? Pushing Megan to perform when she was ill must surely be against God's will. Surely He was now sending Anne a warning, as he'd done once before: *Don't let her out of your sight, or I will take her from you.*

She'd nearly died once, and this had been Anne's second chance. A chance to prove that she could be a good mother. A good woman. She'd cleaned up her act, stopped drinking, dedicated herself to protecting Megan. She couldn't afford to let anyone, even Reverend Rodwell, turn her from the right path for her daughter. No. She would stop it all, the showcasing, the group healings, everything. Only the righteous and faithful would be allowed to see her. Perhaps. When she had recovered enough.

"You've pushed her too hard," she whispered harshly, her face close to Rodwell's. "And it's *not* God's will that she dies. This stops now. All of it. She's done enough."

"Anne," he pleaded. "I can see that you're upset. Of course. We all are. But let's not be rash."

"Get out," she said, flat and calm.

"Anne..."

"Get out!"

He stared at her for a moment, and she saw the resentment and frustration boiling up in his eyes as the scales fell from her own. Things would change around here. Megan may not be able to talk anymore, but her daughter had communicated with her today. Greed had overtaken them all, Anne included, and it had to stop.

If Megan pulls through, Lord, we will both be Your servants, and Yours alone.

"You're right, of course," Rodwell said, hanging his head. "We've pushed her too hard. But it was only ever in pursuit of God's love. The money means nothing, Anne. It's all to help Megan do God's work to the best of her abilities, you know that. But you're right. She needs a break."

- A HOLLOW SKY -

Anne felt herself softening towards him again already. He wasn't the villain here. She shouldn't have taken her guilt out on him. He had always put their best interests at the forefront of everything he did. He was a good man, and she loved him. She knew he meant what he was saying. But, this time, she felt that she had to put her daughter first. He had promised her that it would be fine. That God would always look after Megan. But she needed her mother, too.

"Perhaps," he continued, taking her hands in his and pulling her closer to him. "When Megan is well enough to travel, we can look at going on that holiday you talked about. It would be good for her to have a complete rest. For all of us. What do you say?"

Anne felt a new strength blossoming in her chest. She had never been a woman who could stand up to anyone. She had always lived in fear, letting herself be led by the will or ideas of others. Megan had just made her see that there was only one person in this world who really mattered: her daughter.

"We'll see," she said, taking her hands away and smiling at him. "I need to get back to her now."

She didn't catch the simmering look of frustration and resentment he threw at her as she pushed through the doors into Megan's room. She didn't hear the muttered curses directed at her back. She didn't see the phone come out of his pocket as he marched away.

DESPITE THE COLD numbness creeping over his whole body, Ian felt the slow lapping of the water as soon as it began seeping into the chamber. He had to move faster, but he was struggling. Maybe he should just give up and accept his fate. What was the point of going on without Jane, anyway?

Jane. She would hate to see him like this. And she would be cross with this defeatist attitude he was nurturing. The water was already lapping at his ankles. The tide was rising, and though he had no idea whether it would be a high one, he didn't fancy waiting around to find out.

The narrow chimney up from the sea was already full, and the water had nowhere else to go but the dank space he was trapped in. There was no way he'd survive trying to get down the chimney and out to sea now. It would have been possible, perhaps, before the tide had come in, but not anymore. There had to be a way to access the main burial chamber from this old bathing step though he hadn't been able to find it yet.

He continued his painfully slow search, working his hands, flat-palmed against the stone, feeling carefully for a gap, or a crack that could be the doorway out into the main chamber.

He dredged his memory for a visual map of the site. He had looked it up when he knew he and Jane would be visiting though they hadn't actually made it after all the excitement of their time with Megan. He could remember the odd key-like shape of the main chamber, and he distinctly remembered an old black-and-white image of the bathing step, long since closed off due to regular flooding. Had there been any indication on that website of how the two structures had been connected? He couldn't remember.

Without his glasses his vision was blurry, but he was at least able to see the outline of the space he was in now that his eyes had adjusted to the darkness. The chamber wasn't completely sealed as the odd gust of fresh sea air kept easing in, and there must have been a dim light filtering in somewhere to let him see what little he could.

The relentless boom of waves crashing onto the shore was followed by that mournful wail as the air in the chamber was forced up the narrow chimney to the cliffs above. It sounded like the single, ominous note of a giant pipe organ. The water was over his knees now and freezing cold. If he didn't drown tonight, he'd probably die of hypothermia.

Buck up! He chided himself. *This is down to you now.* As he ran his hands over the rock, feeling and prodding, trying to find a chink in the smooth structure, he wondered if Alex Ripley had discovered he was gone yet. Would she panic? Would she call the police? Of course she would. But they would never think of looking for him here, would they? And what if they had done something similar to her?

The man who'd come for him worked for Anne Shields, he'd recognised the car from their driveway. What if they'd taken Ripley as well? She'd walked right into the lion's den, after all, going to that prayer meeting. It was the first time he'd even considered that

Ripley may be in a similar predicament. She seemed so strong and self-assured; it hadn't struck him until now quite how much danger he'd put her in by asking for her help. If anything happened to her, it would be his fault. He should at least try to get out for her sake.

Another wave pounded the rocks below, sending up a surge of cold water which reached the top of his thighs. He had to try to find some way of getting himself higher. The tide was rising quickly. There wouldn't be much more time to find a way out.

In the darkness, he saw a small reflection of silvery light. Clouds clearing to let the moon shine down the natural chimney from the cliff top, perhaps. Or maybe a rare glimpse of winter sun. Or maybe even the first light of dawn. He had no idea how long he'd been down there. Either way, the chink of light was like a message of hope at exactly the right time. It showed him where the opening to the chimney was. *Of course!* He remembered now, the bathing step was below the main chamber. He should have been searching upwards for his escape route.

Ian reached up and pressed himself into the narrow chimney. It was barely wide enough to fit his shoulders in. The water rushed in again, rising up to his waist and dropping back down to his knees as the force of the wave dissipated. It wouldn't be long before the water reached the top of the chamber. It was a long shot, but getting up the chimney might be his only chance of surviving.

He stood up on tiptoes and stretched up into the narrow space as far as he could go. How the hell was he going to get himself up to the top? He wasn't exactly athletic, and the chimney was at least two meters long, and very narrow. There was no room to move, but he only needed to go upwards. If he could use the water to take some of his weight, perhaps he could use his hands and knees to creep his way up.

He forced himself to slow his breathing as another wave crashed in, pushing the water up to his waist and forcing the air from the chamber to blast up past his face. The wailing sound was louder in the confines of the chimney.

As the water rose in the chamber, the tone got higher and more piercing. When the wave receded this time, he noticed that the water remained at waist level. If his plan to ascend the chimney didn't work, he'd soon be stuck, anyway.

As the wailing sound died away, he began shouting.

"Help! Help me! Help!"

His voice echoed away up towards the cliffs. A scream of reply. But it was just another gull. Another wave forced the water level up to his chest. He felt something solid brush up against his legs in the cold water. *What the hell was that?* It bumped him again, and he stretched his frozen fingers out to try to get a sense of what it was.

He felt something silky, like soft seaweed. He felt something round and solid beneath it. And something else that chilled him immediately. It was a hand! And a head with long, flowing hair. There was somebody else in the chamber with him. That rotten, musty smell he'd noticed. There'd been a body in there with him. But who? Caroline Clifton? No, she had short-cropped hair. Ripley? No, the smell was older.

Ian let out an involuntary cry as another wave forced the water up to his chest again. Some of it funnelled up the chimney into his mouth. He tried to get his hands disentangled from the corpse's flowing hair as the body knocked into him again. He felt sick. He couldn't get away. He was wasting energy.

He screamed again, hoping that someone would hear him above the noise of the sea, above the gulls, above the awful wailing of the wind rushing up the chimney. Was anyone even out there? Was anyone looking for him?

He heard the next wave before he felt it, pushing himself up on his toes to keep his head above the waterline, chin titled towards the sky. As the water slid away, he pushed his hands against the edge of the chimney and pressed his legs as wide as they would go, propping himself up in the narrow column. He slipped a bit, but then stuck and held. His arms shook. Cold and tense. But he was staying put, the water holding some of his weight and his head and shoulders still above the surface. It worked this time but he wouldn't have much longer if the tide kept rising.

HARDING TURNED OFF the engine and listened to the gentle ticking as the car cooled. He had called in a missing persons report, with a description of Ian and what Ripley had said he'd been wearing. He'd also got one of the patrol cars out looking for Caroline's car. He'd told them to check everywhere from the small secret bays tucked down narrow lanes to garages and outbuildings. The car hadn't left the island, but he had a horrible feeling it hadn't even left Rhosfaelog. It had to be here somewhere.

Harding wasn't used to this amount of policing. Usually Rhosfaelog was a quiet place, with its share of petty crime, accidental damage and local squabbles. But nothing like this. Nothing like abduction. *Or worse.* But what was really niggling away at him right now were those missing persons posters that he walked past every day in the reception at the police station.

The most recent, Sally Anne Jones, had gone missing while visiting Rhosfaelog in the middle of November. Not even three weeks ago. Her poster was still up on the station noticeboard though they had already as good as given up looking for her. They'd found her car and some of her clothes in a quiet bay along the coast towards the big caravan park, and the assumption had been that she had walked into the sea.

The Coast Guard had put in a good effort on the search, but they hadn't found her. Of course her family insisted that she wouldn't have killed herself, but then families often do that, don't they? They don't want to admit that there was something they had missed. Something they could have done.

Now, though, Harding was replaying those interviews with Sally Anne's concerned sister in his head. He had been dismissive of her concerns, especially when he'd heard that Sally Anne had recently been diagnosed with an inoperable brain tumour, and that she had come to the village to see Megan, to find a cure. As far as he was concerned, that only backed up his suspicion of suicide.

It wouldn't have been the first time someone had failed to find a cure with Megan and taken the last resort instead. There was a case years before, when Megan had still been in the hospital, where a man had thrown himself off the cliffs after visiting her. He had left a note, blaming her for his death, but his family had all confirmed that he had suffered from terrible depression for many years and that his recent illness was simply the last straw. He had, apparently tried to take his own life twice already that month. None of them blamed Megan, and in fact, they had contributed generously to the early fundraiser as an apology for the damage he'd caused to her reputation.

Harding stared ahead at Anne Shields's house, wondering how the hell he was supposed to ask her if she was involved in the disappearance of at least two people. It had never crossed his mind that there may have been a connection between Sally Anne Jones's disappearance and her experience with Megan. What if there had been others?

He'd known Anne since he was a teenager. Back then, he'd always avoided her and her family if he could—they were always finding trouble. Anne had been a wild child, never far from booze, quick to anger, always in a scrape. Even though she'd been pretty rough back then, he still couldn't imagine her getting involved in kidnap or murder. Or was he being blinded by familiarity?

When Megan had first had her accident, it was big news. It always is when something so tragic happens to a local girl in such a small village. It was a big shock for everyone. As time went on, sympathy changed to support, and Megan's condition became a galvanising force in growing a friendly and supportive community. And Harding had benefitted from that—the close friendliness of the place had given him an easy ride as a police officer.

Anne had been at the centre of that change, and it had changed her too. Megan's charity funded developments and infrastructure that would otherwise not have reached as far as their little conurbation. From play groups, to support for pensioners, from road repairs to connectivity, the God's Gift charity gave freely and everyone benefitted. Anne Shields had become something of a statesman in the village, especially with Reverend Rodwell at her side.

Harding's own mother had been very damning about Anne's transformation from the chain-smoking, heavy drinking, single mum of three tearaways, to the elegant, pious, dedicated mother of a so-called gifted child. He had often admonished his mother for her harsh criticism of Anne, but she wouldn't change her opinion. As far as she was concerned, Anne Shields had always been one for a free lunch and this was no different.

But over the years, Anne had softened. She no longer went to the pub, for one. As time went on, all those incidents of her shouting drunkenly in the streets at someone else's husband had been all but forgotten. She had transformed herself into a pillar of the community, and somehow everyone else had just gone along with it.

Everyone knew that Reverend Rodwell had played a huge part in her transformation and most knew that their relationship went beyond a straightforward business one. Those with longer memories and harder hearts whispered that he must only be in it for the money. Jealous people could be mean though, couldn't they?

Since the accident, Harding had found Anne charming and accommodating, and kind. People could change, he'd always thought. Now he was doubting that. Her recent reaction to Ian Hewitt had been more reminiscent of her old self—bitter, angry and unwilling to hear reason.

He sat up in his seat as the front door opened. Why was he so nervous? Anne's assistant, Simon stepped out onto the path, slamming the door behind him, phone pressed to his ear. He shook his head, annoyed, and said something that Harding couldn't make out.

Harding didn't really know the man, and he knew he shouldn't judge someone he hadn't taken the time to get to know, but he'd never liked Simon. He'd always seemed too snide and controlling.

Reverend Rodwell had brought him in to help Anne as the business grew, and Harding had always felt he'd got his feet under the table pretty quickly. Simon liked to lord it around the village, thinking he was in charge of the ship, always insisting everything go through him. He said it was to spare Anne's feelings, and to ensure that she could focus on protecting Megan, but Harding suspected it was because he wanted to feel important and indispensable. Simon and the Reverend were thick as thieves, too. Always whispering in corners and rolling their eyes behind Anne's back.

Simon paced across the drive. The call didn't last long, and he looked frustrated as he hung up, but his face changed as soon as he spotted Harding's car. He smiled tightly, waved politely, head cocked inquisitively to one side. He strode confidently towards the car, and Harding wound the window down.

"Detective," Simon said, his voice soft and charming as ever. "How nice to see you."

His blue eyes sparkled as he smiled. Maybe it was because he was so angelic looking that Harding didn't like him. He'd always been a big guy, himself. Broad shoulders, big shovels for hands, broad nose, heavy brows. He had to admit being slightly jealous of Simon's fine, model-perfect features.

"Simon," he said, not returning the smile. "I'm just here to see Anne."

None of your business.

Simon gave him a sympathetic look.

"Oh, I'm so sorry, Detective, she's not here. Megan was taken ill this morning at the group service, and the family are all at the hospital. I was just on my way over. Perhaps I can help?"

"No," Harding said, a little too firmly.

Simon's smile fell as Harding's phone rang, making him jump. He held a finger up to tell Simon to wait and answered the call. Harding wound the window back up, shutting Anne's assistant outside. Simon waited a moment, staring through the closed window at him before pivoting on his heel and stalking off to one of the Range Rovers. He lingered again at the driver's door, not climbing in yet. People were always suspicious when the police came calling and wouldn't tell them why. Harding smirked at the thought of how much it would annoy Simon that he was being kept out of the loop.

"Harding," he said into the phone.

"Dylan, it's Matt. Down the coastguards. Listen, you'd better come down to Shillars point. There's a body washed up on the beach here. A woman. It's pretty grim."

Harding fired up the engine and sped out of the quiet cul-de-sac and off towards Shillars point. He was gone before he could see Simon's Range Rover pull out and head off in the opposite direction.

RIPLEY EASED HER car into a lay-by just outside Rhosfaelog, on the road to Four-Mile Bridge. From his description, this was where Ian had caught up with Caroline after she'd been thrown out of the Shields's house.

Ripley shut off her engine and sat in silence, looking out at the open fields bordered by low stone walls. There wasn't much to see from the road. Nowhere to hide. *Where had Caroline gone from here?*

The nearest houses were all the way back on the outskirts of the village. Visible from here, but not close enough to walk to. Ripley climbed out of her car, slipping around the front of the bonnet as a black Range Rover passed close by on the narrow road. One of Anne's fleet. The driver didn't slow at all. He didn't even seem to acknowledge her, staring straight ahead, paying little attention to anything but the road. He had a baseball cap pulled low over his eyes, and all Ripley could see of him were his slender hands gripping the steering wheel. She didn't think she recognised him.

She shrugged on her coat and walked around the front of the car as the Range Rover disappeared round the corner, barely slowing at all. A low wall skirted the lay-by, and she stepped up on to it to get a better view of the surrounding area. She could see all the way to the cliff edge from up here, but there was no discernible path through the fields towards the sea. Hardly the place to stop for a nice bracing walk either, then. The lay-by was little more than a passing place on the narrow road out of town.

Hopping off the wall, Ripley bent down to examine a faint streak of blue on the stone. It was right at the top edge of the wall, on the way out of the lay-by, where the wall joined the edge of the road. On the ground at the base of the wall was a fragment of orange plastic, and another, smaller shard of blue-coated plastic. Part of an indicator light and a sliver of broken bumper, Ripley surmised.

Caroline's car, from her husband's description, was an old model metallic blue golf. 'Old, but in great nick,' he'd said. Did these two pieces of plastic and that small scuff of paint come from her car? Had there been some kind of altercation here? Or had Caroline just clipped the wall when she drove off?

Ripley left her own car where it was and wandered along the edge of the wall, occasionally hopping up to get a better view over the fields. There was nothing to see apart from more of the same bleak coastline, dotted with small bays which would doubtless be beautiful on a rare, perfect summer's day. A few fishing boats bobbed at anchor, no signs of life aboard any of them. An old, faded sign part way down the slope towards the cliff edge warned of dangerous erosion. Someone had tagged it with illegible graffiti.

Looking back towards Rhosfaelog, Ripley realised that she had gone far enough around the headland that she could no longer see the pub. She could still make out the very top of the church tower above the distant houses. Otherwise the landscape was bare. There was nothing at all to suggest where Caroline might have gone or what she had done after stopping here.

She looked the other way, away from the coast and the raging sea. Fields, fields and more fields, bisected by low stone walls, peppered with old barns in various states of repair. Little sign of life, but it wasn't exactly the time of year for farmers to be working outdoors.

She was still wrestling with the idea that both Ian and Caroline had disappeared because of their complaints about the Shields family. Reverend Rodwell, for all his callous money grabbing had seemed genuinely shocked when she'd said that Caroline had been missing since just after leaving their house. Of course, Ripley had seen what kind of showman he was. He was perfectly capable of bluffing his way through her accusations, but she gave herself enough credit to have been able to spot it.

After all, there were still perfectly plausible, rational explanations for everything she suspected. Caroline *could* be hiding out somewhere trying to heal her broken heart. Ian *might* have simply run off to avoid facing his charges. And of course, it *may well* have been some local toerag just trying to scare Ripley away from Megan Shields who'd chucked the rock through the window.

But when she listed all those coincidental pieces in her head, she felt another surge of worry for both Ian and Caroline. *What the hell had happened to them?* She couldn't just leave the island without getting to the bottom of it, but Harding was right—she should get out of the village for now.

She hopped back down off the wall and walked back along the road towards the lay-by. Just up ahead, set back from the road down a narrow double track, was a long, dilapidated barn. It looked like it hadn't been used for years, with great holes in the corrugated roof and open sides where wooden doors would once have hung.

Piles of old farm machinery and rubble, overgrown with weeds and brambles, clustered along one side. Ripley couldn't see inside properly from where she was, but she noticed some relatively fresh streaks of mud leaving the dirt track and joining the road. There was also another, larger scrape of blue paint on the old wooden gatepost which had long since given up holding any gates, but still stood sentry at the end of the track.

She looked up and down the road. There was no other sign of an accident anywhere between the lay-by and the track, but she was convinced that the paint here was the same as that on the wall near her own car. Wishing she had chosen better walking shoes, she set off up the muddy track towards the barns, scanning the ground for any other signs of recent movement.

The tyre tracks looked fairly new and quite wide. Too wide for an old model golf. She took out her phone and took a few snaps of the tracks before walking on, just in case the heavy clouds above ever delivered their payload and potential evidence was washed away.

She hadn't quite reached the barn, but she could already see into the side closest to the road, and what she saw made her stomach fall. A corner of old tarpaulin lifted in the wind to reveal a bright flash of metallic blue. Ripley hurried towards it, knowing exactly what was under there.

AS SOON AS he saw Alex Ripley's car in that lay-by, he knew there would be trouble. It was the exact place where he'd caught up with that Clifton woman. It couldn't be a coincidence. But how had she figured it out? Just when he'd been planning to clear up the last of this mess. He had a horrible feeling this was all going to get even more out of hand.

He'd had no choice but to drive right by her, instead of turning up the track towards the barns as he'd intended. Keeping his face angled away from her so she couldn't quite see his profile, collar up, cap pulled low over his eyes, he didn't dare slow down. He couldn't risk her seeing it was him even if she recognised this as one of Anne's cars. He was glad he'd brought the Range Rover—it was one of several and more anonymous than his own car. As it was, she'd barely looked up as he'd sped past. She'd been too busy looking out at the cliffs. Good. She wouldn't find anything out there.

He didn't like her being here at all. It was far too close for comfort. He should've got rid of Caroline's car in the first place, rather than hiding it, but there had been no time. Besides, he'd covered it well and until Alex Ripley turned up with all her questions, no one had even thought to look for Caroline Clifton or her crappy old car. In his rear-view mirror, he saw Ripley bending down to examine the stone wall. *Snooping. As ever.*

He pulled into a gateway that opened onto the back road down to Hill Farm. The road eventually led back into Rhosfaelog, and even though it was in a poor state of repair, he knew he'd be able to use it if necessary. It wasn't an ideal spot to park, but it was the only place he could stop before the crossroads where the car would be hidden well enough from her line of sight. He turned the engine off, grabbed his coat and kit bag and climbed out.

She was a troublemaker, this one, exactly as he'd predicted from the first time he saw her. He'd recognised her straight away from that television show. She had taken no prisoners then, and he she probably wasn't about to start now. She'd turned out to be even sharper than he had given her credit for. But now she had to be stopped.

He crept back along the wall that lined the road, keeping low, beneath the top layer of stones, popping up occasionally to see what she was doing. He finally made it to an opening in the wall, big enough to see back to the lay-by clearly, and at enough of an angle that he could be completely hidden while he watched her.

She had left her car behind now and was walking along the top of the low wall on the side of the road. She hopped off every now and then, bending to look at things on the ground or on the stones of the wall itself. He knew exactly what she'd found and chided himself for not coming back to clean up better. He had scraped the car against the wall a couple of times as he'd towed it to the barns. He should have cleaned it up, but he'd got complacent. He hadn't thought anyone would come looking for this kind of detail. The useless local cop, Dylan Harding, would never have got this far on his own. He cursed Dr Alex Ripley under his breath. Not for the first time.

His stomach tightened as she hopped down off the wall again and walked purposefully over to the track leading up to the barns. This would not end well.

SURE ENOUGH, WHEN Ripley reached the barn and lifted the loose corner of dirty canvas, she found an old model, metallic blue VW Golf. The registration matched. This was Caroline Clifton's car. Hidden, albeit badly, from prying eyes.

Ripley worked her way cautiously around the barn, removing the tarpaulin lengthways from the driver's half of the car, and flicking it back over the roof. She pulled out her phone and flicked on the built-in torch, cupping her hand to the window to limit the glare. The keys were still in the ignition. There was a handbag and quilted jacket on the passenger seat and a smartphone in a cradle on the dashboard. All of Caroline's essentials were still in the car.

There was no sign of anything on the back seat, but as Ripley pulled the covering back off the boot, she noticed a brownish smear. Dried blood.

With her heart in her mouth, she tucked her hand into her sleeve and tried the latch. Surprisingly, it popped open. As she let the boot door rise, she was hit by a foul stench of metal and rot that she knew only too well. She'd found Caroline Clifton.

When she brought herself to look into the boot, she immediately leaned away, dry-retching, but managing to keep it together. Caroline's body had been crammed into the boot space, jammed up against her small overnight bag. Her mouth was open, her eyes blank and staring, and the smell was overwhelming. Dark blood, sticky and congealed, framed a wound on the side of her head. She'd been struck. Hard. She'd probably died outright, even before her attacker had callously stuffed her into the boot of her own car, and hidden it in this old barn. Left to rot in plain sight. Either her killer had planned to return to do a more thorough job of getting rid of the evidence, or they didn't care if she was found.

Ripley backed away from the boot, scrabbling in her pocket for her phone. She had to call Detective Harding. Her mouth tasted salty. She fought back another wave of nausea. She'd seen enough bodies in her time to get through this. *Pull yourself together.*

She stepped out of the barn, for once grateful for the chill wind whisking that smell away from her nostrils. She pressed the phone to her ear, cupping her hand around her mouth to shield the microphone from the wind. She walked back down the track towards her car as she waited for the phone to connect.

HARDING ARRIVED ON the beach to find a small crowd already gathered. How the hell did news get out this quickly around here? And why did people always want to come and look at a corpse? Macabre. He'd never quite had the stomach for it, and still got ribbed by his colleagues for the reaction he'd had to the first body he'd ever seen on the job.

He strode down the beach, pushing his way through the gawkers and arriving at Matt's side. The old guy had been a volunteer on the coastguard for as long as Harding could remember. His craggy face and no-nonsense attitude made anyone he saved—and there had been many—feel completely safe. He knew the sea. He knew the tides. This wasn't the first time he'd called Harding to report a body washed up on one of the beaches along the coast. Harding noticed that he had covered the body with one of the old grey blankets they kept on the boat to warm people up.

"Hello lad," he said, acknowledging Harding's arrival.

"Matt," Harding replied. "What's going on?"

"Thomas over there spotted her while he was walking his dog," he said.

He bent down to pull the blanket back, enough to reveal a face, bloated and part-decayed. There was a gasp from the small group gathered behind them.

"Give us some room here, please folks," Harding called out over his shoulder, fighting back the nausea that sat high in his throat.

He turned back to the body, examining her face. Despite the bloating, and the partial decay, he recognised her immediately. This was Sally Anne Jones. This was the woman who had disappeared after she had visited Megan. The one whose family had insisted she wouldn't kill herself. Yet, here she was.

"It's her, isn't it?" Matt asked. "That young woman we were all out searching for last month."

Harding nodded.

"I'm pretty sure it is," he replied, covering her face again. "How did she end up here now though?"

"Looks like she's been dead a while, probably around the time we were looking for her. I'd wager she's been trapped in one of the caves up the coast somewhere, and she's been flushed out on the high tide."

"Jesus," Harding said.

His head was spinning. Had Sally Anne killed herself as they'd thought, all those weeks ago, and been trapped in a dark hole, waiting for the high tide to release her body to the sea? Given what he knew about Caroline Clifton's disappearance, and now Ian Hewitt's, he would put money on their being a connection between them. Which meant he had a killer on his hands. He shivered.

His phone rang, shrill and annoying in the strange, choked silence on the beach. He answered on the third ring, cold fingers battling to unlock the screen.

"Harding," he said, his voice cracking.

"Detective, thank God. It's Alex Ripley."

Good Lord woman, just let me get on with my job will you?

"I'm a bit busy..." he began, but she interrupted him.

"I've found Caroline's car. I've found Caroline," she said.

She sounded panicked. Freaked out. *What the hell was she doing now?*

"She's dead," Ripley blurted out.

"Christ!"

His legs buckled slightly. *What the hell was going on?*

"Where are you?" he asked, totally sideswiped.

"I'm just on the road out towards Four-Mile Bridge. There's a barn just before the... hang on a second, will you?"

He frowned as he heard the scratching of fabric on the phone's microphone and Ripley's muffled voice saying; "Oh, hi. What are you..." Followed by a clattering sound as the phone was dropped. And a cry, cut short, as the line went dead.

"Dr Ripley?" he asked, feeling the panic rising. "Alex?"

Nothing. Just the beeps of a lost call.

Shit! This is not good.

He set off at a run up the beach, turning back to call to Matt.

"I've got to go, Matt," he shouted. "Stay here. I'll send someone down."

He was still closing the driver's door as he flung his car in a curve around the car park and sped off in a spray of stones.

IAN COULD NO longer feel his extremities. He wouldn't be able to hold himself up here much longer. His whole body was shaking with the effort of supporting his weight in the chimney. Shaking with cold. Shaking with fear. Exhausted and overcome with desperation. He was sure the tide had stopped rising, but there was no sign of it going down yet.

Just let go.

He felt his vision swim again. A huge wave of black, clouding everything. He pressed his hands harder against the wall. He was slipping.

Don't let go.

A wave pushed in to the chamber. Another rush of water over his head.

I'm coming, Jane.

RIPLEY HIT THE ground with a thud, pain shooting up into her skull from the impact to her nose. Simon hadn't held back on the punch. Her phone had been thrown from her hand and clattered to the ground. For a moment she hoped that Detective Harding was still able to hear, or at least that she'd given him enough to go on to find her.

She scrabbled backward, her hands scuffing on the sharp little stones of the track. He seemed pleased with the power of his punch, flexing his fist open and closed, readying himself for another go. He looked like he was enjoying seeing her fear too. Her eyes watered from the pain and her nose was filling with blood. He'd certainly hit her hard enough to break it.

Simon let her back away from him, smiling sadistically as he watched her. She flipped herself onto her side, starting to haul herself up. She got up onto her knees before he made a run for her, landing a whomping kick to her side, forcing the air from her lungs and knocking her back to the ground.

She coughed, desperately trying to drag air in, though her diaphragm kicked back. She coughed again. He stood over her and laughed. A high little giggle. He was toying with her.

"I *did* warn you to leave us alone," he said. "You should have listened."

Tall, slim and athletic. It was him she'd seen running away from the cottage after the rock had come through the window. Her mind raced back through every encounter they'd had since she'd arrived. From the moment he'd spoken to her outside the chamber, in the car park in the pub, outside the cafe. Simon had been watching her all along. Just as he'd promised. How had she not seen this coming?

She stayed down for a moment, covering her face with her hands, buying herself some time. She could tell he was enjoying seeing her down. At his mercy. It helped her steel herself to strike back. Surprise would be all she had. One chance.

She hacked again, more for performance than necessity. She checked her hands. Sure enough, her nose was bleeding. She felt it gingerly. Making sure to spread the blood across her lips and cheek for added effect, before looking up at him.

"*You* killed Caroline," she said, as though the realisation had just hit her. In reality, she was trying to force him to look at her face, so that he wouldn't see her hand gripping the fist sized rock she'd found.

He laughed out loud. A hearty, cynical laugh.

"They told me you were some kind of detective," he snorted, derisively. "Well done, you."

"Why?"

"She was getting in the way," he sneered. "And she took my money."

Ripley tightened her grip on the rock.

"Where's Ian?"

He crouched down beside her, grasping her hair and yanking her head back, letting her know he was in charge.

"Aw. You think you can still save him?" he asked, laughing as he arched his eyebrow triumphantly. "He's already in the ground. Time and tide wait for no man, Dr Ripley."

He was close enough now. This was her chance. She brought the rock up sharply, smashing it in to the side of his head with all of her strength. He pitched sideways, a look of pained horror on his face—the realisation that he had underestimated her.

As he fell to the ground, screaming in pain and anger, Ripley kicked out, pushing herself to her feet. He made another lunge for her, and she slammed the rock against his head again. He slumped, moaning. A low, animal moan, full of anger and frustration.

Ripley didn't hang around to check his condition. He may be incapacitated, but she wasn't going to risk waiting for him to come round. She set off, running as fast as her damaged ribs and blood-stuffed nose would allow down the track, back towards the road.

She glanced over her shoulder, but he remained prostrate on the ground. She could still hear him shouting, but he wasn't in any position to get up and give chase. Yet.

She burst out of the track onto the road and slowed to a limp, lungs burning, but still holding up. She glanced over her shoulder again. He still hadn't moved.

She slowed completely, gasping for breath and limping to the side of the road. She heard the engine before she saw the car—another black Range Rover, deep and throaty, crested the brow of the hill. There was nowhere for her to run. The car skewed to a stop across the road in front of her and the passenger door swung open. Gareth leaned over from the driver's seat.

"My God, Dr Ripley!" he said, looking appalled. "What's happened?"

Ripley's reply was interrupted by another paroxysm of coughing.

"Lord above," he said, leaping out and shepherding her to the car. "Get in, quickly. Let's get you to the hospital."

"No, I'm fine," she began to protest. She needed to get to Detective Harding. He had to arrest this young killer before he disappeared. She wanted Harding to see what she'd seen in the back of Caroline's car.

"Nonsense," he replied, a heavy hand pushing down on her shoulder to ease her into the passenger seat. "Come on. In you get."

She tried to climb back out, but he closed her door firmly. She yanked on the handle to open it just as he engaged the locks. He paused to look up the track at Simon, struggling to get back to his feet. Gareth shook his head in annoyance. The driver's door was still hanging open and Ripley considered trying to make a run for it, but Gareth was already on his way back round.

"Right, let's get you seen to," he said, lowering himself into his seat.

His voice was entirely devoid of concern now though. Simon was already striding up the track towards them as Gareth closed the driver's door. Gareth watched him for a moment, eyes narrowed. Ripley tried the door handle again. Nothing doing.

"We have to call Detective Harding," she said, urgently. "Simon killed Caroline Clifton. He knows where Ian is."

"Really?" Gareth sounded entirely unimpressed. She turned back to look at him, just as he pressed a cloth over her nose and mouth, pushing her head back hard against the headrest. She tried to turn her face away, but his grip was strong, and she felt the acid tang of the chemical hit her lungs on her first shocked breath.

RIPLEY HAD FEIGNED passing out as soon as she'd detected the chemical on the cloth. She'd held her breath and hoped. She'd flopped quickly but heavily, and he'd fallen for it, not checking properly if she was out or not.

She didn't flinch as he poked her cheek, testing her alertness. She was only grateful he hadn't touched her nose. She was sure she would've cried out and given the game away. As it was, she was fighting every instinct not to sniff as the congealing blood blocked her passageways. Instead, she let her mouth hang open and kept her breathing deep and steady, playing the part of the unconscious victim.

She heard Gareth swear as he climbed out of the car. She didn't dare open her eyes. Her mouth was dry, and she was desperate to close her lips and swallow. But she had to hold out—they could still see her. They were arguing just outside her window. Not arguing, bickering.

"Oh, come on, it's not that bad," she heard Gareth say. "It's barely a scratch."

"Piss off," was the snapped reply. "I thought you said she was leaving."

"And I thought you said you'd cleaned this lot up."

"You're lucky I got here in time, or she'd be gone and we'd both be screwed."

Again, she didn't hear the muttered reply.

"Whatever," Simon snapped. "Look, you finish all this. It's all kicking off back at the hospital, anyway. We should get going."

"Today?"

"Now."

"But…"

"No buts. There's cash in the safe. I'll grab what I can and wait for you by the bridge. Like we said."

Ripley kept her breathing even and forced herself to stay limp as the passenger door opened.

"Help me get her out, will you?"

She was hauled out by inexpert hands. She felt her feet hit the ground, and stayed as heavy as she could while she was dragged, clasped beneath her armpits, head on her chest, along the ground for a stretch before being dumped.

"You take this car, I'll take yours," Gareth said, bending down to haul Ripley up over his shoulder in a fireman's lift. She was grateful they couldn't see her face as the wind was knocked out of her by his shoulder. She felt Simon lean in to kiss Gareth, sandwiching her dangling legs uncomfortably between them for a second.

"I'll see you at the bridge."

"Okay," Simon said. "It's not going to be as much as we wanted, but I'll get what I can. And then we'll go, okay? Just you and me."

"Just you and me."

She heard another small kiss and then Gareth turned and stalked away, with her dangling over his shoulder.

The throaty roar of the Range Rover's engine faded slowly, to be replaced by Gareth's muttering as he stomped into the barn and dumped her unceremoniously on the ground beside Caroline's car. She let out an involuntary yelp. He nudged her with his foot. Exactly where Simon had kicked her before. She had to wince that time.

"Stupid bitch," he muttered.

His foot was right there. She could feel it. This was her chance. She opened her eyes at the same time as she brought her fist up to smack him in the side of the knee. But he was slightly further away than she had expected, his leg had been stretched to reach her ribs, and her punch barely glanced his kneecap.

He was on her, quick as a cat. Two sharp punches to the face and everything went black.

GARETH CHECKED SHE was out cold properly this time. He'd enjoyed hitting her. It had been a rush. Served her right. Meddling cow. Even if his knuckles did hurt now. He got up and dusted himself off. Such a messy business, all this killing. But it was exhilarating too. Was he starting to enjoy it? So what? Perhaps this was the beginning of something new. They could travel the world together, him and Simon, like Bonnie and Clyde. He'd be Clyde.

He smiled at the thought. His life had been so different since Simon had arrived. They'd hit it off almost immediately. Same dark sense of humour. Same tastes. Planning to leave together had come quickly, but Simon had pointed out that, if they were clever, they could leave with a great pile of cash and no one would be any the wiser. And it would be easier to rip Anne off with the two of them working together. No one would suspect a local boy after all.

Megan's fund was being so badly run by Anne and Reverend Rodwell, that Simon was sure they could skim loads off the top without anyone even noticing. And that's what they'd been doing.

Simon had led Rodwell along perfectly, flirting with him, making him think that they could be an item, playing to his ego. He was the one who'd turned the whole shambles into a business. Simon was the one who'd organised the group sessions to bring in even more cash. And he'd made sure that everyone leaving from a one-to-one felt obliged to put a little something in the pot. He was a genius. And Gareth was totally smitten. He couldn't believe that they would be leaving today. Now. He just had to tidy up these last loose ends so that no one came looking for them.

He pulled the heavy canvas tarpaulin off the car and laid it over Alex Ripley. He didn't want to look at her any more than he had to. Sure that she wasn't going to move again in a hurry, he trotted back to the Range Rover and climbed in, driving in a wide circle to turn it round. He wanted to be facing the right way to make a quick getaway.

He opened the boot and took out the jerrycan of fuel that Simon had bought. They'd decided earlier that he would set fire to the barn, rather than risk moving the car with Ripley sniffing around. The old buildings didn't belong to anyone anyway, so no one would be too bothered. By the time anyone thought to check, they'd just assume the burnt out wreck had always been in there. And if they had found the body, it would be too late—they'd be long gone by then.

He unscrewed the cap and began pouring, covering the car with the sharp-smelling fuel, making sure it went in through the open window and all around the tyres. He opened the car's petrol cap, so that the fuel in there would catch too. He held his breath as he forced himself to open the boot and pour some over the decaying body in there.

Finally he doused the canvas that he'd stuffed Alex Ripley under. He wondered if she would wake up enough to feel herself burn, or whether she'd be blissfully unconscious, like her friend would have been when he drowned on the high tide.

He made sure the canvas tarpaulin was completely soaked in fuel and then used what was left in the can to draw a line from the edge of the fabric out of the barn. He flung the empty can back into the barn and took out a box of matches.

Crouching down, he struck one, and turned it round to shove it back into the box, creating a small flare which he tossed onto the fuel line. He grinned sadistically as the flame raced along the dirt and caught the edge of the tarpaulin with a whoosh. As he watched the fire engulf the car and the thick smoke fill the barn, he couldn't help feeling that it had been something of an anti-climax. He'd been hoping for a bit of screaming, at least.

Ah well.

As he turned the Range Rover back onto the tarmac, he heard the explosion as the fuel in the car's tank finally went up. There wouldn't be much anyone could do for Dr Ripley now.

DETECTIVE HARDING COULD see the plume of thick grey smoke from all the way down the hill. It was coming from the fields on the way out of town. On the road to Four-Mile Bridge. Exactly where Alex Ripley had said she was before her phone had cut out.

The feeling of dread only intensified as he crested the hill and saw the raging fire in the old barns that had stood empty and unused for so long they'd become part of the landscape. Dread turned to panic as he saw Ripley's car in the lay-by ahead. He pulled up alongside it and peered across, but there was no sign of her.

He flung his own car into reverse and backed up to the track leading to the burning buildings. Keeping his foot down, he sped towards the inferno. He stopped short of the barns, and stepped out of the car into a wall of heat.

"Alex?" he called above the crackling roar.

There was no sign of her. There was no sign of anyone. He let his car door swing closed and hurried towards the barn. The heat coming off it forced his eyes into narrow slits and made him gasp for air. He'd only gone a couple of steps towards the barn when he saw Ripley's phone on the ground. That distinctive yellow cover he'd seen several times now.

"Dr Ripley! Alex! Are you here?"

He tried to get closer to the barn but it was far too hot. He could see the burning chassis of a car in there. The unmistakable shape of a VW Golf. Caroline Clifton's car. But where the hell was Alex Ripley?

He pulled out his phone and called for the fire service. There was nothing he could do on his own to stop a fire this intense. And if Ripley had been in the barn when it had caught, there was nothing he'd be able to do for her, either. Everything inside the barn was toast by now.

He turned back to the lane, heading towards his car. As he stooped to pick up Ripley's phone, he noticed a bloodied rock, and a few small spots of blood in the dirt. There had definitely been a scuffle here. But who with? And where was she now?

He climbed up over the bonnet and on to the roof of his car, scanning the horizon for a sign of anyone moving. He had taken only a few minutes to get up from the beach to here. Whoever had attacked Ripley and set this fire couldn't have got far. He only hoped he wasn't too late to catch them.

RIPLEY KEPT HUNCHED as low as she could to the wall which led away from the barn, away from the road and away from the safety of her car. She had taken the hits to the face hard but her blackout had lasted a matter of seconds. When she'd come round, she was under a thick covering and she could hear tyres crunching along the track.

Surely he wasn't just going to leave her like this. She wasn't even tied up. It took her a moment to figure out that the car she could hear was approaching, not leaving. She had to move, now.

She shuffled out from under the canvas covering, leaving it hunched and rigid in the middle. Hopefully, it would look enough like she was still underneath to buy her some time to escape. She hid behind the back of Caroline's car and watched as the Range Rover pulled past the barn, circling round to face the road.

As Gareth climbed out and walked round the car to the boot, Ripley seized the moment, sneaking out of a gap in the back of the barn where the old panelled walls had long since rotted away.

She pressed herself against the back wall, straining to hear what he was doing. The second the petrol fumes hit her, she knew. There was nothing she could do to preserve Caroline's body if he was going to torch the barn. The best thing she could do was get as far away as possible while he was busy, just in case he realised she was no longer under the tarpaulin.

She had made it all the way down to the next field before she heard the whoosh of the fire taking hold. She crouched down on the other side of the wall, back pressed into the stones and caught her breath. She had been breathing in short, shallow gulps, trying not to stretch her damaged ribs, but she deliberately forced herself to take a few deep, calming breaths now.

"He's already in the ground," Simon had said. *"Time and tide wait for no man."*

She knew exactly where they'd put Ian, and she was kicking herself for not thinking of it earlier. It was the perfect place to hide a body, alive or dead, and be sure that no one would find it until it was far too late—the burial chamber in the cliff, with its sunken bathing well, long since locked off from the public.

But she had seen the fresh padlock on the doors in the floor of the main chamber. She had seen the scrape marks outside the gated door which had made her think that the chamber had been opened up recently. What if it hadn't been the council, after all, as she'd assumed? What if it had been Gareth and Simon's handy little hidey-hole for getting rid of unwanted guests?

She looked down at the sea in front of her. The tide wouldn't get any higher, but if Ian *was* trapped in that chamber, he'd surely have drowned by now. She couldn't think like that. She had to keep moving. She'd promised to help.

As she set off again, heading for the cliffs and the coastal path which would bring her round the headland to the chamber, she heard the explosion in the barn behind her. The petrol tank in Caroline's car must have just caught fire. There would definitely be little useful evidence now.

She glanced back long enough to see the Range Rover heading out onto the main road and off towards the mainland, away from the village. Gareth wasn't looking for her at least.

It took her longer than expected to reach the cliff path, but once she was there, she had a clear run to the burial chamber. She was out in the open now, and it made her feel even more vulnerable. Especially on foot. On the cliffs. She just hoped they would be too busy with their own plans to imagine she had got away.

From their conversation she assumed that Simon and Gareth were set on leaving the village with as much cash as they could get. *How long have they been planning this?*

She hoped that they wouldn't get away before she could alert Detective Harding to their guilt, but her focus for now was on getting to Ian. If she found a way to get hold of Harding before then, great, but her phone was still up on the track by the barn, and without a phone she was stuck.

Her chest heaved, catching on every breath thanks to her damaged ribs, but at least her lungs were holding out for now. Strange that she hadn't had another attack in all this excitement. She must be getting better.

She could hear the waves crashing against the cliffs as she approached the burial chamber. The water was obviously still too high to force the ominous howling out of the chimney.

"Ian!" Ripley shouted at the top of her voice.

It was highly unlikely he would hear her. It was even less likely that he was still alive if he'd been trapped down in the bathing chamber. But she had to hope.

"Ian, I'm here!"

She stepped into the covered gateway, still barred and locked. She pulled on the lock, but it was shut fast. She headed back to the small, gritted car park area, by the sign explaining the chamber's secrets. She rooted around for something big enough that she might use to break the padlock which held the metal gate to the main chamber closed.

With a heavy, flinty rock in hand, she headed back to the gate and, in three strong blows, smashed the small padlock clean off. The gate scraped on the stone floor as she wrenched it back. She was in.

"Ian!" she shouted again.

Still no answer. She used the same rock on the lock on the metal doors which sealed off the bathing step from the main chamber. It didn't yield as easily, being a heavier lock, but she wasn't giving up now. The floor around the doors was still wet where the recent tide had already begun to recede. The water had been high enough to reach the outside walls of this main chamber. It would have been hell down below these doors.

Ripley brought the rock down again, and the lock popped. She cleared it quickly and, ignoring the stabbing pain in her ribs, lifted one door after the other. The area below was still half full of water. Steeling herself, Ripley dropped in.

The cold water made her gasp. A wave of panic flooded over her and she had only got in as far as her thighs. She was instantly back in that cold lake. Instantly reminded of the feeling as the water flooded her lungs and pulled her under. *I can't do this. I have to do this.*

"Ian!" she shouted again.

Her voice echoed around the chamber, bouncing back at her. A gull cried. Ripley breathed deeper and dropped down another step. The freezing sea water reached waist level. The faint light coming in from the main door didn't give her much to see by, but she cast her hands around, feeling for anything that might help guide her down.

"Ian!"

She heard the tiniest of murmurs. Or had it just been an echo of her own cry? She took a deep breath and dropped down the last step. The water reached up to her chest. She felt everything tighten. *This is not the time for a panic attack. Breathe. Breathe.*

She waded deeper into the cavern and found him, slumped but standing, trapped—shoulders wedged in the chimney, head in the open space. She grabbed his hands. There was no response. She was too late. She wrestled with him, trying to pull him free from the chimney, but she couldn't move him.

"Alex?"

The voice came from outside. It sounded familiar.

"In here," she called out. "Quick!"

"Hang on."

Detective Harding's broad shoulders blocked out all the light from above for just a moment. Ripley had never felt relief like it.

"He's down here!" she shouted.

And then, more quietly, just for Ian, in case he could hear her:

"It's okay, we've got you now."

SIMON SMILED AS he cruised past the service station. He could see the blue flashing lights from the road. Just as he'd planned, the police had responded to his tip off that Gareth would be waiting in the car park there. That's where they'd arranged to meet, once Simon had picked up all the cash from the house.

There had been more than he thought, thanks to the concerned donations of those who'd been at the group meeting. He should feel bad, stealing from a girl in a coma. But he didn't. Her own family were happy to use her, why shouldn't he? Besides, this little piece of revenge had been a long time coming.

His own sister had visited Megan, over two years ago, trying to find a cure for her stomach cancer, and she had seen no improvement. She had felt conned, and when she'd told him about it, he'd promised to help her get her money back. But when he saw the setup there, he realised that he could do a lot more for her. If he conned them better than they conned everyone else, then he could earn her enough to get radical treatment in the United States. He had promised her it wouldn't take him long, and he had been right.

Anyway, Megan would keep pulling in more saps. She would earn this and more back for her mother in no time. They wouldn't really miss it. Besides, he'd earned it. Francis had promised him a bonus after all.

Francis Rodwell. The not very Reverend as it turned out. He'd been happy to turn a blind eye to some of Simon's more creative accounting so long as he got his. He'd been more than happy to line his own pocket to keep quiet. Of course, he didn't know the half of what had been going on. He didn't know about all the people that they'd forced into silence. They couldn't have anything ruining the business.

Once they'd got rid of that first woman, it had got so much easier. It had been Gareth's idea to put her in the chamber. No one would ever think to look in there. And then they'd staged her car and clothes to make it look like she'd killed herself.

Obviously when Caroline Clifton had shown up, they couldn't just do the same thing. And then Ian, and now Dr Ripley. Busybodies, all of them. Trying to ruin everything. But they hadn't ruined him. He'd outsmarted them all.

And now? Well, enough was enough. Mustn't be greedy. With the money from the safe, the money he'd taken back from Caroline that Francis should never have given her, and everything he'd squirrelled away in his own account, he had plenty. It was for a good cause after all. Shame for Gareth he wouldn't get any for himself, despite all his efforts.

It had been too easy to seduce him. To make him believe that there was a future for them. Simon laughed. He wasn't even gay, for God's sake. Gareth had been so desperate to get out of Rhosfaelog, he'd fallen for the line so quickly. A tender touch, a loving kiss. He didn't have to try at all.

Simon slowed, pulling into the car park for a better view. Gareth had tried to run and had been wrestled to the floor by one of the policemen. A fat little officer, knee in Gareth's back, pushing him into the ground as they cuffed him. He wouldn't like that.

Simon pulled into a spot on the far side of the car park where he could watch it all happening in his rear-view mirror. His only regret was telling Gareth about his sister. He hadn't mentioned her name, or anything, but it may be enough to trace him. Would he remember her condition? He wasn't the sharpest knife in the drawer. He had to hope that Gareth would be so embarrassed and devastated that he would forget the details.

He smiled as the officers bundled a protesting Gareth into the back of the squad car, hand on his head like in the tv shows. He couldn't help giggling. Of course, Gareth would tell them all about him, he'd probably blame Simon for the whole thing. But no matter how hard anyone looked, they would never find Simon Butcher. There was no such person.

5th December

ANNE SHIELDS SAT beside her daughter's bed, holding her hand, listening to the monotonous, melancholy beeping. The doctors had already been in and given her the news: It was just the machines keeping Megan alive now. It was only a matter of time until her beautiful little girl would be gone for good. Anne knew she would have to say goodbye soon, but she couldn't bring herself to do it yet.

Outside she could hear more crashes and bangs. Loud voices. Trauma. Crashing. More lives passing. People that may live or die. Nothing to do with Megan. Not anymore.

She channelled all the energy she could muster, trying to push it into Megan, willing her to come back. Wishing her strong again. She prayed and pleaded until there was nothing more she could do. She had thought she would want Francis with her, but when he'd come he'd seemed distracted and at odds, so she'd sent him away. She alone would be here for her daughter. She, and God, of course.

EVERYTHING FELT VERY far away now. Even Mummy. Always there. Trying to hold on to her. She could feel her warmth pulsing in and out. It wouldn't be enough though. Not this time. Megan had been holding on to the darkness ever since the boy had visited. She'd nurtured it, keeping it close like a small pet. But now it had grown big and strong.

She had also worked hard on that wall. Whose wall? That woman had brought it. Dr Alex Ripley. It was her wall. And Megan had broken a part of it down. She was sure of that much. She'd seen the light shining out through the hole she'd made. But she had no more strength to break it down further. She hoped it would be enough.

She could feel the last of her energy like a small ball, no bigger than a golf ball. Not even very warm any more. The beeping grew louder.

She pushed that little ball into her mother's hand. It was time to go. The darkness flooded back in and she let it take her. Finally, she sank, deeper and deeper, until she was gone.

RIPLEY SAT BY Ian's bedside, watching the monitors tracing the life that the doctors had managed to pound back into his half-frozen body. He had miraculously managed to keep himself wedged high enough in the chimney to stop himself from drowning, but he'd been able to do little to stop the hypothermia.

The doctors had told her that if he hadn't been wedged into the cramped space when he'd passed out, he would have died in the water below. He had been lucky, though he wasn't out of the woods yet.

She looked up as Detective Harding poked his head round the door.

"Can I have a word?" he asked.

Ripley joined him in the corridor.

"We've arrested Gareth Williams," he said quietly. "Bron's absolutely raging."

"What about Simon?"

"Gareth's told us everything he knows about him," Harding said. "Says it was all his idea. Says he was in love with him. Who knew? Anyway, we've searched everywhere, but there's no sign, yet. The name doesn't show up on any databases or anything. So we're none the wiser. We'll keep looking though, obviously. He's made off with nearly sixty grand in cash from the safe. But according to Gareth they had well over a hundred grand stashed in an account. No sign of that either, needless to say."

So Simon had tricked them all, Gareth included. Ripley couldn't quite bring herself to feel sorry for him. She did feel sorry for Bron though. She obviously didn't know as much of what was going on as she had assumed.

They both looked up to see Anne step out into the corridor. She looked exhausted. Lost. The twins crowded around her. She bent down to their height and said something, and both of them wrapped their arms around her.

"Megan passed away a few moments ago," Harding said solemnly.

Ripley watched as Anne scooped up her babies and sat down on the hard plastic chairs with them both pressed into her chest. It was their turn now.

"She and Reverend Rodwell are going to have some questions to answer, but Gareth has assured us that they knew nothing about the killings. The Rev knew about the fraud though, and the fact that Simon was creaming money off the top. Gareth says he's been taking handouts of his own. Had his head turned by this Simon character too, by all accounts."

Greed and fear and love.

"That's awful," Ripley said.

"I wanted to thank you, Dr Ripley," Harding said, shaking her hand. "If it hadn't been for you and Ian, I don't think I would have even noticed any of this."

"Don't be too hard on yourself," Ripley smiled. "Simon—or whoever he really is—seems to have had everyone fooled."

"How is Ian?" he asked.

"He'll be fine," she said. "I'm sure."

And she was sure. He would find a way to move on now. It may take a while, but he would be fine.

RIPLEY HAD SAID her goodbyes to Ian after he'd woken up, promising to keep in touch. She'd offered her condolences to Anne and wished Harding all the best for a return to the quiet life.

Just as she was crossing the bridge to leave Holy Island, her phone rang. She pressed the receiver on her bluetooth speaker to answer as she drove.

"Alex Ripley," she said.

"Alex, it's Neil Wilcox."

She almost swerved the car off the end of the bridge.

"Hang on Neil," she said as she guided the car over to the hard shoulder. A few hoots from other drivers, but otherwise she was safe.

"Okay," she said. "I'm here. What news?"

"We've found him, Alex. We picked John up last night. We're bringing him home."

"Is he—?" she found she couldn't finish the question. *Is he alive?*

"He's not in great shape, he's been through a lot, but he'll be all right. He's alive."

The relief floored her. She sat in silence for an age after she hung up. Cars whizzed past, buffetting her old Audi. She couldn't move. The one thing she'd most wanted had happened. They'd found John. She'd got her miracle.

ACKNOWLEDGEMENTS

For his constant and unwavering support, my heartfelt thanks, always, goes to Richard—my husband, friend and emotional rock. None of this would be possible without you.

For their advice, inspiration, and constructive criticism, my thanks go to my friends and 'first readers' Mandy, Tim, Zoe—your gentle criticisms are always welcome, as is your attention to detail.

A huge thank you always to my mother, Carol—the source of my creative genes, and the first person to tell me I could do this, if I worked hard enough.

As always, an honourable mention must go to the Red Dogs. Dylan, Max and Oscar—you're crazy, but you help to keep me sane.

ABOUT THE AUTHOR

M. Sean Coleman lives with his husband in the Oxfordshire Cotswolds, UK, where he writes novels, and television and film scripts. He has three dogs to keep him fit, and when not writing or walking the dogs, he spends his time gardening.

Readers can contact him in any of the following ways:

Web: www.mseancoleman.co.uk

Twitter: @mseancoleman

Facebook: mseancoleman.author

- A HOLLOW SKY -

Lightning Source UK Ltd.
Milton Keynes UK
UKHW041148120922
408725UK00001B/34